ACCLAIM FOR GERMAINE SHAMES'

YOU, FASCINATING YOU

"Germaine paints a vivid and accurate portrait of the world of ballet in pre and post-war Europe. The epic drama expected on the ballet stage is dwarfed by the tragic real life events of her ballerina heroine, Margit Wolf. Penetrating descriptions of political brutality and the prepossession of romantic love, an ever present theme in classical ballet, make for a page-turning, impelling read."

—Janet Panetta, Ballet Master Tanztheater Pina Bausch, Int'l Guest Teacher NYC & PARTS

"An epic story and a true story. Margit Wolf's life is the kind of character journey that makes for great movies."

—Howard Allen, "the Script Doctor"

"A love story reminiscent of that of my grandparents. I could not put it down."

—Kinga Nijinsky Gaspers

"In this heartbreaking and original novel based on the life of Hungarian ballerina Margit Wolf, Germaine Shames has crafted a story that will absorb readers fascinated not only by history and art, but romantic obsession. From Wolf's touching point of view, we see a valiant Jewish artist swept along by a combination of political horrors and her unfailing passion for her husband, famed Italian composer Pasquale Frustaci, who refuses to help her and her son escape from brutal life under the Nazis occupying Hungary. Shames' faithful, carefully researched portrayal of Wolf's blindness and history's cruelty makes this a compelling read."

—Elizabeth Evans, author of *The Blue Hour*

"Shames captures the essence of a ballerina with such expertise in her riveting story. Dancers succeed by creating beauty from effort; this book, too, shows that exquisite art can be made from history's hardships."

—Elana Altman, soloist dancer, San Francisco Ballet

"Germaine Shames' beautiful depiction of the life of Margit Wolf and Pasquale Frustaci is told with such vivid and haunting detail, it's as if the reader is propelled back in time to witness a devastating journey of shattered dreams, juxtaposed with the strength and courage of the human heart. A tragic story, beautifully written."

—Susan Jaffe, "America's quintessential ballerina"

"They say love is blind, and so is a ballerina's resolve—in *You, Fascinating You* Germaine has captured both. The fact that Margit gave up everything—everything—to protect her son and defend her choices broke my heart. I have never read what happened to the Jews of Hungary told from this perspective, with evil seeping in like a shadow no one could detect. This beautiful story made me give gratitude for all the freedoms I have in front of me, and for the freedom to dance wherever, and whenever, I please."

—Georgia Reed, actress and dancer

"Compelling, heart-wrenching, and heroic."

—Jim Bencivenga

ALSO BY GERMAINE SHAMES

BETWEEN TWO DESERTS

"Shames, a former Middle East correspondent, handles the complexities of Eve's visit to war-torn Jerusalem with a subtlety seldom seen in this genre. She is careful not to pass judgment on either side of the political equation as she skillfully intertwines the lives of this diverse cast of characters to produce a tightly executed, emotion-filled work."

—Publisher's Weekly

"(The novelist) creates the intense atmosphere of an unstable world with grace and a sort of lyric power."

—National Public Radio

"One might expect the journalist and novelist to approach this story quite differently, but in *Between Two Deserts*, foreign correspondent Germaine Shames has realized a combination of these crafts, lucidly capturing those immutable qualities that speak to our souls."

—Rain Taxi

"An evocative plea for the power of love in the heart of Middle East turmoil."

—Kirkus Reviews

"In Jerusalem where rhetoric and revenge rule, Shames shows us humanity and insight."

—Bloomsbury Review

You, Fascinating You

Based on the true story of Hungarian ballerina Margit Wolf
and Italian composer Pasquale Frustaci,
aka "the Italian Cole Porter"

Germaine Shames

Pale Fire
Press

First Print Edition

Library of Congress Control Number: 2011913138

ISBN: 978-0-9838612-0-1

Cover image by Stanislav Belyaevsky: www.artballetphoto.com

You, Fascinating You online: http://palefirepress.com

Germaine Shames online: http://germainewrites.com

For information about subsidiary rights, bulk purchases, or author events, contact biz@palefirepress.com.

In memory of Margit Wolf

And for all the artists—dancers, musicians, singers, actors, painters, playwrights, authors, filmmakers—whose oeuvres were cut short by the Holocaust and whose loss history has yet to reckon.

In the final weeks of 1938, in the shadow of *Kristallnacht* and imminent war, a heartsick Italian maestro wrote a love song called "*Tu Solamente Tu.*"

Its lyrics lamented his forced separation from his wife, the Hungarian ballerina Margit Wolf, in the wake of Mussolini's edict banishing foreign Jews from Italy. The song, first recorded by Vittorio de Sica in 1939, catapulted to the top of the Hit Parade and earned its composer the moniker the "Italian Cole Porter." The German version, "*Du Immer Wieder Du,*" would be performed by Zarah Leander, the foremost film star of the German Reich, and its English counterpart, "You, Fascinating You," by the Glenn Miller Army Air Force Band.

Twenty-two years would pass before the maestro and his ballerina again met face-to-face. This is their story.

"You are, you are
That love I was waiting for all my life…"

"Ho Travato L'Amore"
I Have Found Love

One

They say ballet chooses the dancer. I, Margit Wolf, am twice chosen.

My father Mano Wolf worked as master tailor to the Hungarian State Opera. We lived a few doors away at 28 Andrássy út, an elegant address despite its dearth of plumbing. At every window flocked hosts of pigeons blown inland by a moody Danube, and in the parlor, between the spinet piano and my mother's heirloom curio cabinet, stood the sewing machine that dressed half the Romeos east of the Alps. All the greatest actors, the greatest dancers of the day would come to our flat to be suited out as princes, satyrs, sylphs … The sewing machine occupied the center of the living room. Clients would disrobe behind an oriental screen and step out transformed, standing tall with self-importance while my father crawled at their feet on all fours, his mouth barbed by straight pins.

"Make like you're on the stage."

The players would strut a soliloquy, the baritones belt out an aria, the ballet dancers camber and curtsey testing the reinforced seams, inspecting the flawless drape of the fabric. The tailor was no less an artist than his clients, yet he received no accolades, only more orders. He seldom left his machine. All the perfect little stitches, the dull and niggling little stitches, and the contraption chirring, always thirsty for oil.

I hoarded the scraps—silks, velvets, damasks. The feel of them spoke to me of worlds stitched together not with thread but light. Let others wield the needle, I would wear the fine costumes, I would make the hemlines sway and billow like a nimbus.

At the age of four, while my brother József learned the leather trade and my sister Rosa fine stitchery, I began training as a ballerina. At seventeen, having attained the swan-goddess ideal— spine elongated, execution flawless, ambition forged— opportunity trod on my heels. His name: Pippo Buffarino. Buffarino of Milan, who had the gumption to call himself an "impresario."

A commanding figure the Italian was not. He had the dimensions of a milk crate with legs poking out. He parted his hair down the center and smoked pencil-thin cigars from an ivory holder the length of a billiard cue. Having no business with the administration, he loitered at the stage door. "*Scusi*! *Scusi*!" When we dancers walked out he would charge forward, bow in reverence, and proffer a card monogrammed in gilt letters. Then came the one Hungarian phrase he had rehearsed to perfection: "*Kezitcsokolom*." I kiss your hand.

My companion Karola and I stepped out together that night linking arms, radiant after a second curtain call. Finding no way around the little man, we took his card and studied it in the scant light of streetlamps: *Impresario, La Scala, Milano* ... words to quicken the pulse.

"I was in the audience tonight, *signorine*." The stranger spoke a patchwork of languages punctuated by hand gestures. "I have seen you dance. Such talent, it humbles me. Wasted here. In Italy we know how to appreciate exquisite ballerinas like yourselves, we worship at the altar of your talent. That is my business."

"You work at La Scala?" Karola replied in the archaic French of classical ballet.

"Let us say I have connections. If I say, give this goddess an audition, she gets an audition."

"Whether we dance like goddesses or scrubwomen makes little difference," said Karola. "However hard we work, we languish in the chorus."

"A waste, a waste…"

"We have trained from the time we could walk, we have had no life apart from ballet, and what can we look forward to? A dancer's prime lasts no longer than a few seasons."

"What role do you covet, tell me?"

I stood by while my friend, her dimples deepening, plucked a bit of lint from Buffarino's lapel. "Any role will do, so long as I am prima ballerina. But it's starting to rain. Why don't we discuss this over a coffee? The Lukács' nearby."

"With pleasure, *signorina*, but I'm not a man to make small talk. I return to Milan within the week. I have space for four ballerinas. Accompany me, both of you, and I will strew your path with roses. You will have all Italy at your feet."

I could keep silent no longer. "For a chance at La Scala, I would dance the Firebird on a tightrope!"

Karola and the Italian turned to look at me, but I couldn't see their faces. The streetlamps cast them into silhouette, dark masks behind which comedy and tragedy mingled.

Buffarino gabbled rather than laughed. "A tightrope, eh? Why not? I can make something of a girl like you."

He gave a parting bow, faintly clicked his heels, and hurried off on his ten-pin legs, puffing smoke into a sky bare of the palest star. Gazing after him, Karola breathed into the fox collar of her coat, "This is it, our ticket out of here."

"And your family?"

"My mother will cry, my father will get drunk, and in the end neither can do a damn thing to stop me. I'm eighteen. I pay my own way."

A year her junior, I could only wonder at her bravado.

She turned to me and said with complete assurance, "My

parents would run off themselves given half a chance."

Unloved Budapest. People were always leaving—to escape hunger or persecution, to seek their fortune. Somehow I always knew that I would leave, too. The winters were endless, the summers a mere glimmer, and everywhere the same weathered facades, averted eyes, locked doors.

There was no question of sleeping that night. Beside me in the trundle bed we shared, my sister Rosa curled like a drying leaf. I lay awake and thought of my first ballet master, Nicola Guerra, whom I'd known only briefly but whose face I pictured vividly with its meteoric changes of expression, brooding one moment, playful the next. *So, little mouse, you want to be a ballerina? I will make you one, but first you must bring me the moon. It's closer than you might think.* At six, I heard my mother rouse from sleep and pad to the kitchen to start the hot chocolate. Minutes later, my father followed, silent but for the shuffling of his leather slippers. I rose from bed, washed, and took my customary place beside him at the kitchen table.

"Up so early? How was the performance last night?"

"Nothing special."

"Szidonia," he said to my mother, who stood stationed at the wood stove, "come feel her head. She looks flushed."

"I'm fine. You'd think I was an invalid the way you pamper me."

"The late nights, and you hardly eat."

"There's something you should know. A man came to the theater last night, an impresario, and he's offered me a place."

"An impresario? In Budapest?"

"A Milanese from La Scala. He's offered me a place at La Scala." This wasn't entirely true, of course, but why trouble my parents with nuance, why torment them with doubt? They had little enough to believe in.

My mother turned from the stove with more than her usual gravity, both hands already wringing her apron. "Can we trust this man?"

"Perhaps he has references," my father, shrug-shoulderd in his worn dressing gown, suggested.

"I could ask."

"Fine. Good. Ask."

He drank his cocoa hurriedly, fussing with the cuffs of his robe. My mother busied herself with breakfast. They would never stand in my way, I knew, would never pit their loss against my ambition.

I saw Buffarino again after the next performance.

"So, my firebird, what have you decided?" He stood, cigarette holder in hand, looking more theatrical than foreign.

"For me, there is no decision to make, but my father—what have you in the way of references?"

"Your father, I take it, has never traveled? Anyone in Milan, in Paris, in Vienna could tell him about Buffarino and his ballerinas. Name any of the grand opera houses and my girls have danced there."

"Of course, but is there someone he might wire? Someone familiar with your reputation?"

At that moment Karola stepped out from the stage door, and his attention fixed on her like a precision lens. "The goddess herself! Breathless you leave me."

Whether or not I joined the troupe mattered little to the Italian, who could easily have left Hungary with a dozen dancers as avid and well trained as I. The slightest hesitation might have lost me my place.

"This Buffarino is no small fish," I told my father at breakfast the next morning. "Colleagues say he launched Grisi—Carlotta Grisi, the Italian prima ballerina—and also Fanny Elssler, the Viennese. Took her all the way to America."

He sat expressionless.

"Your chocolate's getting cold."

His eyes fastened on my hands, which had acquired grace without losing a natural restlessness. I strained to hold them still. Having given me to ballet, my father could only admire its effect.

"I don't like to think of you so far away," he said.

"You won't lose me, *apa*. I know my way home."

"Go, Margit." He looked so small across the table, emptied of whatever it is that gives a man stature. "Go as far as your talent will take you. I'll be here."

By week's end, our quartet of hopefuls—Karola, Teréz, Ilona and I, known throughout the ballet academy as the *Pas de Quatre*—had cast its lot with the itinerant Buffarino. Four girls who had entered the school awkward and unformed, and gravitated toward one another for no apparent reason. We had nothing in common apart from ballet—but then, what else was there? Long hours at the barre, at rehearsal, waiting in the wings... we seldom saw daylight. The same rigid alchemy had been worked on us all. Ilona, double-jointed with slanting eyes, could be moody; bottom-heavy Teréz stubborn; Karola, dimpled, everyone's favorite, vain. But at night, when we lay down to sleep, we dreamed the same dream: to dance center-stage with all eyes upon us, to receive the bouquet of roses, to be *loved*. To be loved as only a Giselle or Juliet could be.

Having rent the family fabric and said our goodbyes, we piled into Buffarino's waxed Fiat. Its roof sagged under the weight of all we could not leave behind. Pushcart vendors shuffled past, street sweepers with their boar-bristle brooms. My brother József came to see me off, carrying the tin trunk that held my favored possessions. He took in the Italian through narrowed eyes, shook his hand with some reluctance, and said, "Take care of her. We know people in Italy."

We didn't, of course. Buffarino emitted one of his gabbling laughs. "Relax, relax, I treat your sister like the Queen of Sheba."

The car engine backfired and we lurched forward. József stood in the middle of the street with one arm in the air, not waving, still as a paving stone. I called out to him, "Kiss mama, kiss papa..." but we were all shouting something, all sobbing and giggling, and the engine drowned out everything but the fanfare inside my head.

♪

It was late on a Sunday night when we pulled into our first Italian city of some size. All the buildings stood shuttered. Prostitutes posed on the curbs. The sky was tinged fuchsia and warm rain seeped from it. Having been motion-sick from the time we left Budapest, I slid to the pitted sidewalk and swayed on my feet.

"This is it?" Ilona said, sounding as deflated as the Fiat's tires.

"We must be on the outskirts."

"The guy's a pimp," muttered Karola, "he's brought us to the red light district."

As if on cue a woman in stilettos and a lace petticoat glanced in the Italian's direction and spat.

"That must be one of his harlots."

Buffarino, oblivious of our mounting panic, began to offload luggage. "You like risotto? How about a nice veal cutlet? I got an appetite like a herd of charging bullocks."

Ilona's chin rose in the direction of a seedy hotel. "That must be the brothel."

"Let him go first," whispered Teréz. "If you see red satin, make a run for it."

"You girls got your figures to worry about, but not me. We'll start with antipasto—you like anchovies? I like anchovies. Washed down with a little *vino bianco* ..."

"I'm going to be sick."

"If he tries anything, go for his male parts."

"You like tripe soup? Nothing like it. Secret's in the oil. And Gorgonzola, I've known Hungarians to swoon over the Gorgonzola..."

"Excuse me, Mr. Buffarino." Karola tapped him on a shoulder.

"Pippo," he corrected her. "Call me Pippo."

"I've seen photographs of Milan, Mr. Buffarino. We've all seen photographs. They don't look like—like *this*."

"Smart girl," the Italian said with condescension. "You're right, Milan is bigger. Milan's got the Duomo, etcetera. We're not in Milan."

"Not in Milan?"

"This is Novara, my goddesses."

"But I've never heard of Novara."

"Never heard of Novara?" The Italian let out a gasp. "Some of the greatest ballerinas of all time got their start in Novara: Taglione, Duncan, Pavlova... and then on to Milan! The critics are already lining up. Never fails."

We looked at one another, doubting.

"Why the long faces? I'll put you in a nice pension, get you a hot meal. Tomorrow you'll wake up and say, 'That Pippo, what a prince!' You'll thank me. Now, could you just give me a little hand? What do I look like, Charles Atlas?"

Not knowing what else to do, we gathered up the luggage and tramped after him into the dank lobby of the *Ostello Buona Notte*. The night clerk roused from a nap and eyed us with a brand of lechery that stung at first but would soon become familiar.

"Your latest?" he said to Buffarino.

"Mind your business," rejoined our protector, jabbing at the hotel register with a leaky Ancora. "And wake up the cook. I got an appetite like the Huns storming Constantinople."

"Wasn't there a famine in Constantinople?"

"Smart guy. Just get me the cook."

In daylight Novara looked less threatening, a town not without charm, but our spirits had deflated and could not be buoyed by promises. Buffarino drove us to what he called the "opera house," a boxy edifice with posters glued to every inch of wall. Inside, a motley assortment of entertainers—singers, actors, a trained poodle—moped in the wings, waiting for a chance to rehearse. An orchestra tuned up. The stage bore the scuffmarks of every foot that had ever crossed it.

"Excuse me, Mr. Buffarino," Karola started in again, "but this isn't an opera house. We all know what an opera house is, we grew up in one. *This*"—she made a sweeping gesture not unlike a *rond de bras*—"this is no venue for a ballet."

"Not an opera house? But only last month I attended an opera under this very roof." The Italian broke into a pout. "If it's not an opera house, what is it?"

"A music hall," I said flatly. "You promised us La Scala and brought us to a music hall."

"I brought you out of Babylon to the Promised Land! You've been so long in a backwater that you don't recognize culture when you see it. Your sensibilities aren't attuned. Drop your airs, my goddesses. They'll do you no good here."

We saw no more of our deliverer that day. The conductor, a jaunty figure with hair like Valentino's, winked in our direction, and I had the impression that he was amused by our plight, had been a witness to it countless times before. Indeed, no one seemed inclined to offer the least sympathy. A wardrobe mistress, whose name we didn't catch, led us through a massive storeroom, gradually disappearing behind an armload of gaudy costumes.

"I won't be seen in these bits and bobs," said Ilona, swiping away tears with a lace-edged hankie. "We're classically-trained ballerinas, not can-can dancers."

"*Were*, you mean." Karola's voice went glassy. She took a hand-rolled cigarette from her satchel and lit-up. "We've got no ticket home. We don't even know where we are. That this place—call it what you will—lacks category, who but Buffarino would think to debate? But even if it's nothing but a fleabag, when that curtain goes up I'm going to dance."

"You'll disgrace yourself, disgrace the art, and for what?" Ilona was weeping openly by then, her tartar eyes dark as drowning pools. "We'll never see the inside of La Scala. We'll be less than whores."

"You talk like my mother. This is 1928."

"Some things don't change."

Karola dragged on her cigarette and turned to follow the costume mistress. "What the heck else can we do? If you're so virtuous, tell me what to do."

We spoke no more about it.

♪

Have I mentioned Pasquale? The orchestra leader. Maestro Frustaci, a native of Naples, was working at that theater in Novara when the four of us arrived. Not a braggart exactly but unabashedly Neapolitan, the maestro held sway from the first note of the overture until the final ovation, at which time he'd promptly vanish from the theater, always with a woman on his arm. He favored dancers. That much was common knowledge. He treated me no differently from any other: a polite nod to my face, a discreet glance at my posterior.

"Watch out for that one," counseled Karola, who from her first performance in Italy was besieged by suitors. "A wolf and penniless besides. Just look at the women he goes with."

Teréz, already on a first-name basis with the industrial scion she was fated to marry, took a more indulgent view. "Have you seen the way he ogles Margit? Poor boy's smitten."

At seventeen, I'd had no experience of men. What I knew about love I learned from ballet librettos: two people are brought together through circumstance, the imps work their magic charm, and one is struck senseless—like a sleeping beauty, like a sculptor succumbing to his own creation. Choice plays no part. Had it been otherwise, I would not have chosen Pasquale Frustaci, who aside from his cockiness had already begun, at twenty-six, to lose his hair.

Those first days in Novara, the maestro formed the hub around which the production, such as it was, took shape. The dance director, a former circus owner whose idea of ballet was to send us donkey-kicking across the stage with our skirts in the air, seldom made an appearance. The maestro ruled his orchestra with a seemingly light hand. His perfectionism would rear up only at dress rehearsal, which stretched on into the night until every note satisfied. He did not limit himself to overseeing the music but kept an eye on us dancers, gently coaxing a synchrony of melody and movement. Whatever polish our performance gave off must be credited to him—which is not to excuse his peccadilloes, thick and public as they were.

I took Karola's advice and avoided him. After the show, while the others went out to clubs, I would linger at the theater to do floor exercises and then walk the few blocks back to the pension, where, if my timing was right, the proprietor might warm-over that evening's dinner. Another month, I told myself, and the maestro would fade from my life like confetti in a scrapbook. One month, the time it would take to fulfill my contract and bring down the curtain on a dream in shambles.

"Working at this hour?" The maestro, fedora in hand, spoke from the wings. "I stopped back for my wallet. Never could hold on to money." Which explained his presence, if not his sudden attentiveness. "But what's wrong, eh? Homesick?"

"What means homesick?"

"You miss a sweetheart, maybe?" He joined me onstage, assuming a role of his own making. One footlight had been left burning and he positioned himself in its beam. "It's a lonely life, the comedies. And you, a stranger—but you're learning. Your Italian is good."

"Not so good."

"Okay, contradict me. But tell me what's wrong? I walk in and find you crying. You should be out celebrating with the others. Come, I'll take you to them." With practiced gallantry he extended his arm.

"I have not the party feeling."

"I'm not much for parties myself." The arm dropped soundlessly to his side and he looked, for a moment, boyish, shy of his limbs. "Don't believe the things you hear about me."

"About the women?"

"Okay, so I like women. I respect them, too. But I'm not the bohemian people take me for. I've got ambitions."

"I, too."

"Do you?" He did not dissemble his interest but studied me

11

as one might a futurist painting. "Tell me about them."

"This dancing is not art."

"So, that's why you're crying?"

"Because the men, the way they look at me. Is not art."

"But you mustn't be ashamed. Why, you grace the stage! You're above it all."

"The men, they make whistle."

"It's what they know. They come to be entertained. Me, I make music, songs people hum while they work, songs that make their day a little lighter. Why ask if it's art? If my music makes people tap their toes, then that's enough for me."

"I do not believe you."

"So, call me a liar." He threw up his hands, a stage gesture. "Sure, I'd like to be Arturo Toscanini, but I'm a practical man. There's nothing noble about starving. And besides, show me a livelier audience than at the comedies. People lose their cares here."

"Is not serious."

"Exactly, is not serious."

"You make the fun of me."

"Not at all. I just wanted to see you smile. We're friends now, eh? What's your name—not your stage name, the name they call you at home?"

"Manci."

"Around here they call me maestro, but to my friends I'm Pasquale. We are friends, aren't we, Manci?"

I couldn't feel offended by his presumption.

"But you're a *bambina*, a baby. When were you born, eh?"

"Nineteen-ten."

"The same year as Markova. Come to think of it, you look a lot like her."

Admirers never failed to note the resemblance. Markova had the good fortune to be born British. Her father was an Orthodox Jew and her mother Irish, converted. Yet Markova danced everywhere, and the Queen conferred upon her the title *Dame*, which made her royal in her own right. Marvels like that could happen elsewhere.

"Come, let me play something for you." Again the maestro extended a hand, and this time I took it and allowed him to lead me down into the orchestra pit, through a maze of music stands, to the grand piano. "Chilly, no? Here, take this." He draped his big-shouldered suit jacket across my back, took his seat on the piano bench, and patted the place beside him. I sat. A moment's stillness, and then his fingers began to dance along the keys with contained frenzy. The familiar strains of "Hungarian Rhapsody" filled the theater.

"You know Liszt?"

"Not personally," he said and gave me one of his maddening winks. "But I know his country, and yours"—he paused for effect and then added, "*babuci*." An endearment meaning little doll.

"Is not bad your pronunciation. How you learn this?"

"You know the New York Café in the seventh district?" There was not a more elegant venue in Budapest, nor one more infamous. The most flamboyant artists and writers of our day congregated there to rub against the status quo. "I played piano for a while, got to know the city. It felt like a second home." His hands leapfrogged each other, building toward a crescendo. "You like Italy?"

"I like. La Scala very beautiful."

"I see, so you've got your sights set on La Scala. You *are* ambitious. Me, I keep my ear to the Atlantic." And for a moment he seemed to gaze out through the walls toward that aqueous horizon I had yet to glimpse. "Now, you tell me, what is the difference between this and *this*?" "Blue Skies," I believe the song was. Mindful of being watched, he played it stylishly, wrists arched, mouthing words he could not have understood. "Irving Berlin," he pronounced with gusto, "*Americano*. Is art, is not art?"

"Is modern—is good."

"And this?" "Make Believe," also popular at the time.

"Jerome Kern, *Americano*. How about this?" "Someone to Watch Over Me" with all the flourishes. "George Gershwin. Is good, no?"

"Thank you, but I prefer Liszt."

The maestro's fingers jarred silent. I could feel his eyes trace the downward slope of my torso, discreetly, one might even say reverently. Mustering resolve, I slid to my feet and narrowly escaped my first seduction.

"Don't go." His hand closed on my wrist.

"I think, Pasquale, it is you the lonely one."

"One day," he promised, "I'll compose a ballet just for you, a terribly serious ballet, and then you'll see who I am." He stood up, whisked his jacket from my frame. "Lonely? Me? I've got more friends than a mutt's got fleas."

"Too many friends can be no friend at all."

"What time is it, eh? I'm expected at the Paradiso." He hesitated and could not keep the disappointment from his voice. "Goodnight, *babuci*."

♪

Our *Pas de Quatre* arrived windswept for a final performance in the city that was not Milan. Having strolled around the town square and tried on hats at a local milliner, our mood was airy. The theater pulsed with laughter. We entered our dressing closet, greeted the costume mistress (who had grown fond of us despite our tantrums), and began at once to strip off our day clothes.

"*Momento, signorine!*" the mistress trilled, snatching a feather boa from my hands. "Have you not heard?"

Karola turned to be zipped. "Heard what? Has anyone seen my scepter?"

Outside someone pounded at the door. "Have you heard?" called a male voice we didn't at first recognize.

"*Eccolo,*" snapped the mistress, "the mouthpiece of providence." She stood aside to make way for maestro Frustaci.

Once inside the door, the conductor struck a businesslike mien. "Your dance director is in hospital with a hernia. They say

he'll catch up with us in Rome, but good riddance to him."
Surprised less by the news than by the identity of its bearer, I
grabbed whatever came to hand and covered myself. The maestro
stifled a wink, bowed toward the others, and went on, "If you
would like in the director's absence to substitute numbers—that
pastoral romp, for example—what's it called? The program
wouldn't suffer without it."

The mistress made to shoo him from the room. "But
maestro," she scolded, "that would be mutiny."

He showed his palms. "All art is mutiny, so what? Let the
ballerinas decide."

There was no time for deliberation. A crowd had begun to
gather in front of the theater; we could hear their footfalls on the
cobblestones, smell their mothballed finery. A stagehand paused
at our door to drone, "*Twenty minutes to curtain ... twenty
minutes ...*"

I pivoted to face my sister ballerinas. "If you have no
objection, I would like to dance the "*Pizzicato*" from *Sylvia*."
Guerra had assigned me the solo as a parting gesture, and
although I danced it onstage only once, its mesmeric
choreography had left an imprint.

Teréz stopped slathering greasepaint onto her cheeks.
"Without a rehearsal?"

"I could dance *Sylvia* in my sleep."

The maestro seemed to mull this. "Delibes, isn't it? I have
the sheet music. The ballet I have never seen danced, but the
music... so seductive, a haunting score."

"Can your orchestra play it?"

He pulled on his white gloves with more than the usual
aplomb. "If you can dance it," he said, "I can conduct it."

In memory I do not feel the stage beneath my feet; I do not
hear the music but breathe it; I do not dance so much as soar,
trailing my gossamer veil after me. When the suite ends, the
ovation stuns me.

I catch sight of the maestro. White gloves at his sides he has turned to face me. What expression he wears I cannot know, the spotlight blurs it. A single yellow rose torn from his lapel and dispatched like a carrier pigeon lands at the toe of my ballet slipper. Cradling its petals, I dip low at the knee and curtsey, my hands trained toward the orchestra pit as if to render tribute.

♩

Milan, Turin, Venice ... The revue made the rounds of second-tier theaters, playing to audiences large and small.

We were thirty or so dancers, singers and actors, a family of sorts, into which our *Pas de Quatre* was gradually absorbed. Pasquale kept an unnatural distance, pursued his conquests on each town's far fringe. The gossips attributed his aloofness to a leggy Polish soubrette whose driver sometimes collected him at the stage door, but I gave little importance to the stories. I knew something the others didn't: that the maestro's seeming flippancy was but a means to the success he coveted. An ambitious man keeps his course.

Bologna, Florence, Rome ... Italy, viewed from the fogged window of a sleeping car, seemed to wind on forever, the cypress-studded hills, the vineyards, the periodic monument to modernity—a factory, a smokestack. Not the Italy of today, but a land on the brink of something. Mussolini might have called it greatness. A fine crafter of words was the Duce. I taught myself Italian by reading the newspapers; his speeches, reproduced in full, transported me to a world where black was white and every barefoot child a harbinger of glory.

My eyes might have told a different story, but I was young and wanted to believe.

I have photographs from that era crammed to the margins with eager young artists joined by the arm, smiling down from steamer trunks—not that I can put names to the faces. We moved as a band, the natives chattering in Italian more quickly than I could follow. They introduced me to wine and cigarettes. By sifting their expletives, I learned the names of the saints. Admirers would wait at the stage door as Buffarino once had, proffering bouquets of orchids, invitations to fine restaurants, promises of more and better to come. As the calling cards accumulated and my scruples eased, I began to enjoy my own foreignness.

By May we had reached the capital, where everyone, it seemed, had a favorite haunt, a secret sweetheart. No one slept. Meals were black coffee and pastries, taken in whichever café stayed open latest. In a fortnight we would be gone, reason enough to linger in the piazzas until dawn. And on the periphery, melting in and out of a black limousine, maestro Frustaci bided his time. I saw the glances he cast my way, sensed the pique my outward indifference caused him. There was nothing between us, and yet I felt bound to him by an invisible cord that tugged me back each time another man raised his glass in my direction or tried to smooth-talk me onto the dance floor.

In the claustrophobic world of the comedies we could not long avoid each other. On an unseasonably cold morning in a drafty theater whose name I have forgotten, Pasquale, early for rehearsal, poked his head in the open door of my dressing room. "Where is everyone? I call a rehearsal for ten and they dally at table, licking their fingers."

"It's only 9:45." I continued lacing my ballet slippers, had yet to apply my lipstick.

He ignored the remark. Not waiting for an invitation, he stepped across the threshold, squared the lapels of what appeared to be a brand new suit, and began to pace. "So, you've been getting out."

"Karola insisted," I said, adopting the overconfident tone I had learned in the company of faster girls. "And even if she hadn't, it was time I stopped sulking and mingled. You said so yourself."

"And the flowers?" His eyes fastened on a gaudy bouquet crammed into an old kerosene can.

"Oh, those... Pasquale, could you help me with this hook? It's in such an awkward place."

Obliging, the maestro positioned himself behind me. "You're growing up." When had he troubled to notice? "In the worst sort of way," he added gravely.

"I turned eighteen yesterday."

He took me by both shoulders, firmly, his hands manlier without their white conductor's gloves, and spun me around. "Why didn't you tell me? My favorite ballerina enters the bloom of womanhood and I'm the last to know." He backed off like a kicked puppy.

"You appeared occupied."

Again he gazed toward the greasy bouquet, his jaw faintly quivering.

"Nearly ten," I felt compelled to point out. "The orchestra will be arriving."

"Let them wait. These people you're *mingling* with, I worry about you. I've seen young women attract the wrong sort of attention, fall in with a bad element, lose their heads..."

"You are welcome to take the flowers with you, maestro."

He faced me squarely then, looking more parental than gallant. "Whoever he is, ditch him. I'm taking you to the opera for your birthday. I'll wait for you at sunset in the Piazza Venezia."

"The girls will talk."

"Let them," he said, knitting his arms in a parody of defiance. "Let them chatter like mother hens. I know what can happen to young innocents on tour. For your own sake, *babuci,* I'm taking you in hand."

♪

To keep company with a man is an act of faith—at least it was during the era of rising hemlines, when my courtship began in earnest. In the comedies young people had both more freedom and less privacy than was the norm, which tended to make us secretive even when we had nothing to hide.

It all began in the Piazza Venezia... The maestro surprised me by being punctual. I arrived and found him straining to read his wristwatch by the dwindling light. In one hand he held a small bunch of violets, which he cradled against the night breeze. Having come south without his scarf, he wore the collar of his new suit jacket upturned.

"Pasquale?"

He hadn't seen me approach. "So, you've come," he said, looking for a moment as if he might burst into song, but he contained himself, held out the violets almost apologetically, and stood in the middle of the pavement breathing into his palms.

The opera we saw I don't remember. The theater was grand and the seats plush, and the maestro whispered in my ear rather than speak above the din. When the curtain came down, he leaned close and said, "I hate sad stories."

We stopped for coffee somewhere on a back street, a family place unlikely to attract our fellow artists. Pasquale offered me a Silk and we made a game of blowing smoke rings, first small, then large, one consuming the other. He was good at it, but soon grew short of breath.

"*Brava*, Manci, you've picked up some talents in Italy."

"As you once said, maestro, I am a quick learner."

He threw back his head and laughed, a full-throated cackle that stunned the room to attention. "But we've an audience here. How about a stroll? It isn't every night a man finds himself in Rome with a beautiful woman."

Back on the street, we linked arms and no longer felt the cold. We walked, our footfalls echoing through the forums thick with shadows and stray cats. "So much history…"

"Leave it to the fascists to tout past glories," rejoined Pasquale, suddenly serious, "it's the present an artist has got to contend with."

"Would you topple the monuments, blast away the foundations?"

"Things topple in their time. What does it matter to a family man that some Caesar conquered Abyssinia umpteen years ago? Give him a decent-paying job. And at the end of the day, give him music, spectacle… for a couple hours let him sit in a darkened theater and imagine himself—the King of Siam. A man's entitled to his fantasies."

"And you, maestro? What goes through your mind when the house lights dim?"

"Me, I don't need to fantasize. I've got the songs. The rest is a matter of knowing the right people—and luck."

"An intelligent man makes his luck."

He paused, too proud to admit he was lost, a stranger casting about for a landmark. "How right you are, *babuci*," he said and absently nodded. "How right you are."

♪

Our first tour was drawing to a close. There was talk of next engagements; those lucky enough to have them boasted of fifty-piece orchestras and sold-out opening nights. The *Pas de Quatre,* neither booked nor bound, danced with abandon. Ballet had taught us a sort of faith. If Aurora could escape a spell and Nikiya conquer death, surely four young ballerinas at the height of their pluck might tempt destiny to their door.

The night of our last show Buffarino barged into the dressing room, his ten-pin legs ending in elevator heels that increased his height without adding stature. Ignored, he nonetheless looked inordinately proud of himself.

"Gather round, my goddesses," he bellowed, though the room could not have been more than six feet square. "Uncle's got your new contract. *Ecco*, the Carlo Felice, the Reggio, the Comunale… Moving up in the world, eh?"

Having taken the measure of the "impresario," we continued our toilette.

"What's a matter? Too dazzled to talk to old Pippo?"

Karola paused her powder puff to ask, "And La Scala, Mr. Buffarino?"

"Always the troublemaker!" he erupted. "I rescue you from the Carpatian backwoods, put your name up in lights, and not a word of thanks do I get. Do you think it's easy?"

Karola stared through the Italian and glided off with her chin in the air.

"What's wrong with *her*?"

Teréz promptly followed.

"I could strangle this little meatball," muttered Ilona in Hungarian.

"Let me deal with him," I said, getting up from my dressing table with calculated calm. Even in ballet slippers I towered over my adversary. "As I recall, *signore*, you're a man of few words, so I'll come to the point. We may be young but we're not stupid. You've been making out like a bandit at the box office. If we move up, so do ticket prices. How much are we to be paid?"

A testy smile curled the Italian's lips. "Same as before. Which is plenty good, considering. With times the way they are, a person's lucky to have work."

"It wasn't enough last time and it's not enough now."

"You want to work, you sign."

"Forty thousand lire each," I said. "And first-class train tickets—we need our rest."

"This is a joke, right?" He gave a fraught little laugh that might have been a seam ripping. "You Hungarians, so full of yourselves. Look, I'm a busy man. I could have couriered the contracts, but no, uncle wanted to look in on his goddesses, make sure they're comfy…"

"Those are our terms."

"Since when do you speak Italian anyway? Smart girl. I don't got time to argue. Forty thousand lire." Mustering dignity, he drew himself up.

"And the train tickets," I said evenly.

He made for the exit, his tiny arms flapping in the air like a signalman's flags. "*É troppo!*" He looked from one of us to the other, and as one we returned his gaze. "You're giving me heartburn already. Just be ready to pull out of here in two days. And if you see me in the dining car, I don't know you. Meals are on your own tab."

♪

The scene was everywhere re-enacted: Buffarino set upon by four clawing ballerinas, pummeled with powder puffs, and sent on his way bleeding lire. The *Pas de Quatre* earned a certain notoriety, deserved or not.

We all had sweethearts by then, Teréz her rich industrialist, Ilona a mysterious fencer rumored to be tight with the Duce, and Karola the heir to an empire built on dictionaries. Between shows, I often found myself alone in the pension, my friends having removed even their luggage. It was natural that I spend more time with the maestro. We continued to meet in out-of-the-way places, though our discretion fooled no one. It was simply our habit to hide.

The tour took us north to Cortina, south along the Adriatic, and loped circuitously west arriving at its height on the Amalfi Coast, not far from where Pasquale had grown up. One morning he rang me at the pension to say, "Rehearsal's been canceled. I'm taking you home."

He came for me in a dented taxicab whose driver, Enzo, he had hired for the day. That the engine had no muffler who would have thought to remark? While we settled into the back seat, the two men rattled off the names of foreign actresses and relatives who lived in Brooklyn. Grinding gears, the cab snaked through town to a two-lane *superstrada* and headed for Naples.

"Haven't been home in ages," the maestro thought aloud.

The driver's eyes glinted in the rearview mirror. "New road, new harbor—you'll hardly recognize the place."

Pasquale draped an arm across my knees and lowered his voice. "My father owns the American Bar overlooking the pier. I grew up there. People would stop in for a last Sambuca before boarding the boat for the New World. I watched them leave in droves."

"Didn't you ever want to follow them?"

"Me and boats don't get along. I did a stint in the Navy. From the moment we'd leave harbor, I was sick as a poisoned rat.

The worst kind of sick. I put in for a discharge, but the lifers laughed at me, until one night we had the king on board, Emmanuel himself, for a big bash. I was to lead the band. In full dress uniform I turned to His Majesty, bowed, raised my baton—and puked. Right on his royal shoes."

I could only laugh.

"Let the world come to me," Pasquale said, cocking a thumb beneath his chin.

"There's only so much you can see from the road. I'd like to fly."

"If God wanted us to fly, he'd have given us propellers. Me, I'll take the streetcar. I'll walk. What's the hurry anyway?" Spoken like a man born in the path of a live volcano. "Are you happy you've come?"

"Ask me after I've met your family. What time are they expecting us?"

"They're not. Who am I, the holy Pontiff, that I've got to announce myself?"

"Let's stop at a florist, at least."

"*Fermati,* Enzo," he told the driver. "Let me out here."

Before the car could come to a halt, the maestro bolted to the roadside and began to forage—lady's mantle, yarrow, columbine. Whistling a melody unlike any I had heard, he doubled back, deposited the bouquet in my lap, and we continued on our way. The tune would become my favorite of the maestro's early songs, "*Ho Trovato L'Amore,*" a slow beguine rich in counterpoint. Perhaps you know it? "*You are. You are that love I was waiting for all my life, that splendid joy to love the rest of my life, this life of mine that is blooming.*"

In memory we are driving down that road for hours, for hours... cars did not race along as they do today. There was time to mull our words.

"Pasquale," I felt obliged to confide, "you might as well know: I'm Jewish."

"Doesn't surprise me. I never heard you invoke the

23

Santissima Virgin."

"Religion isn't something I talk about."

"Nothing to be gained by talking about it," he concurred. "No one needs to know."

"*You* know."

"Doesn't make a goddamn bit of difference to me. Just let's not broadcast it, eh?" He angled his chin toward the driver, though the car engine drowned out any conversation. "It's nobody's business. Like being Neapolitan—better they think I'm Italian."

"But you are."

"Depends who you talk to. Mussolini considers us southerners a different race. It's treason to speak dialect anymore. The Neapolitan song is dead. You can't get it published. The only composers with work have signed-on with Cesare Bixio, who between you and me can't even read music. He rents a big office in Milan and suddenly he's a songwriter. Me, I was writing songs in the cradle."

"Your parents gave you lessons?"

"My sisters took the lessons, I hid in the closet. At night, I'd sit at the piano playing without ever striking a key. But I heard the music. The melodies were in my head even then."

"It must be wonderful to have a head full of songs."

He cupped his temples, as if to stem the flood of notes. "Doesn't leave room for much else."

"Any gift has its price."

We arrived at the outskirts of the city and Pasquale leaned forward in his seat to give directions. In an instant, the road crowded with vendors hawking rosaries, decks of cards, fish still thrashing in the net... Vesuvius came into view. The maestro held out his arm like a hussar leading the charge. "And here we are, my innocent, in the fields of fire. Keep a grip on your pocketbook."

♪

The Frustacies lived in a spacious flat in the Vomero district overlooking the Bay of Naples—not far from where I sit. The view from their balcony was not so very different from this.

Mamma Rosa, perfumed in oregano, her apron neatly ironed, met us at the door. "Always he arrives in time to be fed. Maria, Elena, Emilio... your brother's here!" The rest of the brood— Titina, Anna and Giacomo—had started families of their own by then.

"Say hello to Margit." Pasquale nudged me across the threshold. "We work together in the comedies."

"Another dancer?"

"A *ballerina* classically trained at a respectable opera house."

"Like I said, another dancer. Your father's waiting for his soup. Go sit down."

"I'll help in the kitchen, *signora*." The offer disarmed her long enough for me to add, "Is that *baccala fritto* I smell?"

Rosa veered and poked a finger into her son's ribs. "She's got a good nose, your *innamorata*."

The maestro's brothers and sisters began to pour into the parlor, some balancing children on their hip, others dressed in school uniforms. Emilio, baby-faced in his starched black shirt, greeted Pasquale with the fascist salute, something of a novelty back then.

The maestro held out his arms. "Stop being a knucklehead," he chided, "and give your brother an *abbraccio*."

The boy shrank back. "It's not hygienic."

"Have I got lice or something? We're in family."

"The Roman way is more manly," Emilio insisted.

"More manly... what's manly about letting some politician tell me how to behave in my own home?"

"*Basta*, Pasquale," intervened his father Salvatore, limply waving a hand, "we'll miss the latest on Nobile." The fate of General Nobile and his arctic expedition would rivet Italians to the wireless for months, but these were early days, heady days, and we dared to hope that the dirigible might right itself and the

25

expedition succeed. Such was our faith that we half expected to glance out the window and see Nobile, unflappable, drift by.

With Rosa and assorted daughters I retired to the kitchen, where pots the size of kettledrums emitted fragrant gusts of steam. "So, Margit, you're not from here? Let's see if they've got cooks where you come from," said the mother, steering me toward a cutting board. "The sauce could use more garlic."

"Unfortunately, *signora*, I'm allergic. But please, hand me a broom and I'll sweep up."

Rosa raised her whip of a brow." So, the ballerina doesn't cook. I should have known." Turning to her youngest she said, "Elena, show our guest how to mince."

"I suppose you were raised with servants," said the older girl, Maria.

"Not at all. In Budapest, where I grew up, my mother and sister did the cooking. We lived quite modestly."

"Does your sister dance?"

"Rosa her name is—like you, *signora*. No, Rosa doesn't dance. She sews for my father." I thought it best not to mention that my sister played the violin (ardently, if not professionally), which would only have aroused her namesake's suspicions.

"A hard worker. She'll have plenty of marriage proposals."

Elena aimed her chin at her older sister. "Maria's had two this year—three, if you count the married butcher."

"Butchers can be stingy with the prime cuts."

"You'll have your hands full with Pasquale," Rosa said, not unkindly. "Likes his food, his wine, does whatever he pleases... I could tell you stories. He would never go to school. He'd sneak into the cinema and stay there until all hours."

"When he wasn't practicing with his band—"

"Or skulking around the music shops—"

"Papa forbade him to play the piano. The piano was for girls."

Rosa clucked her tongue. "Your father wanted his eldest son to earn a respectable livelihood. Any parent would have done the same. But Pasquale—well, you'll just have to see for yourself, Margherita, and good luck to you."

We rejoined the men. Salvatore had not budged from the wireless.

"Any word on Nobile, *signore*?" I asked.

The old man only upturned his palms.

Pasquale reached across his father's lap and shimmied the dial. "Nobile, Nobile... what was he doing up there anyway? What's to see in the arctic? Ice. Snow. And for that they die." A blast of static followed by Bernardo De Muro's all-enveloping tenor. "That's better, isn't it?"

Salvatore's fist came down on the armrest. "Don't say that. Don't say that they're dead. No one has said they're dead."

"A blimp falls from the sky into a frozen wasteland and no one dies. Fine."

"Just don't say it."

Father and son looked away from each other.

"Some welcome. My own brother won't shake my hand."

The women, busy with pepper grinders and baby rattles, left the pair of them to sulk.

"Lunch is ready," said Rosa, stepping back from the table to scrutinize her handiwork. "Emilio, get another chair. Margherita will sit beside me."

The family arranged themselves in no discernible order. Platters were passed up and down the length of the table—antipasto, macaroni, fried cod ... The men tucked napkins beneath their chins. The women fed the children from their own hands.

Rosa inspected my plate. "I suppose you're on a diet."

"Not today, *signora*."

"So, what do you hear from Vittorio?" De Sica she was referring to, her son's childhood friend.

"He's in Rome getting chummy with the *Radiotelefoniche*, doing some plays, some recording. Rome is the place to be now. Mussolini wants the American imports out—music, movies.

Someone's got to replace them."

"You," I said. "Why Vittorio and not *you*? If Rome's the place to be, then you need to get a foothold there."

Mamma Rosa tapped a finger to her temple. "She's got horse sense, your *innamorata*.

The maestro took a generous swallow of Chianti. "No argument there. I'm making her my manager."

Time passed pleasantly enough, but no sooner had the plates been cleared from the table than Pasquale glanced at his wristwatch and said, "Enzo needs to get back. Where'd I put my jacket?"

"Always the same," his mother said, raising her chin to mask the umbrage heavy on her features. "He eats, he goes."

Pasquale, already kissing cheeks en route to the door, pretended not to hear her.

"I'll bring your son back to you, *signora*," I promised her. "If I have to box his ears, I'll bring him back."

The Frustacies, prodigal with good wishes, shadowed us to the landing. As the maestro detached from them and took a first step down the staircase, his mother clamped a hand to his shoulder and tugged him close. Into his ear she whispered something that, for an instant, seemed to bring him to the brink of tears. Years would elapse before I learned (from Rosa herself) what had passed between them. "This is the one," she had told him. "Marry her."

♪

Fire consumed the next theater the troupe was to have played (omen or chance?) and we landed back in Rome for an overnight. I hadn't seen the fire, had only smelled the smoke as we re-boarded the train. By the time we disembarked, the incident was forgotten, the air bracing and clear. The troupe took to the streets in loose formation. Somewhere along the Via Veneto in a squall of pigeons, the maestro fell into step beside me.

"Trying for a new world record?" he said, short of breath, his fedora precariously angled. "I've been trotting at your heels up and down the length of Italy." My companions walked on, trailing amused glances. "What, I got egg on my face or something?"

A distance opened, a distance measured not in meters but whispers.

The maestro waved off the few stragglers. "Run along, *ragazzi.*" He bounded from the curb toward an arriving tram and grabbed hold of the door handle, letting it pull him the last graceless paces. "Aren't you coming?" he called.

All eyes turned in my direction. The carriage gave a slow lurch forward. Abandoning caution, I broke into a run, took the maestro's hand, and let myself be lifted aboard.

"Where are we going?" I asked.

"Let's see if Vittorio's at home. I owe him a visit."

We rode to Parioli, an elegant district disproportionately populated with show people where Vittorio lived with his first wife. The building in which he rented a flat gave off a scent of old leather and freshly minted banknotes. An elevator had lately been installed, marring the symmetry of its twin stairwells. We rode up one flight. Pasquale knocked at a broad door waxy with fresh paint and I heard a woman's voice call out with obvious irritation, "Who could it be at this hour?" A moment later Vittorio appeared and ushered us inside.

"Hail Caesar! Where have you been hiding?" The two men embraced. Our host, his smoking jacket stiffly new, turned to me with a lopsided grin, "And this lovely lady?"

"Vittorio, meet my fiancée, Margit. Best thing to come out of Hungary since paprika and she's got talent besides."

From the next room the invisible wife ribbed him, "Another dancer?"

Vittorio shrugged, an apology. "Mouth on that woman. Never mind."

He led us through a dark foyer into a parlor decorated in the modern style. The flat had a certain understated elegance: small rooms, high ceilings, floors of cracked and faded tile. Newspapers and glossy magazines lay scattered.

"Please sit down, Margit. What can I get you? I know better than to try to make a dancer eat, but how about grenadine? And you, Pasquale, the usual?" By which he meant wine, the most ordinary in those days. "I was just saying to Marotta, where in hell is that Pasquale? There's no keeping tabs on you."

"I go where the work is. Can't remember the last time I stopped in a city for more than a fortnight."

"And our Hungarian guest—is she also with the comedies?"

"She speaks Italian."

"You might say my life has become a comedy of late."

"Thanks to a two-bit con-artist," added the maestro, casually circling the room before taking a seat beside me. "Handed her his usual line."

Vittorio gave a knowing nod.

"Oh, Buffarino isn't so bad."

"Maybe, maybe not," rejoined Pasquale. "Anyway, I owe the scoundrel. How else would I have met the most divine ballerina ever to grace a stage?" He raised his glass. "To Buffarino, the lying bastard!"

"To Buffarino!"

"To Italy!"

"To Hungary!"

"To us!" Pasquale took a lingering sip of wine. "God, I'm beat. Man in the train kept bellyaching about his kidneys all night. All night. If I ever get like that, promise you'll shoot me. Mind if I stretch out on your sofa for five minutes?"

"Make yourself at home."

"Take your shoes off," called the wife.

"Don't mind her," said Vittorio, walking to the door and noisily closing it. "Have you heard the rumors? Turin may lose the film industry to Rome. Everyone's talking about it."

"Just as well, Turin has no heart." Pasquale laid his head in my lap and slung his legs across the cushions, looking like an overgrown boy. "Let them make cars."

"Italians have always had a natural affinity for film. Something about the medium excites us, but have we tapped its full potential? Not nearly. And in the current climate, we won't. We don't dare."

"What, they giving you problems at the *Radiotelefoniche*?"

"It's the same litany everywhere. Look at Toscanini."

"Spare me. He'll make a bundle in America."

Vittorio let the remark drop. When it came to politics, the two friends walked the same uncertain line. "Don't tell me, Margit, that you've cast your lot with this old troubadour? One bad night on a train and he can't even sit up. I suppose he's mesmerized you with melodies."

The maestro yawned in protest.

"We're artists," I told Vittorio. "We want the same things in life."

"May it always be so, *amica mia*." He gave me a smile tinged with melancholy—the look I associate with him still, though he would later evade the invisible wife and find happiness with another woman. He spoke haltingly, as if faced with a puzzle. "Life has a way of pulling people in opposite directions. You wake up one day and there's a wall between you. Pasquale's a good sort, but restless. Listen to him, snoring. He's got a smile on his lips. Must be dreaming of you. In fact, I'm sure of it, Margit. A beautiful woman can dance her way into a man's very dreams."

♪

Ballet did not seem much on the minds of my fellow ballerinas the autumn of 1929. Enrico Cecchetti, the ballet master under whom we had dreamed of studying at La Scala, died suddenly the same year we arrived in Italy. A year later, the great Diaghilev followed him. Upon what personage, what stage, were we to pin our hopes? Europe's classical school had lost all direction.

To outside eyes, we had come up in the world. After one or another lackluster performance Karola, having more pocket money than the rest of us, reserved a table at Savini's. We walked together from the theater to the Galleria Vittorio Emanuele, linking arms as we used to as students. Even with the lights discreetly dimmed, the restaurant's foyer glowed with cut glass and silver. Tucked into a far corner, a tuxedoed pianist played "Honeysuckle Rose." The maître d' led us to an elevated alcove. He addressed Karola by name and asked after her fiancé, whose claim to a privileged view we enjoyed by association.

"I've dined here three times this week," said Karola, svelte in a fitted jersey dress, her hair ironed into marcel waves that slyly framed her dimples. "See that man two tables over, yellow cravat. Sets the program at La Scala. Zingarelli hunts with him." She took a gilt cigarette case from her purse and passed it around the table. "Zingarelli knows everyone."

Teréz eyed the man with his proud yellow throat. "I've seen him at a party somewhere. He likes boys."

Ilona giggled.

"Don't laugh. They say Diaghilev was the same way. Look what it did to Nijinsky, poor lamb."

"Shall we order?"

Of the meal I remember little. We sipped wine between courses, talking of trifles—the Duce's war against the swimsuit, the latest in face creams, the craze for Latin dances ...

"What do you hear from Hungary?" asked Karola, a common enough question among the four of us.

Ilona yawned. "My mother says prices have gone through the ceiling."

"And the opera house?"

"Nothing ever changes at the opera house."

I had had a letter recently from Margit Horvath, a ballerina of some standing with whom we had trained. "A few male dancers have come on board. Boys, but with potential."

"How I shall miss playing Romeo!" quipped Karola, puffing out her chest in a burlesque of masculine ardor.

Having emptied a bottle of expensive wine, we laughed more than the joke warranted, laughed becomingly, aware of being watched by the men around us, and then fell oddly silent.

Teréz pushed away her dessert plate, cleared a space, and inclined forward with her wrists primed on the table edge. "I've had it with touring, and anyway Boselli's asked me to marry him." She turned the gold ring on her finger, revealing a diamond the size of a hundred-lire piece. "I'll be staying in Milan."

What was there to say but congratulations? We made much of the engagement ring, admiring it from all angles.

"My, but you're dripping diamonds, *Signora* Boselli."

"Just don't let him lord it over you. Men think they can buy a woman's submission."

"It will take more than diamonds to tame Teréz."

"But what will you *do* without dance, without the life?" The wrong question to ask, the wrong moment, but wine has a way of loosening the tongue.

"You talk as if there were no other," Teréz said, forcing a smile, "as if life ended at the footlights. Perhaps that's where it begins."

In vain Ilona tried to match her levity. "You'll find out soon enough."

Again the table fell silent.

Karola stretched in her chair, looking like a pedigreed cat. "You might as well know," she purred, "I won't be continuing on either."

"Zingarelli?" we said in unison.

"None other."

"These Italians can't resist us," gloated Teréz, her four carats flashing. "Had we arrived sooner, Rome might never have fallen."

Unwound by then, we laughed more than before, shaking like putty against the upholstery. For what seemed a long time our nerves kept us bobbing and tittering until, emptied of whatever it was that had brought on such hilarity, we went still. In the background the piano played a medley of old parlor songs. Karola tapped time.

Ilona gazed across the distance with the beaten smile that would seal her spinsterhood. "That leaves just the two of us. I guess we're the *Pas de Deux* now, Margit."

My sister ballerinas turned to look at me, but it was Guerra's face I saw, its Mediterranean ardor, sparks flying from his flint lips. *One does not dance on air, Miss Wolf. Even a ballerina must tread this hard, cold earth...*

"This is no time for glum expressions," Karola scolded, sweeping the tabletop of its crockery in a single deft stroke. "We've everything to celebrate." Our arms intertwined, drawing us into an embrace whose symmetry no longer mattered. We clung. "The champagne's on Zingarelli, girls. Waiter!"

♪

The production folded with a reluctant curtain call that lasted only long enough for the audience to locate the nearest exit. The troupe clipped its bows. In the dressing room we shed our costumes for the last time, gathered our few possessions into satchels, and arranged to meet at the *Carioca*, an after-hours club notorious for its sweaty conga lines. Teréz and Karola said a hurried goodbye, promising to stay in touch.

"You'll come, Margit, won't you?" Ilona wiped the pancake make-up from her face with a scrap of chintz. "Last nights can be so maudlin. I don't want to go alone."

"And your sweetheart?" She seldom spoke of the fencer, but some days earlier I had seen her leave the theater in his glinting Alfa Romeo.

"Ferretti? He's away on business." She looked at me in the mirror as she spoke, cold cream rimming her heartbreak eyes. "Come with me. We won't stay long."

I sent word to the maestro via a stagehand and he agreed to meet us at the club.

Ilona, dribs and drabs of cream still dappling her face, slung her satchel over a shoulder. "I hate empty theaters. Nothing but echoes."

We walked briskly out, stopped at the pension to leave our

things, and the night being mild, continued on foot to the *Carioca*. No sooner did we make our entrance than a group of musicians, acquaintances of the maestro, pulled us onto the dance floor. My eyes scanned the room for Pasquale.

"He's not here yet," whispered a timpanist, moving his hips to a Latin tempo, closing-in pelvis first.

I left the floor and wove through the crowd to position myself near the entrance. I took a table. The music, heavy on brass, had everyone swaying, grinding. An actress I vaguely knew dropped into the next chair to fan her face.

"I suppose you'll be returning to Hungary," she said.

"One day."

"Then it's true what they say about you and maestro Frustaci?" She shook a finger at me as if to rebuke a child. "Naughty, naughty," she said and lumbered upright to drape herself across a man with gold teeth.

Into the vacated chair flopped Ilona, flanked by the timpanist and a frizzy-haired youngster missing a front tooth. "This is Giuseppe," she said, tousling the boy's wiry curls. "He's run away from home to become an actor."

"I found him outside the theater. Kid just hangs around on the street."

"You mustn't encourage him," I scolded the timpanist. "The boy belongs with his family."

"Go home, kid. You heard the lady, scram!"

Wearing the same vapid grin, Giuseppe and the timpanist sidled off together in time to the music, which had grown louder. Ilona took a glass from the man with gold teeth, sipped deeply of a fluorescent pink liquid, and handed it back. "Naughty, naughty," I heard the actress chide her companion. "Naughty, naughty," he parroted back.

To my relief I looked up and saw the maestro, pausing alongside the table to survey the havoc. "I must be late, party's in full swing," he said distractedly. Then turning to face me, "My wallet, again."

35

He commandeered a chair from a nearby table and joined us.

"Aren't you going to dance?" said Ilona, rising unsteadily to her feet.

"Later maybe. You be my warm-up act, eh?'

"Dance? *Ballare?*" Ilona, randomly tapping shoulders, shimmied toward the dancefloor.

"I don't like this place." Pasquale sat erect in his chair, legs crossed, nostrils pinched. "Bad crowd."

"Something's wrong with Ilona. I've never seen her like this."

"She's drunk."

"Ilona doesn't get drunk. She barely touches alcohol."

We watched her bump about the dance floor, passed along from one set of arms to another. "Only thing to do is take her home," said Pasquale. "Keep an eye on her while I get a cab." He made to stand up but was shoved back into his seat by a man in black.

"Hey, watch it," the maestro protested, springing back onto his feet with his arms poised to strike. By that time the man in black had penetrated farther into the club, shadowed by ten burly youths, similarly uniformed. The dancing continued. "*Mambo, que rico mambo ...*" crooned a quartet, trying to sound like Perez Prado.

The lead blackshirt raised a megaphone to his lips. "*Silenzio!* In the name of the fascists, I order this den of iniquity closed. All present will produce their papers."

"The hell we will," said the maestro.

"*Silenzio!* In the name of Il Duce—*maledizione!* Block the exits, boys!"

The maestro pulled me from my seat into a crush of bodies. "Hold on tight," he ordered, beginning to maneuver through the crowd like a tank.

"We can't leave without Ilona."

"There she is!" With his free hand he gestured toward the deserted bandstand, where trumpets and conga drums lay scattered like the debris of war.

The ballerina had stepped onto the stage where, fists in the air, she loosed a babel of invective into the microphone. "*Puritani*! *Hypocritak*! Who are you to judge me? I came to this country a virgin…"

We pressed toward her and mounted the stage, arriving a scant step ahead of the blackshirts.

"*Disgraziati*! Go home to your illiterate mamas…"

Pasquale encircled Ilona at the knees and bundled her over his shoulder. "*Brava, amica mia*! A real firebrand you turned out to be, but be still now. A retreating army doesn't sound a fanfare." Then deadpan, like a colonel to his lieutenant, "Get that door, will you? There's a service exit down the corridor. I'm glad I got my wallet. If they've stationed more thugs outside, flash some bills."

"Filthy hypocrites," muttered Ilona. "Offer them a few lire and they prostitute themselves like anyone else."

"Right you are, *amica*." The maestro staggered forward under his load, eyes twinkling with merriment. "In the name of the fascists," he intoned, a poor imitation, "I declare the world a den of sin, a garden of earthly delights, a delusion… "

"Don't drop her."

"Not to worry, she's light as a feather." He took a few zigzagging dance steps. "*Mambo, que rico mambo …*" Ilona gave a low moan, and Pasquale reached up and burped her like a baby. "A night to remember, Manci," he sighed. "One goddamn beautiful night."

♪

I paid a week's rent at the pension. There were cheaper places in less desirable neighborhoods, but an artist could ill-afford to appear down on her luck.

"We could economize by moving into one room," suggested the maestro, already anticipating my response. "I wouldn't take advantage."

"Of course, you wouldn't. But I might."

He laughed with a moderation that was not like him. He had

bought a new fedora and absently nudged it this way and that. "I suppose you envy your friends, getting hitched to rich men who can butter their bread on both sides."

"Men they don't love. What's to envy?"

"I've got nothing, Manci, but if there's an express train to *la vita frou-frou*, you bet I'll be on it."

"Save me a seat, will you?"

We walked to a nearby café and ordered coffee with biscotti. It felt strange to be alone together without a pretext for stealth. Our acquaintances from the comedies had gone their separate ways, the chosen ones to begin rehearsals on a new show, and the rest to scavenge for work, as we were left to do.

"How's Ilona?" the maestro asked, pushing away his cup.

"Sick. I put her to bed in my room. She thinks someone tampered with her drink—the pranks men pull. Ferretti gets back today. It's best that he not hear about it."

"Word gets around."

"I'll take her some breakfast. She'll be fine."

Pasquale gazed into space, lit a cigarette, and drummed his fingertips against the clothless table edge—his way of composing music. Only later would he go to the piano and tap out the melody all of a piece. Having my own thoughts to occupy me, I kept silent until his hands had gone still and his attention returned.

"Drink your coffee." I watched him down the rich expresso in a single swallow. "Buffarino is off to Hungary for fresh recruits. We've fallen out, he and I."

"You don't need Buffarino."

"Maybe not, but I need to dance."

"You still miss the ballet." He said this accusingly, jealously, as if searching the closet for a rival.

"I miss what ballet *was*. The only remnant is the Bolshoi, no place for a Hungarian. The comedies may be all the audience I ever have."

He hid his relief behind a prow of noble intentions. "We'll

find work."

"Karola has given me some leads, one here, the others in Rome."

"Let me follow them up," he said, taking charge with an air of grim determination. "And I'd better look into renewing your papers. They're not so friendly to foreigners anymore."

We parted at noon, stealing a kiss in the vestibule of a ministry building rank with shoe leather and printer's ink. Drab suited clerks crept past shuffling papers. "Trust me, I'll have them treading grapes," the maestro said and strode off.

With storm clouds gathering at my back, I returned to the pension. Ilona had gone out. Laundry hung from every hook and pillar. I opened the door and peered down the corridor—no one. I walked to the window, wrenched open the casement, and could see nothing but a gray sliver of alley. I tried to read the newspaper, but my mind would not focus. The bells atop the Duomo chimed noon, the doorknob turned, and Ilona, damp-haired, backed into the room, her arms heaped with dresses and perfume bottles.

"Feeling better?" I asked.

My friend spun on her heels to face me. "You shouldn't go scaring people like that." Breathless, she leaned against the door as if to blockade it.

"What happened to you? Your face…"

"Nothing. An accident."

I made my way toward her. "Here, let me help you with these things. Sit down. I'll get a cold compress."

"Is it bad?" She cupped a hand to her blackened eye. "It doesn't hurt, not really."

"But you're trembling."

"Ferretti—I think he has me followed. He knows where I go. He knows every moment of my day."

"We'll leave Milan."

"Leave Milan?" She curled in on herself, cradling her own ribs. "But Teri and Karcsi are here. I couldn't bear to go home to

39

Hungary, the only one not to…not to… Perhaps Ferretti will take me back. Yes, I think he will. He was just a little upset with me."

I sat beside her on the bed remembering the affecting little girl she had been, moodier than the others, prone to extremes. Guerra had once called her "the Tempest." Had she but learned to harness her passion, what a brilliant dancer she might have become!

"My Ferretti's got a temper," Ilona said with a sort of pride, "but that's because he cares." She drew herself up with wounded dignity. "A man's got to love a woman to care that much. Yes, I do believe the old boy's in love with me."

"Of course, he loves you. We all love you."

She threw her arms around me and hugged until it hurt. "Then he'll take me back, won't he? Won't he, Manci?"

♪

While we searched for work, I arranged for Ilona to stay at Karola's flat in Magenta, a tree-lined district north of the city. The idea was not to hide her from Ferretti, an impossibility, but to give her a few days' respite, a chance to reflect. Karola sent Zingarelli's driver to the pension. Ilona, her bruises hidden behind a coating of pancake, donned a broad-brimmed hat for the ride. I went along, intending to stay only long enough to get her settled.

Karola came to the door coiffed and perfumed in a white peignoir, her face radiating pleasure. "My poor Ilonka, poor dear… poor, poor Ilonka. Men are beasts."

"It's not Ferretti's fault." Ilona pouted, her makeup cracking like old varnish. "They spiked my drink. They made loose with me. I barely remember."

"But to hit you—the man should be castrated."

This being a first visit, Karola led us about the flat, pointing out its modern features—a gas cooker, a flush toilet—saving for last a large mirrored room with a polished mahogany barre running the length of it. "Zingarelli fitted the studio out himself. I don't use it nearly enough."

"I miss taking class," said Ilona. "The routines. Knowing what was expected."

Karola pirouetted across the floor in her satin bedroom slippers. "It was prison. We never played like other children, never expressed ourselves. The steps were imposed on us."

"Imposed? It's natural for a child to take instruction."

"We were lumps of clay, hardly children at all."

I ran my hand along the barre, so solid and steadying. "But look at the discipline it's given us. Look what it's made us."

Karola glanced toward Ilona, who eclipsed by her own hat brim stood staring into the mirror at the shadow she had become. "Come, let's get out of here." She led us back through the parlor to the overstuffed settee piled high with silk and brocade pillows. "It's the maid's day off, but there's paté, cheese ... music, we could listen to the gramophone. How about a nice bubble bath?"

I made my excuses, rode back to town as the afternoon began to dim, and arrived at the pension to find the maestro pacing the corridor outside my room. Slow to notice me, he continued to circle, rattling the coins in his pocket, tripping over a loose floor tile.

"Waiting long?"

"An eternity," he said and leaned hard on the doorframe as I inserted the key in the lock.

"I left as soon as I could." This seemed to placate him, although he said nothing. "How did things go today?"

He stepped into the room after me and hurriedly closed the door. Starved for an audience, he launched into his account with obvious relish. "I'd forgotten how long a day can be when you're not working. Stand on this line, stand on that line. Signor *Il Pezzo Grosso* will be right with you. And what does he do? Sends you to another office. Rigamarole starts all over again."

"And?"

"Always impatient, my *babuci*." He drew me close and stroked all the way down. My buttock fit in the palm of his hand. "I thought of you all day long. I ached to touch you—"

41

"Don't." If a woman aspired to marriage, the line had to be held.

"You just pretend you don't like it. It's a game with you." He turned away as he always did when aroused. He had the delicacy not to let me see him that way. "Hell, I'll buy you a cup of coffee," he said, already reaching for the door handle.

"Sit a moment."

"I can't. I can't be alone with you. Get your hat."

We left the pension in single file and spoke little until seated at a café several streets distant. Trolley cars streamed past, carrying people home from work. Stray cats prowled at our feet. The maestro, choosing his moment, inclined across the wrought-iron tabletop and said with the utmost nonchalance, "How would you like to play Paris?"

"Don't joke."

"Who's joking?" He reached inside his jacket, paused, studying my face, and finally extracted a manila envelope. "Our contract," he said, waving it aloft. "What Frustaci promises, he delivers."

"Paris! I didn't dare to hope."

"That's just the beginning. From Paris we head south to Marseilles, from Marseilles to—ah, I forgot Lyon."

"Spain, will we see Spain?"

"Barcelona…"

"Flamenco!"

He struck a pose: arms in the air, fingers playing imaginary castanets. "A finale in Madrid, and then home—second-class, unfortunately. I don't have your knack for haggling."

"No matter, maestro," I blurted, giddy with good fortune, "I could sleep in a cattle wagon!" One of those things we say without thinking. Years later, traveling in just such a wagon, I would recall the remark, the setting, and how the maestro laughed. No ordinary laugh, which would have been souvenir enough.

"A cattle wagon," he repeated, slapping his sides with mirth. "Ah, *babuci*, the things you come out with!"

A man in uniform. An officer of high rank, judging by his many-colored medals and epaulets: *Capitano* somebody—Panciotto? Panciuto?—under whom the maestro once served aboard the battleship Galileo. He sat washboard-stiff in the audience when we played Madrid, Pasquale having procured him a front-row seat.

"But what is he doing in Spain?" I asked.

The maestro waved the question off. "These military types. Always poking their noses where they don't belong."

After the show, we took our guest to an after-hours club, where the cast often gathered for a late supper and a round of cards. We chose a table in a far corner. The captain surveyed the room before seating himself, back to the wall. Although the place could not have been more of a rumpus, he remained buttoned to the chin.

"So, Frustaci," he said, "has your stomach finally settled?"

Normally, the maestro would have returned the ribbing, but instead he laughed it off. "Some men leave their hearts at sea, I left my entrails. Who'd have thought we'd survive the Straits of

Messina? That squall, and the slop they fed us."

"I don't remember a squall."

"Okay, I imagined it. How is the old crew—Franco, Gianni, that skinny kid with the tonsils?"

"Shipped out, most of them." He lowered his voice. "Little disturbance in the colonies."

"Say hello when you see them."

"Likewise, my regards to your family."

"My mother still asks for you, that dashing officer with the mustache. Your facial hair alone endeared you, but when you accepted second helpings you entered the pantheon of gods. Stop by when you're in Naples."

A waiter took our order and left behind a plate greasy with finger food.

"*Prego*," the maestro said, motioning for the captain to help himself. "I prefer the food back home. No one eats like us Italians."

The meal passed in small talk and jokes whose punch lines carried the addendum, "You had to have been there." By the time coffee arrived, conversation had lapsed altogether.

But the captain was only biding his time. "That discharge of yours, Frustaci—"

"I owe you for that," the maestro hastened to say.

Our guest raised a hand. "I'm not here to call in favors but to give you a piece of advice. The climate has changed, *is* changing. When the Navy let you go, we had all the hands we needed. Things were quiet. We could afford to be humane—do you see what I'm getting at?"

The warning could not have been plainer, but the maestro played dumb.

"What I'm saying, *amico mio*, is don't expect that discharge to hold forever. If it were up to me, I'd leave you to rot on land— you're a lousy sailor—but the Navy has gotten less selective lately. I've got men in my charge with no teeth and one thumb."

"Teeth I've got. Just tell me who I have to puke on to get out of this outfit."

The captain, unmoved, sipped his coffee. "My advice is, take out insurance, make a gesture. With so many of our men stationed abroad, it's tough to maintain morale. Put yourself in their place: the heat, the flies, the smelly natives. What they need is—"

"Women."

"What they need is diversion. They would love this revue of yours, the orchestra, the charming dancers." For the first time that evening he acknowledged my presence. "Wouldn't you like to entertain the troops, *sorella*," he prompted me, "to dance for men who are risking their lives for the glory of Italy?"

"It would be an honor." Having yet to grasp Mussolini's grand design, I could say this sincerely. "We Hungarians have always considered Italy our second *patria*."

The maestro faintly rolled his eyes. "Look, I'd like to do my bit, but put me in the water and a squid's got better rhythm."

The captain flicked his brass wrist buttons. "*Basta*, Frustaci, comparing yourself to a jot of blubber." He folded his dinner napkin into a precise triangle and slapped it onto the tabletop. "The Navy would provide transportation, of course."

"Where to?"

"Why, Tripoli, of course. I'm headed there myself tomorrow morning." He pushed back his chair but did not get up. "You've been thrown a lifeline. This little junket will stand you in good stead. I'll see that the right people hear about it."

We all rose in unison, and the maestro gave his old acquaintance a mock salute.

"See you in Tripoli, *Capitano*," he said with the bitter sangfroid of a condemned man.

♪

Today there is a sameness about places: the hypermarchés, the arrow straight highways, the pidgin English. Not so in my day, when Italy was still Italy and France, France. Spain, Moorish despite its boulevards, might have belonged to another continent altogether. Theater was the only constant. To dance, to make music, to draw the audience into a dream ... with the Depression bearing down and all Europe re-arming, never had people been more avid to lose themselves in spectacle.

The maestro and I were at a café somewhere near the sea, I watching the passersby, and he, sickened by the smell of fish, bemoaning our impending voyage. "It will be like a holiday," I tried to reassure him. "We'll see the sights. I've read that the Italians have built a lovely esplanade along the waterfront, paved roads, excavated ruins ..."

"Whole country's a ruin. What the hell are we doing there anyway?"

"Restoring the Empire." A phrase I had read in a newspaper editorial.

He threw up his hands (the same gesture, the same bodily vim, with which he conducted overtures). "Government's sucking us dry, and what for? So some Arab can ride his fly-infested camel along an esplanade."

"We have no other engagements," I felt obliged to remind him.

"I'll find work." The response had become automatic. He'd ball a fist each time he said it.

"Karola will know someone. She's always been a magnet for the right people."

He looked stung. "When are you going to learn? You can't count on friends. Me, I've always made my own way, I don't owe a fig to anybody."

"You've seen the queues in front of the cinemas. Talkies are what the public wants. When did we last play to a full house? Look at all the theater people pounding the pavement— musicians, actors, dancers." Indeed, it was the dancers who appeared the hardest hit of all. "And who gets the attention? Josephine Baker. Must we strip naked and convulse like crazed primitives for a moment in the limelight?"

"Baker's a novelty."

Something Hungarians no longer were in Western Europe.

"The way I see it, you've got two things going for you. One, you can dance. And two"—he thumped himself on the chest—"Frustaci. Have I ever let you down?"

I picture him at that table with his puppy-brown eyes swimming, seasick on dry land. "Am I asking too much, Pasquale? I just want to dance."

"You will, *babuci*," he said, making fists of both his hands. "This is Italy, home of all things beautiful—and what's more beautiful than a great set of legs?" He laughed at his own joke, but the cackle had gone flat. "Work I can always find."

♪

Ilona and I packed for our return trip to Italy. My sister ballerina, whose mood throughout our travels had alternated between giddy elation and cavernous despair, clicked shut her suitcase only to open it again. "Have you seen my red garters?"

"Under the bed."

"My sleeping draft?"

"Have you eaten today?" I took an apple from the windowsill and handed it to her. "We'll get you a proper dinner on the train." I doubled back and glanced down at the boulevard with its gray stream of pedestrians and low-hanging clouds. A black Alfa Romeo pulled up to the curb of the hotel and began to honk its horn, to honk loudly, piercingly, like a half-slaughtered goose.

Ilona veered. "If I didn't know better…"

"Stay where you are!" I kept my eyes on the car, recognizing the fencer at once. He had slid out the driver's seat door and stood in the middle of the street, craning his beefy neck.

Ilona leapt forward, tripping over her suitcase. "It's him, isn't it? He's come. I knew he would."

The honking began again.

"Stay down! He hasn't seen you. I can tell him you've gone back to Hungary."

"Where's my red dress? Ferretti always liked me in red."

"I can tell him you're engaged to a gangster."

"My hair could use a washing and I've lost weight—Ferretti hates it when my bones poke out. He was always sending me chocolates: the round ones with cherries, the little bricks with rum and raisins..."

I got hold of her shoulders. "You don't have to take him back, Ilonka."

"Don't be silly, Manci," she said and pecked me on the cheek, "it's only a lover's spat. Loan me a dab of your Chanel?"

"Help yourself."

"You're a darling. I'll have Ferretti invite us somewhere swank."

"Some other time." I resumed my packing. The train was scheduled to leave within the hour.

Ilona slithered into a flame-red jersey dress and doused herself with eau de toilette. Rehearsing a smile, she pirouetted to the window and called out, "*Ciao, caro!*"

Ferretti shouted back, directing her to meet him in the lobby.

"Come with me," she said, fumbling in her purse for powder and puff. "I think he's a bit afraid of you."

The cad could wet himself with terror for all I cared.

"Come, hurry. I can't wait to see his face when he sets eyes on you."

"His Excellency Ferretti can wait. We'll collect Pasquale on the way."

That the two men had never liked each other was apparent: they were too polite, too quick to light each other's cigarettes. The fencer wore showy clothes of a cut I had not seen. The maestro could have used a shave. Ilona had applied enough perfume to stun a herd of bison. We were the only patrons in the small dining room. In every corner a waiter stood with his back turned, noisily sorting cutlery.

"You're keeping well," Ferretti said to Ilona and bowed stiffly from the waist.

She looked as if she might strike him—there was fire in her tartar eyes, fire in her jutted hips—but instead she kissed him on both cheeks and fell lightly into a chair. "I have always admired a man who can lie. A well-told lie can be very useful."

Ferretti laughed, revealing his one defect: teeth that might have belonged to a fishmonger. He did not laugh often.

"Where have you been?" Ilona asked with forced nonchalance.

"America. The summer games."

"Ah."

If Ilona had expected Ferretti to say more, he disappointed her. A liar he may have been, but he was more apt to lie by omission than embellishment. He sat back preening his cuffs.

Pasquale signaled the headwaiter. "What shall we have?"

Too late for lunch, too early for dinner, we ordered coffee— Ferretti had his with a jigger of brandy—and lit up cigarettes. The men made small talk about yoyos and Mickey Mouse, American imports then new to Italy. Trivia spared them from saying anything of substance, about which they would surely have disagreed. I watched Ferretti's hand slide beneath the table to rest on Ilona's knee.

"It's getting late," I said.

Ilona pushed away her cup, got to her feet, and said coolly in the fencer's direction, "I guess we'll run into each other back in Milan."

Ferretti, still seated, his athletic chest pressing at the seams of his expensive foreign shirt, waved the remark away. "I've booked us a suite for the night. We'll leave in the morning."

"I don't know..."

"What's the hurry? No one's expecting me back home, I've seen to that. We'll spend a few days at the coast, hire a motorboat, maybe try our luck at the casino."

The anger melted from Ilona's features, leaving her face as bright and dewy as a spring thaw. "Oh, *caro*! Who's in a hurry?" She slid back into her seat and helped herself to a drag from her lover's cigarette. "You don't mind, do you, Margit?" she said in Hungarian. "You have other company." She angled a penciled brow toward the maestro. "And besides, the train can be so tiring."

♪

The maestro and I stepped off the Simplon at the central station, surrendered our luggage to a porter, and trudged out to the street where a cabbie leaned against his Fiat, whistling "*O Dolci Mani.*"

"So you like Puccini?" the maestro said amiably.

The cabbie did not lift but swung our bags into the trunk. He opened the rear door with the same brute vitality. "I was weaned on Puccini—*Tosca, Madama Butterfly, Aida...*"

Once we were seated, I whispered in Pasquale's ear, "The man doesn't know Puccini from Verdi."

The maestro shrugged. "He knows what he likes.

It was dusk. The streetlamps fluttered on, turning the sky an iridescent mauve, the streets a steely blue. A glowing ribbon of rainwater edged the tram tracks. We followed it to the Brera district and returned to the same pension we had left the month before. Recognizing us at once, the proprietor wrenched himself from a plate of polenta and hastened to his post behind the reception desk.

"*Bentornati!* Signora Karola has been calling for Signorina Margit—not once, not twice ... a most persistent woman. She finally sent her driver with this message." He plucked a monogrammed envelope from the key slot and handed it to me.

I thanked him and tucked the envelope into a coat pocket.

Again we took two rooms, though we could barely afford one. Because the hostelry was booked to near capacity, the rooms did not adjoin. Setting down our luggage, we opened the door of the first.

"No view," said the maestro glumly.

"I'll take it. You can have the other."

Minutes later he returned to sulk, "Brick walls to every side. Bricks to high heaven." Still wearing his fedora, he collapsed full-length onto the bed. "So, what did Karola have to say?"

I reached into my pocket and drew out the envelope, which

had strands of linen running through it and smelled of rosewater. "Perhaps it's an invitation. She had promised to introduce us to that Austrian count."

"I wouldn't mind playing Vienna. The Viennese feel their music."

The note said only that I should get in touch the moment I returned.

"If that isn't Karola all over," the maestro jibed. "What are we supposed to do, read her mind?"

"Forget about it. I'll take the tram there in the morning." I opened the wardrobe and began to hang dresses.

"Leave that for now," he said and patted the space beside him. "We haven't been alone in ages."

"You exaggerate, and besides, we have a busy day tomorrow. What a bear you can be after a long train ride."

"There's no rest for me without you in my arms."

I took a step toward him, drew back, not trusting myself to close the distance. "I'm sorry, Pasquale."

The maestro swung his legs over the side of the bed and hunched forward, cradling his head in his hands. He held this posture. When at last he spoke, his voice poured out so slowly it might have been paraffin. "How long can we go on like this?"

The very question I had been asking myself.

♪

"Come in, darling, come in. Let me look at you. New cloche, isn't it? And your hair—didn't I tell you the stylists in Paris were out of this world?" Karola stepped back for a fuller inspection. "You're becoming quite the sophisticate." We kissed cheeks and walked with arms linked to her plush settee.

"And you, you've never looked more radiant."

"Does it show? I've been keeping it to myself, but you might as well know. Zingarelli has popped. We'll be married this June." She extended her hand to display a postage stamp-sized diamond encircled in sapphires that shone the same blue as her eyes.

"A jewel for a jewel." The expression came readily to my lips.

My father had said it when he bought me my birthstone, a single pearl on a fine gold chain. I wore it still.

"Thank you, darling. But I didn't ask you here to bask in my own happiness. It's yours that concerns me. No doubt you've heard by now, Diaghilev's old company is regrouping under Rene Blum." Could my surprise have been more apparent? "Blum, of the Monte Carlo Opera? Zingarelli knows him. In fact, we'll be paying a call on him this coming week."

"You'll audition?"

"Me, no. The opera house is keeping me busy enough. And there's Zingarelli to consider, the figure he'd cut abandoned at the altar while his bride races for a steamer. But you, Margit, do you think I don't know how you've suffered lifting your skirts? Refinement like yours doesn't belong on the popular stage. Blum could be your ticket."

"I've lost form."

Encircling my waist, she tugged toward an enormous beveled mirror. "Nonsense, you're trim as a reed," she said and traced the line of my torso along the glass. "You've kept your discipline. You could be ready to audition in a matter of weeks. I'll arrange it. Balanchine's already on board."

"Balanchine! To dance under such a genius…"

"Blum's staking everything on him."

"No risk there—"

"And I'm staking everything on *you*." There is no yoke as binding as another's faith.

"What's the matter, darling? Stage fright? We came to Italy with such dreams, the four of us."

"We came to Italy pie-eyed as children. What did we know?"

Karola walked to the casement and gestured out. She looked so fragile from behind, as if her bit of flesh clung to a skeleton of crinoline. "You can see La Scala from this window. That's why I took this flat, so that I won't forget what brought me here."

"Forget? It's what we've lived and breathed."

"Then dance, Manci! Dance like a firebird on a high wire.

Take your own dare. There won't be another chance."

I looked down at my feet, feet that could not have looked more common in their buckled shoes. It seemed suddenly extraordinary that such appendages had ever propelled me across a stage.

"Surely you don't doubt yourself?" whispered Karola. She had left the window and crept up behind me, propping a near-weightless hand between the blades of my back.

"No, it's not that."

"Look, if you're concerned about practice, move in with me until the audition. You can chain yourself to the barre."

"It's good of you, Karola, but—"

"Pasquale. I know what you're going to say. Don't be naive, my friend. Your maestro is like a parasitic vine, he latches onto any woman who gives him the time of day. Twenty years from now he'll still be pounding away at the keyboard, and you? What will be left for you?"

"I'll talk to him."

"Don't talk, *tell* him."

"Pasquale is an artist himself. He'll understand."

"Here's the key to my flat." She clapped it firmly into my palm. "Make yourself at home. And dear, it only hurts for a little while, leaving a man. One night in the spotlight outshines a thousand between the sheets."

She was wise in her way, Karola. Zingarelli gave her his name, surrounded her with every luxury, opened doors. I might have done worse than take her advice, but it was too late for revisions. Imagine a wind so strong that your feet leave the ground. You're carried along... carried along until there's no going back to where you started and no knowing where or when you will land. That is love, a one-way ride to the brink.

♪

Each day I waited for the right moment to broach the subject of Blum. The maestro, bowing to necessity, spent mornings poring over sheet music at Azzura; evenings he taught at their choral school. Better a pigeon today then a hen tomorrow, he rationalized, and who was I to argue? For me, no work had been found at all. Before long my funds would run out and I would be dependent on him for the roof over my head, for my next morsel of food.

"Not to worry," he assured me, "I'll work like a beaver. Just leave it to Frustaci. And besides, I've already cut a deal with the *Capitano*. If I can put together a first-rate revue—say, two dozen artists—there might even be a few lire in it. We sail for Tripoli at the end of the week."

"Assemble a troupe in *one* week?"

"Easy." He brushed palms, once, twice. "Half the artists in the business are out of work."

No sooner had the maestro left for Azzura than the pension's proprietor knocked at the door. "A message for you from Signora Karola," he said with ill-concealed irritation and held out another of her perfumed envelopes.

The note consisted of a single line: "*Have you told him?*"

I put on my most becoming hat and went out. There was still enough daylight by which to read the marquees. I waited for Pasquale in the piazza nearest the choral school, waited on my feet, pacing, and watched him approach in his dandyish suit, humming a tune only he could hear.

"But *babuci*," he chided, assuming his parental stance, "why aren't you at home resting?"

I said the first thing that came to mind. "The pension ran out of coffee."

"I'll invite you for a cup but only one sugar, and then I'm seeing you home. When did we last get a night's sleep? One of the actors has found us a place to rehearse, a relative's warehouse, but we can't start until midnight—they're expecting a shipment of bananas. Why I let you talk me into this trip…"

"Would you prefer another stint in the Navy?"

We took a table at a popular café not far from the pension. We sat outdoors and let the night air nip at our faces. The maestro's smoke rings hovered above his head like a jester's cap.

"I've got this great number for the revue, all I need is a singing camel." He waited for me to laugh and then drew me close and nuzzled my neck. "When we get to Tripoli I'll buy you a silk veil and have you dance the "*Pizzicato*" for me. Me, alone."

"Pasquale, I can't go on this trip."

"Don't tell me you're getting butterflies, too? Rough seas, uncharted shores. If it weren't for the troops, I'd take you home to Napoli and fatten you up."

"Listen to me," I said more sharply than I had intended. "Please. These shows we perform, they're all the same—the stunts, the dances. The standard does not change, only the costumes."

He recoiled as if thumped on the chin. "It sells tickets."

"If I had a chance to return to the ballet—"

"The ballet's dead in Europe. You said so yourself."

"I was wrong. Rene Blum is reviving Diaghilev's *Ballets Russes*, bringing the finest artists back to the Continent."

"What are you saying?" A cocked index finger rose and fell in time with his breath. "The rest of us don't count, eh? Are you walking out on me, is that what you're saying? After all I've done."

"I am a ballerina."

"What am I, eh? An organ grinder?"

"If I had a chance to dance again, to dance as I was trained to do, you would want that for me, wouldn't you?"

"Don't ask. Don't ask me to be noble and let you go. I can't, damn it. Don't even ask."

"But, Pasquale—"

He brought both his hands down hard on the tabletop and then pitched forward, palming the cups of coffee as they hopped from their saucers. "Don't! Rene Blum—who's Rene Blum? I've got all the big names lining up for me: Toto, Montalbo, Osiris ... A few more years and I'll be flying high with De Sica."

"Of course you will. You've got the songs."

"Damn right. And it won't mean a thing if you're not there beside me." Without warning, he sank to his knees on the dusty cobbles. "Marry me, Margit."

"Get up."

"Marry me right now. Marry me or I'll crawl after you all the way to Monte Carlo. I'll do worse: I'll commandeer a fighter plane and smoke bomb the theater. I'll drop tomatoes. There's no telling what I'll do ..."

"Get up."

"I'll stand atop the Eiffel Tower crying out your name. They'll have to drag me down and put me in a cell. They'll have to shoot me."

We might have stemmed the course of events with a simple "*Come now, let's be sensible,*" but we were artists, lovers, and what was the art of love if not to risk all?

"Marry me or I'll haunt every stage you ever touch. I'll compose my own dirge and broadcast it to kingdom come. I'll open my veins and rain blood on your ovation. My ghost will stow away in your tutu ..."

I raised him up and kissed him full on the mouth. "My dear maestro, when have I not been your wife?"

♪

The boat docked in Tripoli harbor. The cement esplanade, drenched in torrid orange light, sprawled long and low. A flurry of white parasols streamed toward us, followed in close formation by a marching band, whose members advanced flit-eyed as if awakened by lightning. The captain stood frosty as a block of ice on the pier. But it was the Arabs in their flowing robes and headdresses and sandaled feet that riveted our attention and let us know that we had arrived somewhere very strange indeed.

"Don't get too close to them," cautioned the maestro, peaked from the voyage. "There may be insurgents. Fighting's still going on."

"They look friendly enough."

"Friendly enough to slit your throat with a scimitar," he

muttered under his breath. "Let the others go first. What's all the shoving?"

I stifled the urge to cartwheel down the gangplank. Joking and jostling, the rest of the troupe filed past us. "Who would have expected such a modern city?"

"Only along the waterfront. Like a stage set."

"The hotel looks real enough. You'll feel better after a bath."

"I'll feel better without these natives gawking at me."

"If you're nice, I'll wash your back."

A furtive grab at my derriere. "Just don't make plans for tomorrow, eh?

"Why not?"

"We're getting married, that's why not. I've lined up the *Capellano*—you don't mind, do you, a military wedding?"

I had always imagined myself marrying in a synagogue beneath a *chupah*, as my mother had done and her mother before her. For all my independence, I wished to marry correctly, though what that meant I was no longer certain. "There must be no mention of Christ. You'll tell the chaplain?"

The band struck up the *La Giovinezza*: "*Youth, youth, springtime of beauty...*" Waving from the esplanade, a group of friends cried, "Come along, Margit!"

In memory I am gliding down that gangway with my skirts billowing, my legs bare, and the green oasis sprawling before me like a carpet of plumes. The maestro's lips move silently. In time I will learn to read their melodies. I will hear the music inside his head.

We wed in full sunlight. The captain had arranged a private room for the ceremony, but once the wedding party assembled— the chaplain, our fellow artists—the maestro drew us out into the courtyard, where a donkey grazed on sparse grasses and palm fronds swayed above our heads. A pair of parrots strutted on their perches, chattering in a language I had never heard. I wore white—white dress, white shoes, the camellia in my hair. The maestro held a straw boater. Leaning close, he whispered, "Isn't this perfect?"

How to explain that a wedding divorced from tradition, *my* tradition, seemed like make-believe, that I played a role not my own?

We said our vows, exchanged rings, and the parrots preened and went on chattering. There was a piece of paper to sign, long lost, and then, back in the private room, a champagne toast. The captain, starched from his eyebrows to his cuffs, raised his glass and bellowed, "*Figli maschi!*" May you have male children.

"*Figli maschi!*" echoed all present.

Having fulfilled his mission, the military man excused himself with a trim salute.

"Where'd you dig up that two-bit actor?" said the maestro's timpanist. "Miracle he didn't exit goose-stepping."

A second toast, to Italy's fighting men and their safe return home. A third to the parrots. We were quickly running low on spirits. And then one of the singers slipped out a rear exit and returned carrying a large brass cage. "On behalf of the troupe, I'm pleased to present you with—"

"What's a good name for a monkey?"

"For chrissake!" The maestro began to roil with laughter. "Smile for Frustaci," he cooed to the creature, tapping at the cage's brass bars. "That's one beautiful mug, *piccolino*."

"Arab guy we bought him from might have been one of the Forty Thieves."

"Thief nothing, the guy was a *babi*—you know, a disciple of the Bab. This monkey's holier than the Three Kings' ass."

I crouched beside the cage, the better to see the little one's baby pink face. "But he's trembling." The creature twitched and jabbered, his twiggy limbs pressing at the walls of his prison. I opened the cage door and he leapt at my bodice. He clung, smelling of wet grass. "*Ne félj*, Bábi" I whispered. Don't be afraid. It seemed natural to speak to him in Hungarian, a language as cryptic and mellifluous as his own. I cradled him like a child, soothed him with caresses. "*Ne félj*, Bábi. There's nothing to be afraid of."

A few months later, once Vittorio had found us a flat in Parioli, the monkey, grown by then, would swing from the balcony onto a high-tension wire and die instantly, electrocuted. I would retrieve his remains from the street below, and having nowhere to bury the corpse, wrap it in brown paper and place it in the trash bin.

♪

We returned to Rome within the week, playing four tepid performances to an audience primed for new sensations. On the next street Gennaro Righelli's *La Canzone dell'Amore*, the first Italian talkie, was making its debut. Outside the cinema, people queued for hours only to be told that the house had sold out. The maestro used his connections to procure two tickets, and we were admitted through a rear entrance to view a late matinee.

The film was no masterpiece, it had nothing over Hollywood, but the story was taken from Pirandello and dramatized by Italian actors—indeed, when the dialogue ended and the credits rolled, there was not a foreign name to be seen. But only one name interested the maestro. "Did you see?" he brooded. "Cesare Andrea Bixio. Always Bixio. He's credited for the score."

"His publishing company certainly does well. The man must have talent."

"The man's got one talent: making money." The maestro, having spent the brunt of his ire, gave a one-shouldered shrug. He got up from his seat and helped me on with my wrap. "When I won the *Sagra Di San Vicenzo*, did he have a kind word for me? There I was, a kid of fourteen with nothing going for me but these songs. He was a few years older and fancied himself a poet. Suddenly he leaves Naples, buys a couple second-hand pianos, and sets himself up in the music business. Bixio, a composer? A lyricist?"

"He's no Liszt. Still, there might be something worth learning from him."

The cinema had emptied around us. A man in coveralls

worked his way along the aisles, sweeping hairpins and cigarette butts into a tin dustpan.

The maestro's eyes lingered on the blank screen. "He had to have heard my songs—'*Varca Napulitana*,' '*Addio Santa Lucia*,' '*La Vela*'..."

"Any Italian knows your songs."

"You think he'd give his *paesanos* a foot up?"

"The score was nothing special. You could do better."

He slung his jacket across a shoulder with the élan of a toreador entering the ring. It took so little to puff him up.

"When we're next in Milan, why not pay a call on Bixio?" I had learned by then to wield the measure of influence he allowed me. "A social call. Let him bring up business."

We left the cinema as the sun began its slow melt over the Vatican. For a few moments, the city shone like amber. I can recall nothing more beautiful than that fleeting last light, its reflection skimming down the Tiber. We strolled a long way without speaking.

As darkness fell, the maestro tightened his grip on my arm and murmured, "A social call, why not?"

"Keep it casual—shoptalk, chitchat. Let your songs do the selling."

"And if he plays cool?"

"He won't. He's too shrewd to let a winner get away."

My husband's chest seemed to broaden. He looked out over the water, up at the sky, and emptied his lungs. "Hell, a married man can't afford to let the future dart ahead of him. I know my obligations."

♪

The maestro gave notice at Azzurra and we moved to our flat in Parioli, two stark rooms in search of a rug, just down the corridor from Vittorio. Whenever we were in town, he and Pasquale would spend evenings together at the kitchen table. Give them a deck of cards and a bottle of wine and they would amuse themselves for hours. Ageless together, they might have been back in Naples, watching the boats set sail from a table at the American Bar.

"I hear you subdued the savages of Tripoli," said Vittorio upon our return, "came, saw and conquered. What the Italian military failed to accomplish with heavy artillery, you clinched with two-part harmony and a chorus line." He kept the tone light but could not entirely mask his distaste.

"Hardly," the maestro was quick to counter. "We entertained the soldiers and colonists, all of them stupefied by the heat, desperate for any reminder of home. Play '*O Sole Mio*' and they weep like widows."

"Where will you strike next, great white conductor? They say the Duce has his eye on Ethiopia."

The maestro topped-up Vittorio's glass. "Me, I've done my bit for the *patria*. I have a wife now, time to work on the nest egg."

"The economy's not good." Vittorio took a silver 20-lire piece from his pocket and flipped it in the air. "Better to live one day as a lion," he recited aloud, "than one hundred years as a sheep." Every coin bore the slogan. "Easy for the Duce to say, he's got a key to the coffers."

"The only lions are on celluloid. The rest of us, artists no less than laborers, will always be sheep. We've got families to feed."

And so it was. With the rent coming due and the icebox empty, the maestro paid a call on Cesare Andrea Bixio and returned home with his neck bunched and the fedora low on his brow. He slumped dead weight into the flat's one armchair. "It's done," he said, his voice gone to gravel, "I start on Monday."

We took a second flat in Milan, not far from the Galleria del Corso where Bixio kept offices. Some of the best popular songwriters of our day—Cherubini, Fragna, Ruccione—plied their trade there, shut away in cubicles barely large enough to accommodate a spinet piano. A gay cacophony of dance tunes, love songs and brash improvisations buzzed through the walls. Someone was always whistling—someone other than the maestro, who to the end composed stone silent.

Early on, I'd visit my husband at work. Bixio was friendly enough back then, the benign benefactor meting out praise and paychecks. "Married life becomes you, *Signora* Frustaci," he would say with a bow and hurry down the corridor, moving from room to room like a worker bee.

I knew better than to correct him: *Signora Wolf.* The maestro had not offered his surname, reasoning—rightly, no doubt—that flaunting a foreign wife could only hinder his career.

Having time on my hands, I wrote long letters to my family in Budapest, memorized saint's days and metro stops, tried out Mamma Rosa's recipes... Leisure was a discipline like any other, Teréz assured me. With practice, I would master boredom as I once had gravity. Why, then, did the days only seem to grow longer?

"Pasquale, isn't it time I go back to work?"

We were seated on a new sofa, delivered only that morning. It smelled like the bolts of brocade with which my father once dressed kings and courtesans.

"What's the matter, don't I keep you well?"

"Of course, you do," I hastened to assure him, "but I didn't come to Italy to be a housewife."

"You don't want to cook? Fine, we'll eat on the street."

"It's not that. You miss conducting, don't you? It's no different for me, that feeling of bringing a stage to life."

"I know." He sank low into the upholstery. "You think I like punching the clock, putting in time like some pencil-pushing hack? I do it for us, so we can start a family. Don't you want that?"

A ballerina who bore children was finished, I knew. Women of my generation did not lead lives of infinite choice.

"Don't you want to bear my child?" he repeated.

"Eventually." Surely this was the logical answer, if badly timed. "First, we make our mark. We see the world. We put something aside."

"How right you are, *babuci*. Only…"

I waited for him to go on, but instead he dimmed the lamp.

"You'll make a good father."

"The best," he said with utter faith in himself, and scissoring a knee between my legs, eased me down onto my back. His lips found my ear. "Only let's not wait too long, eh?"

♪

Keeping my promise to Mamma Rosa, I coaxed the maestro home for the Christmas holiday. At no time of the year is Naples so entirely itself, prodigal in its piety, a battlefield of processions through streets seamy and smelling of fish. Inside the Frustaci home, the entire family had gathered. There were more mouths to feed, more babies to coddle and clean up after.

It was my first visit as a member of the family, yet the domestic commonplaces, the proprieties, the private jokes already felt familiar. Rosa's gaze fixed on the gold wedding band that had yet to be resized to fit my ring finger.

"For once he's acted with sense," she said, giving Pasquale an ecstatic pinch on the cheek before dissolving in tears. She took me in her arms. "*Figlia mia, figlia mia*… Elena! Maria! Anna! Come embrace your sister. Salvatore! Your son's finally got his head screwed on straight."

Salvatore dragged himself from his armchair and took a few uncertain steps toward the maestro.

"Go on," prompted Rosa, giving Pasquale a nudge forward, "give your old father a *bacio*."

The two men eyed each other, the elder pale, the younger flushed, neither willing to take the last step.

"Go on."

"*Complimenti*," stammered Salvatore, bypassing his son to plant a single kiss on my cheek. "We must drink a toast to your health." He turned quickly away, resumed his seat, and signaled the girls to bring glasses.

"Later," said Rosa. "We will wait for the others." She had not let go my arm and now began to tug toward the kitchen.

I would have liked to have taken my husband aside, but he fled the room, tugged in the opposite direction by his brother Emilio. Salvatore, alone in his corner, switched on the wireless.

An ornate nativity scene covered the top of the buffet. Missing was the baby Jesus, who would be added before mass. Not far from the manger a jug of Chianti. Arrayed throughout the kitchen were more pots and platters of food than I had yet seen, the traditional seven-fish meal lavishly slathered with oil and garnished.

"When did Pasquale last join us for Christmas?" Rosa said to no one in particular. "You'd think he was an orphan." She took up her wooden spoon, lifted the lid on a cast-iron pot. "Maria, the oregano. Elena, the new oil—it's been a good year for olives."

The girls, tying on aprons, jockeyed for my attention.

"How did you get him to propose?"

"Did he get down on his knees?"

Rosa mopped steam from her brow with a scrap of cheesecloth. "Let your sister rest. She's had a long journey." A stitch formed between her dark, generous brows. "You married in a church, didn't you?"

She was a pious woman, my mother-in-law, and I would not have wanted to disappoint her. "An army chaplain married us, a Catholic."

"A religious wedding. *Bene.*"

Dinner preparations proceeded: anchovies added to the vermicelli, the eel fried, chestnuts roasted... Having yet to learn the fine points of Neapolitan cooking, I was handed a lacquered tray and left to arrange the dried fruits. Once the meal was nearly ready, Rosa dispatched the girls to their room to change into Sunday dresses. The kitchen went silent except for the undertone of garlic sizzling in a skillet.

Rosa glanced up. "You mustn't think badly of your husband." Her hands, graceful despite their chipped fingernails and chapped knuckles, worked independently of her mind. "The way he behaves with his father, with Salvatore, he has his reasons.

Salvatore has a hard head about some things, especially when it comes to the American Bar. A business is supposed to pass to the eldest son, that's the way it is here."

"Which is why your husband didn't let Pasquale take piano lessons?"

For a moment Rosa's hands knit together, and then they began to whip the egg whites, to whip them so fiercely I feared for the glass bowl. "Salvatore did more than refuse him lessons. He wrecked the piano—keys, pedals, everything. With a sledgehammer."

The old man glued to the wireless seemed incapable of such an act. Obstinate he may have been, but where was the passion?

"That should have been enough," Rosa went on, "but no, Salvatore couldn't leave it at that. He wanted his son out of Naples, separated from everything and everyone that had put ideas in his head. He wanted to drive the music out of him. A customer had a relative who worked in Parma at the government reformatory—that's where Salvatore sent his son, to a school for delinquent boys. And that's where Pasquale learned to hate his own father."

She set down the bowl, and a mountain of white froth oozed from it. She had to have seen the spill but did not wipe it away. Slowly, the stiff peaks fell.

"You're a Frustaci now, Margherita," she said, jutting her proud jaw. "You're one of us, and you should know."

♪

The New Year came in gusting a clean wind. We returned to Milan on Epiphany and watched the faithful carry their crosses to the Duomo. The nuns in their habits inflated with air, birdseed blew from their hands. It seemed the church bells would never stop ringing. When they did, routine resumed like dullness after a heavy meal.

"I'll need ironed shirts," the maestro murmured, reaching for a newspaper he spread across the kitchen table but did not read. Within moments, he was asleep.

Next day, he arrived home from work at the usual hour, coat slung over a shoulder, the remains of a baguette tucked beneath the arm. "*Babuci!*" he called needlessly (I was already en route to the door to greet him, as was our custom). We embraced. I took his coat, intending to hang it in the foyer closet. "Leave that," he said. "Leave everything."

"Dinner will burn."

"Let it. Let the building burn down. I want to kiss my wife." He backed me against the wall. "You're as beautiful as the day I first saw you—no, more beautiful. You've ripened like a plum."

"And you, maestro, you've aged like fine Tokaji."

He laughed and twirled me across the floor to the sofa, tripping over his own feet. "I miss seeing you dance, looking up from the orchestra pit at those milky thighs with all the gauze about them flying."

"It's been so long, why speak of it?"

"Why?" He began to grin like a cornetto. "Because you are about to return to the stage. Because—here, have a look." He reached into his jacket pocket and pulled out a scrolled paper covered in small print.

"Bravo, maestro!"

The contract was in German, a language I knew like my own, but its legalistic claptrap stumped me. Pasquale made a show of tossing the scroll into the nearest ashtray. "We're going to Austria: four performances in Vienna, two in Salzburg. Top-notch bill." He paused to smarten his lapels. "First-class tickets, of course."

"Keep this up, and I'll treat you to a sleeper. But tell me, what do I dance?"

Pasquale got to his feet and tautly zigzagged. "From what I could make out—the agent had an accent thick as schnitzel—no program's finalized yet, but the dancers are already on board. If any of them doesn't show, you're in."

"*If?*"

My husband stopped pacing. The room fell silent. One could have heard a soap bubble collide with a ball of wool.

"Look, it was the best I could do. The dance director had already closed up shop."

"An understudy—is that what I'm to be? Waiting in the wings while you work."

"Look, I only heard about it today. I'm not exactly a first choice myself. They had some big cheese maestro from Germany, but he keeled over. Bum ticker. I saw the obituary on Bixio's desk, got the afternoon off, and hi-tailed it to the agent's office." The performance finished, he dropped deadweight onto the sofa. "Okay, so I'm not a miracle worker. It's a job: you rehearse, you get paid. I tried my damnedest. I thought you'd be happy."

The smell of charred meat spared me from having to hide my disappointment. Letting the matter rest, I made a beeline for the kitchen.

Pasquale followed, kicking off his shoes as he went, and drew up beside me as I took the roast from the oven. "If it were up to Frustaci, you'd be the Rani of Sarawak."

"And who would you be?"

"Your *marito*," he said simply. The word seemed to stun him, as if he had invented a new language. "Your husband. Yours."

♪

No one was waiting for us when we arrived at the Suedbahnhof. We had been told to expect a driver holding aloft a placard with the maestro's name. As we gathered our luggage, dozens of such placards bobbed into view: *Herr Schwartzkopf, Mr. Smith, Cook's Travel...* The horde of arriving passengers made their connections and drifted off.

"I thought the Austrians were sticklers for punctuality," the maestro muttered, making to glance at his wristwatch but choosing the wrong wrist.

"The train got in late. Perhaps the driver gave up on us."

"Some welcome. We'll have to get a taxicab." He hailed a porter, Vienna being one of the few places where a new arrival is not set upon like carrion. The first comer loaded our bags onto a hand trolley, and we followed him out to the street. Traffic stood in silent rows, the motorists having switched off their engines. "Damn, not a single cab!"

"Strike," said the Austrian, first in German and then in French.

The striking cabbies had barricaded the city's major arteries, paralyzing everything on wheels. Angry words pealed from megaphones. Armed soldiers marched in tight formation along the sidewalks, leaving pedestrians no choice but to weave among the cars.

"You'd think it was a war." The maestro clapped a handful of coins into the redcap's upturned palm.

"It is, I assure you."

"So, what do we do?"

"The metro is not far from here. I would take you, but..." The porter gestured without object. The impossibility of maneuvering the trolley through the crush of bodies could not have been plainer.

And then a single voice rose above the din, crying out in an expansive baritone, "Maestro Frustaci? If you can hear me, maestro, kindly raise a hand!"

"*Ecco,* Cecil B. DeMille." Pasquale took the handkerchief from his pocket and waved it in the air.

A ruddy-faced gent in cashmere and gators parted the crowd and emerged larger than life. An arresting figure both in height and width, he spread his arms as if to shelter us. "Maestro? Mrs. Wolf? I do apologize. With conditions what they are..."

"Is the limo nearby?" the maestro said rather too abruptly.

The stranger looked offended. "The driver is stranded in traffic, as is half the populace. I'm the manager of the Theater an der Wien, Gabriel Saunders."

I extended my hand. "It's so kind of you to come, Herr Saunders."

"But your German is flawless, Frau Wolf."

"My mother had family here. She insisted on speaking

German at home, believing it more refined than Hungarian."

"Of course, one language for the street and another for family." A fleeting look of recognition passed between us. We were Jews, however assimilated, and knew our own by instinct. "Fortunately, your hotel is quite nearby. I've rung the reception and a bellman should be along any moment."

"Very kind. I trust the theater is having a good season?"

"One can't complain. For now. And yet—I won't bore you with politics. All Vienna has become a theater of late."

The maestro, understanding little German, took Saunders' commentary as a joke and laughed politely. "It's the same in Italy."

Our host looked doubtful but mustered a laugh of his own. "Let's hope the politicians don't steal our audience entirely. The German elections have been commanding more than their share of attention—politics again. Forgive me."

"Traffic seems to be moving."

The Austrian's relief might have filled an arena. "I hope you will not be further inconvenienced during your stay."

"Is that the bellman I see scrapping his way toward us?"

"None other. Good. Marvelous. Movement." The big man craned his neck in all directions, and then, drawing in his elbows, bowed. "Now I must leave you. Our *chanteuse* arrives from Paris at five. If you'll excuse me."

The maestro clicked his heels. "See you at the theater, *capo*."

Herr Saunders received the homage with a straight face and promptly vanished into the crowd, leaving a void the size of a baby grand. His mighty baritone drifted back, "Rehearsal at eight. English time."

♪

"*Ausgerechnet bananen*... we have no bananas today." The chanteuse, satisfied with the An der Wien's acoustics, gave the maestro a coy thumbs-up. Her name was Zarah Leander. No one had heard of her back then, she was just another Swede trying her luck. "At your service, maestro."

Pasquale hadn't the gift for languages. He liked to joke that he had chosen music as a profession because, regardless of where it was played, the notation remained in Italian. But Hollywood he could speak, the verbal shorthand of the talkies. "From the top," he said and the orchestra leaned to attention.

"*Ausgerechnet bananen...*"

A stagehand sighed, "With melons like those who needs bananas?"

I made a friend of the Swede. Touring throws people together who might otherwise stay strangers, the need to share impressions, to sit opposite someone at a table.

"How do you stand it?" she said, offering me a flamboyant red Sobranie only to beg a light. "Surely an understudy can't help but think, if only the prima ballerina would turn an ankle or suffer an attack of hiccups. It's only human."

"Let her dance her part."

"I don't have your generosity. Who comes to this business wanting to play second fiddle? One is either a star or nothing."

Her candor both refreshed and appalled—in this she was fully a woman of her times, single-minded, free of scruples. She also happened to be beautiful.

"Have you gone for a screen test yet?" she asked.

"Not yet."

"Acting lessons?"

"No."

She touched a pinky to her lower lip and removed a speck of tobacco. "Dance can be a hard life and where's the future in it?"

"I don't think of life in terms of hard or easy. To a ballerina dance *is* life."

She brought her ringed fingers down on the table edge with an eloquent resonance. "You've got moxie."

I never forgot the remark, though so much else has gone by the wayside—the names of Zarah's various husbands, her face powder, the corset shop she swore by... We corresponded for several years. True to type, she rose to stardom, amply filling the gap left by Marlene Dietrich.

The production came off smoothly until the penultimate performance, when minutes before the curtain was to rise, the second soloist had a lover's quarrel with the choreographer and stormed off the stage.

"Here's your chance," whispered the maestro. Giving me the wink I knew so well, he pulled on his white gloves and vanished into the orchestra pit.

There was barely time to lace my toe shoes. The costume mistress thrust a wand into my hand and out into the footlights I glided. *"Don't think, little mouse,"* chided the voice of memory. *"Dance!"*

A cambré. A pirouette. Chassé right, chassé left. It is not my feet that carry me but my soul. I am La Sylphide, casting my spell on the sleeping bridegroom, enveloping the room in light...

The maestro would later tell me that my eyes shone like burning coals, that I spun so fast and surrendered to the role so completely the string section dropped their bows.

"A harmless entertainment not lacking in sequins," opined the *Neue Freie Presse,* adding, "The surprise of the evening was provided by stand-in Margit Wolf, who, it seemed, had taken flight." The troupe basked in encores and set out, overconfident, for Salzburg. Herr Saunders dispatched us to the train station in a fleet of hired cars. Too much of a gentleman to take his leave at the theater, he insisted on accompanying us for the ride.

"It has been a pleasure to have you with us, *Frau* Wolf." He towered over me, more mountain than man. "You must come back soon," he said in his lush baritone.

"If there were work, I'd return on the next train."

"Talent like yours—not since Elssler has Vienna seen the likes of it! New productions are forming all the time. I'll call around."

I felt my husband's eyes on me, probing. He could not have understood our conversation but sensed my mounting excitement. "*Paroles,*" he whispered, waving away Herr Saunders' words like so much smoke.

The Austrian gave me his card. "Check back with my secretary in a week or two. Don't wait too long." We exchanged pleasantries for a time before noticing that the car had come to an absolute halt.

"Not again!" exclaimed the driver.

Herr Saunders leaned forward in his seat. "*Was ist das?* Don't tell me the cabbies are still acting up." Coloring, he unwound the cashmere muffler from his neck. "There's no order anymore. No order and no sense."

The driver rolled down his window. "Listen, *mein herr,* they're singing."

"Let them serenade someone else. These good people have a train to catch."

"Do you hear? It's '*Die Wach am Rhein.*'" A song all too familiar now. "*There sounds a call like thunder's roar, like clashing swords, like surging waves...*" The driver sang without self-consciousness, drumming with fury on the steering wheel. "To the Rhine, to the Rhine, to the German Rhine!"

"Enough!" Herr Saunders rasped, wrestling free of his overcoat. "Raise the window. Sound your horn. Get us out of here."

"No chance of that. They're marching."

"Marching, singing—you'd think they were an army."

The driver sat awed. "The Lord's own. So many torchlights. A stirring sight, *ja?*"

A wall of fire rose in the distance, fanned out, and snaked slowly toward us. Powerless to cross it, we could only watch the tongues of flame lap at the metallic night.

Herr Saunders hunched toward my ear. "Stirring? The Nazis strut victorious through the streets and this fool bursts into song. We are witnessing the death of Austria. Mark my words, Frau Wolf." He yanked open the door. "The bags, Smuts. Just get the bags."

♪

Consult any history book and you will know that Herr Saunders was a sort of prophet—not that anyone listened to him or would have acted differently if they did. The war had never ended, it had just bled itself dry for a decade or two. Behind the smokescreen of peace, Europe's vanquished were staking new claims. The Duce promised us wheat and glory. Empty our stomachs may have been, but our heads were brimming with Fred Astaire "Puttin' on the Ritz," slide trombones, showgirls bursting out of frosted cakes... Buy a ticket in the *Lotteria di Tripoli* and win six million lire! Who had an ear for doomsayers?

The Nazis wasted no time in spreading their gospel to Hungary, but Horthy wasn't having it. Karola often traveled to Budapest in those days, dancing her pick of roles at the opera house. After each engagement, she would return in triumph to her villa in Milan and host a soirée, dozens of mismatched guests in evening clothes snapping their fingers to Count Basie, moving to the forbidden rhythm—*gez*, we called it—and the gramophone records brand new, not yet out of their wrappings. Zingarelli kept the champagne flowing. After a midnight buffet Karola had a liveried houseboy roll out the waxed Steinway, and the maestro took his cue and played requests.

"Righelli's here tonight," he would whisper in my ear. Or Garinei or Rascel, men who had hitched their wagon to a star and could, if they chose, pull those less well-known along with them.

"I'll have Karola introduce me." We had been friends too long to stand on ceremony.

I would like to think those meetings planted the seeds of my husband's eventual success. At the time, they seemed merely an exchange of small talk with the din forcing strangers into ever closer proximity. I could have named the bath soaps of half the film producers in Turin—which is not to say I knew them. Strangers we arrived and strangers we parted, but knowing one another's scents, primed for the hunt.

The random Hungarian with enough talent or money to make a name in the arts would sooner or later land an invitation.

You could pick him out of the crowd by his outmoded clothes.

Karola would take up the refrain, "Nothing ever changes in Hungary…"

Which, true or not, did nothing to assuage my homesickness. My sister ballerinas would carry gifts back for my family, from Milan fine confectionary, from Naples painted ceramics, trifles bought on impulse to salve a guilty conscience.

"They were at my last performance," remarked Karola one evening, "your mother and Rosa."

That would have been in thirty-four, a period of relative normalcy, the same year my brother József married and opened a leather shop opposite the Terézvárosi Church.

"They came backstage."

"How did they look?"

"Szidonia, sturdy as an ox. And Rosa… Your sister has never seemed part of this world, the weight of her gaze and the rest of her so feathery she seems to float. She gave me something for you. Wait, I'll get it." Karola crossed the room on tiptoe, lifted the lid of a music box—"*Clair de Lune*" it played—and removed a filmy silk handkerchief lavished in appliquéd calligraphy. "Have you ever seen such delicate handwork?" She surrendered the gift with apparent reluctance. "But what does it say?"

I studied the myriad stitches, stitches as tiny and precise as the pores of an egg. It was in German, a quote from Goethe: "*A great talent finds its happiness in execution.*"

Karola turned away, but not quickly enough to hide her look of pity. "Isn't it time you make a visit home?"

"Pasquale can't get away."

She tossed back her golden waves. "So? Just get on a train."

"It's not that easy." For her it was, everything was, she had forgotten what it meant to steer among flawed choices. "Pasquale would give me the money, but my papers have lapsed."

"Why didn't he take care of all that when the two of you married?"

The marriage had yet to be registered. "It was a religious

wedding," I tried to explain, "not long after the Lateran Accords." Mussolini's dirty deal with the Pope legitimizing marriages made in the church.

Her blue eyes narrowed. "Tell that to the *carabinieri* when they escort you to the border."

"The maestro, naturally, will arrange the papers. It just takes time."

"Let Pasquale drag his feet, talk to Ferretti." She brushed her hands together, a theatrical one-two, as if the matter were decided. "When Ferretti says jump, people jump."

I told her I would, if only to put her mind at rest.

And then Herr Saunders reappeared, a foreigner walking alone on the streets of Milan, peering hungrily into storefronts, craning his head to read the marquees. I barely recognized him, though nothing obvious had changed, at least not at first. He remained a bulky presence, impeccably dressed, overdressed, but the brio had left him. His proud head seemed suddenly too heavy for its stem.

"*Guten tag*," I greeted him, extending a hand. "Don't you remember me, Herr Saunders? Margit Wolf. The maestro's wife."

He took the proffered hand, kissed it, kissed it again. "You? Here?" His voice had diminished by half.

Was I still naïve enough to hope he might have a role for me?

"Of all the coincidences…"

"What brings you to Italy?"

"Hitler," he said flatly.

"If you're alone, if you have the time, I'd like to speak with you. There's a park nearby."

He followed in silence, seated himself at a polite distance, and then turned to survey the surrounding benches.

"No one can hear us."

He looked unconvinced but began at cautious volume to speak. "Your husband is Aryan, Frau Wolf, is he not? Better for you." He paused, took another look around. "I like the Italians. They've lost any inflated sense of destiny. No one can lead them by the nose."

"And your family?"

"I've sent the children to a school in Switzerland. My wife is presently packing up house. I'm on a reconnaissance mission, you might say, assessing prospects."

"But the An der Wien—"

"My dear Frau Wolf," he said with the lugubrious courtesy of a mortician, "Austria is no different from Germany. They have a plan for us. What we have seen is only stage one: bring down the highest, take away our livelihoods, make us grovel."

I thought him, not mad, but under too much strain to judge events soberly. My first thought was to calm him. "A man of your experience will surely find prospects good in Italy."

"I'd like to think so, and yet ... "

"You mustn't lose heart."

"How much clearer it all is in hindsight! A person would have to be blind not to have seen it coming: the Austrians feared the Nazis, but they feared the Communists more. The middle ground couldn't hold." He emptied himself of breath and began again. "Along comes Hitler—high school drop-out, failed artist, author of that rabid book. Who could have expected my countrymen to take such a *schmendrik* seriously?"

The Italians had barely noticed when the Duce met with the Fuhrer in Venice earlier that summer. It was rumored that the meeting had gone badly, one endless clash of personalities. The advent of Flash Gordon had caused a greater stir.

"Do you know people in Italy?"

"A few," said the Austrian.

"Let me give you my address. Please. We'll stay in touch."

Herr Saunders seemed for a moment to disappear into his own chest cavity—ponderous head, gizzardy neck—but his voice grew, indeed seemed almost the operatic baritone of old. "That is kind, Frau Wolf. You do my heart good." He took the calling card in both his hands, examined it under a lorgnette, and tucked it snugly away. He bowed. I could see a bald spot starting at the crown of his head.

"You needn't worry, Herr Saunders, with so many theaters…"

Upright once again, his face flushed, he nodded without conviction. "Of course, why worry? *Abi gezunt.*"

♪

I felt sorry for Herr Saunders, never suspecting that I daily skirted the same trap door down which he had fallen. That I would soon return to the stage seemed certain—hadn't they applauded me in Vienna? Hadn't the critics sung my praises? My moment in the spotlight had been too brief. A dancer who cannot perform feels the blood dry up in her veins.

I still began each day with practice, using a towel rack as my barre.

"The roof could cave in," the maestro liked to say, "and you wouldn't miss a *battement.*"

It was a question of preparedness, I told myself. Youth was then the fashion in ballet—all eyes were on Balanchine's "baby ballerinas"—but tastes change and talent endures.

The morning of my twenty-fourth birthday I began practice at the accustomed hour, in the brief silence between midnight prayers and the soft drink truck. Any moment Pasquale would awaken and call for his coffee. So little time.

"When you're a hundred years old, you'll still be coaxing your poor body into these contortions." My husband was up early. He leaned in the doorway, rubbing his sleep-swollen cheeks. "Surely you've earned a day off?"

Without deigning to look up, I inched to the floor in a full split. "There are ironed shirts in your bureau."

"Forget work," he said, sinking down onto the floor beside me. "Let's celebrate. I'm taking you to Turin, to the Ambrosio" (as elegant a movie house as had ever been built). "The *avanspettacolo* there is something you should see."

"You know how I feel about those two-bit revues."

"Yes, yes, you once compared them to an indigestible

goulash, but the category has come up. Consider it research."

We caught the express train, which moved not much faster than the donkey carts it displaced. Between the two cities people lived as they had for centuries, oblivious of urban development schemes and the Fiats rolling off the assembly line. Turin's film industry was in eclipse. Spurred by the Duce himself, ground had already broken outside Rome on Cinecittá, and anyone in the know could enumerate its marvels: fourteen sound stages, three water pools, 40,000 square meters of walled complex...

The Ambrosio was showing Camerini's *I'd Give a Million*. Vittorio starred in it, playing by turns a rich man and a pauper; having been both in real life, he could not have given a more convincing performance. But when I think of that day, the screen is mere backdrop. Center-stage stands a line of scantily clad amazons, the Bluebell Girls, once the toast of the *Folies Bergeres*. English most of them, dressed in little more than feathers, they kicked so high that their platform shoes might have brought down the chandeliers.

"That's Margaret Kelly over there," the maestro whispered, motioning with his chin toward an elegant woman in the front row. Illumined for a moment by a spotlight, she kept an airtight self-possession. "You can pick out her girls anywhere, the way they tower above the crowd. I suppose there are men who like that, to be dwarfed by a woman, but most Italians... well, it's no secret what Italian men like."

"Enlighten me."

"Just look at Teréz."

A generous derriere had done nothing for my friend's ballet career.

"Bring back a troupe of foreign dancers like Teréz," insisted the maestro, "meaty where it counts, rump like a pair of sun-kissed muskmelons, and you can write your own ticket."

Until that moment I had not thought about assembling my own company, but the notion seemed suddenly a lifeline. Kelly was Irish, a dancer at the end of her career, yet she moved freely on the Continent, fêted by those who might otherwise snub so unexceptional a talent. "My troupe will have technique, line, not just voluminous derrieres."

"Line can't hurt."

"There's no substitute for classical training."

The Bluebell Girls high-kicked in unison and then flounced off the stage to thunderous applause. Called back for an encore, they shimmied until their boas flew. I searched the darkened theater for Kelly, only to watch her twirl a chiffon scarf about her shoulders and slip out a rear door.

The maestro kept his eyes stubbornly on the stage. "*Is not art*," he conceded, mimicking to perfection the Hungarian accent I still labored to efface.

"But they have a certain—what's the word? *Balzo.*"

"A rubber ball's got bounce. These gals could kick your teeth in and fry your eggs without a skillet."

"Dancers I can find, but the red tape..." New government ministries seemed to sprout every day, regulating everything from stage names to skirt lengths.

The curtain came down, the lights up, and the audience started and shielded its eyes. I lingered in my seat, nursing a small, fierce hope. "My bet's on you," Pasquale said, giving me first a wink and then a glancing punch on the arm, all the encouragement I needed. "But these gals have the market cornered on legs. Forget legs."

♪

It began with a stomach upset. A twinge in my lower abdomen would awaken me just before dawn, too late for a warm cup of milk, too early to put on coffee. The maestro, a light sleeper, would breathe into my ear, "A bad dream?"

"Go back to sleep."

My husband, a natural skeptic, propped himself on an elbow to study my face. "You've been like this every morning—for how long?"

"It's nothing. Dinner didn't agree with me."

His expression held equal parts ecstasy and terror. He lowered the sheets, raised my nightdress, and cupped a hand to my stomach.

"Flat as a board," I felt obliged to point out.

"I'm taking you to the doctor."

Soon, I was round with my son. The flesh came on suddenly, thrusting at the seams of my dresses, announcing to all and sundry that my body was no longer my own. Women stopped me on the street to recommend midwives, onion poultices, the proper saints to consult when home remedies fell short.

"Naturally, you'll have the child in Naples." In Milan the maestro worried about the air, in Rome the excitement. "My family will take care of you. They have experience in these matters."

Mamma Rosa soon wrote to say arrangements had been made. It was decided that I would join her in my seventh month, until that time my husband and I would stay in Milan, living as quietly as possible.

My sister ballerinas, none of whom would bear children in their lifetimes, stopped by most days. My belly was a source of wonder to them, its sheer size and the way the skin went on stretching to accommodate its load.

"Remember when we danced the role of fairies in *Sleeping Beauty?*" reminisced Karola, then at the peak of her career. "The entire company filled the stage to celebrate the birth of Princess Aurora—what pageantry! What magic!"

"We had only to wave our wands, " said Ilona, "and the future was whatever we willed it."

Not since the Dark Ages had women had so little say over their own bodies (let alone their lives), but why scuttle my friends' illusions? In a country that revered motherhood alongside all the Popes, the stigma of barrenness hung over them. Mussolini's cronies had gone so far as to call birth control a crime against the state.

Back in Budapest, my family received the news of my

pregnancy with an outpouring of good wishes and the hand-sewn layette handed down from mother to daughter through the generations. I wrote to thank them, wrote again, but weeks passed without a response.

When at last a letter arrived, I recognized my brother's handwriting, schoolboyish in its correctness, *i*'s dotted, lines ruler-straight. The same careful script with which we, as students, had filled composition books. Greedy for family news, I tore open the envelope and began to read on the landing. The next I knew the maestro, his nose red from cold, still wearing his topcoat, called from the doorway, "What's the matter? Something the doctor said?"

"*Nem.*"

The letter was in my hand, as was the door key, and I was standing at the window, the casement open, leaning hard against the sill.

"Cold as a crypt in here," said my husband, tossing his coat onto the living room sofa.

I held out the envelope.

"But this is in Hungarian."

"About my sister—" I returned to the first line: *Something unexpected has happened...*

"Rosa? Don't tell me she's found a husband!"

"She's dead."

Pasquale's face disappeared into his palms.

"She died in her sleep. She would have been twenty-two this month."

He raised his head, glanced anxiously at my waist, and began to sob—stopped just as abruptly. "You mustn't let this affect you."

"I can still hear her violin ... she had no other voice, Rosa."

"It's unnatural being a spinster. A woman needs a husband."

I walked blankly about the room. "I must get home."

"Home? Your home is with me. You're having my child."

"My father isn't taking it well. He's ill."

81

"Your brother will look after him. *Certo*, we'll send a wire. Here, write down what you want to say and I'll run it to the post."

"Not enough. My sister is dead. My family needs me."

The maestro lowered the casement with a thud. "*I* need you. Your place is with your husband. You'll stay in Naples as arranged. My mother and sisters are expecting you. The air is best in Vomero. Your family can come and visit, eh? They'll see how well I keep you."

"*Tumbala, tumbala...*" The melody seeped like blood from a wound. "*Tum balalaika, shpil balalaika, tum balalaika, freilich zol zein.*"

My husband fumbled in his pocket for a Silk and lit up. I found my way to the sofa and folded in on myself, breasts distended against my belly, belly leaden atop my thighs. A tank could not have budged me.

"*Sing balalaika, let us be merry.* She played her heart out. She played herself into an early grave, and who listened?"

"You mustn't upset yourself like this."

"*Tumbala, tumbala ...*"

He smoked the cigarette to ash and let it drop onto the floor. We owned no rug. "Naples is the place for you. Puts color in your cheeks. Our son will be robust as a sailor, eh? Eh, *babuci*?"

Does an unborn child feel its mother's mourning? I'd like to think not and yet my son has always had a melancholy streak, from the womb, from the moment I felt him swim within me like a tiny merman. My sister became an absence and he that much more of a presence, commanding my attention with the aquatic vigor of his kick.

Italian winters do not last. The redstarts nested, butterflies flitted from bush to bonnet. It was hard to stay indoors. I would walk to the Galleria del Corso and trace circles, waiting for the maestro to emerge from work. More than once, I crossed paths with Herr Saunders—what else had he to do but roam the streets? He had not found a position, subsisted on the occasional translation or lesson (he tutored not only German, but classics, art history and music). His wife painted miniatures. I had yet to meet her.

"Frau Wolf, what a surprise!" The Austrian's standard greeting. He would bow over my hand, never quite touching his lips to it.

I would ask after his family, and he after mine. It gave us a bond, this distance from our roots and the people we loved, the fear we felt for them.

"Hitler goes to an astrologer and asks, 'When will I die'?" Herr Saunders recited his jokes with a fitting gravity. He kept an arsenal of them larger than any the Reich might amass. "The astrologer responds succinctly, 'On a Jewish holiday'. Hitler, dissatisfied, asks, 'But *which* holiday'? Says the astrologer, 'Any day you die will be a Jewish holiday.'" He never laughed at his own jokes, only threw up a hand as if to say, draw your own conclusion.

German and Austrian refugees, not only Jews but dissidents of all stripes, had continued to stream into Italy after the burning of the Reichstag, some seeking visas to America, others simply lying low. They were hard to spot at first, but slowly their shirt-cuffs would begin to fray.

"If you don't mind my saying, Frau Wolf, you appear— excuse me, but—you're with child, aren't you?"

I had to have been in my sixth month by then, my cargo bulbous and uncontainable. One might have expected congratulations, but the Austrian's face held nothing but care.

"These are difficult times to raise children. Questions of identity."

"My child will be Italian, naturally." If he was expecting me to declare allegiance to a tradition I had neither studied nor practiced, I disappointed him. "We will give our son an education."

"Of course, an education," he echoed sadly, "that is the most important thing."

"A person must believe in the future." What any expectant mother would have said.

The Austrian stepped closer and lowered his voice. "A future *where*? My relatives have left Vienna, Berlin. We are all trying to chart a course through this *mishegas,* but alliances keep shifting. Who will have us? I have applied for a visa at half a dozen consulates."

"You're safe here."

"For now." He surveyed the piazza with a fugitive's agile eye and added, "Perhaps."

There was no convincing the Austrian otherwise, I knew, no anchoring him to anything but reason. As I turned to go he said sadly, "No one would fault you for raising your son Christian, the way events are unfolding ... "

I stretched my coat across my belly and trudged home.

♪

In May, the maestro took me to Naples and left me in Mamma Rosa's care. Relieved to be among women for whom motherhood came as naturally as breathing, I gave in to my body's demands.

"Don't believe what you hear about baby formulas and suchlike," Rosa clucked, peeling clove after clove of garlic. "*This* is what you need. It will give you good milk."

The local midwife felt my stomach, my breasts, and said, "You're too thin."

Mamma Rosa heaped my plate with double-helpings for the *bambino*—a son, naturally—and sent me back to bed at intervals with a ginger poultice across my ribs.

I accompanied the women to market each day. There was a building we passed on the way, a stony old place I might not have noticed except for the unreadable brass plaque set in its façade. The engraved characters were in Hebrew, a language I recognized but could not decipher and that exerted a primeval tug each time I walked by. One day, needing to mail a letter, I ventured out while the Frustacies took siesta. On an impulse I walked to the synagogue, touched a hand to the high iron gate, and felt it open without resistance.

"*Prego, signora?*" A voice at my back, friendly, if guarded. "I'm a little late today. Were you waiting to go in?"

A bearded man in a black skullcap, neither old nor young (younger, in either case, than his palpable gravity suggested) drew up alongside me.

"No—yes. If I may."

"I don't recall seeing you at *shabbos*. You're not from Naples?"

"No, but I have family here."

"You're visiting then? Welcome." He waved me ahead into a shadowy courtyard, talking as he went. "My wife can help you with the *mikvah*, if you'd like."

"Thank you, but it's the rabbi I've come to see."

"I am the rabbi." Without ceremony, he held open the door to a small office.

I stepped inside. My host patted a chair, purled his beard, and waited for me to arrange my bulk.

"I'm not sure if you can help me, or even if I have the right to ask."

"These are troubling times. Unburden yourself."

"As you can see, I am soon to become a mother. My husband is not Jewish. I'm wondering what to do."

"Do?" A hardness entered his voice. "The Law is plain. A child born of a Jewish mother is also Jewish. That is the *way* in Judaism, has always been."

"I see. And there are no exceptions?"

"There can be no exceptions. That is the nature of law." His forehead creased like a page out of a ledger. "You're not observant, I take it?"

"I'm here for my child. I want to raise a child worthy of his heritage."

"You should have thought of that when you married." The rabbi drew in his breath. We might have been sitting on opposite sides of an iron vault.

"*Yossi? Yo-ossi?*" A woman's voice. Into the room bustled a Jewess of the orthodox stamp, long-skirted, her dark hair hidden beneath a kerchief, and no less pregnant than myself. "I brought you coffee, Yossi." Noticing me, she gave a shy smile. Wordlessly, we acknowledged each other's bundle. "Ah, you have company. Shall I bring another cup?"

"Don't trouble yourself, *signora*. I was just leaving."

"You needn't rush off," said the rabbi and followed me out into the foyer. "I haven't told you what you wanted to hear, is that it?"

"Your wife…"

"Yes. Soon, like you, we will be parents. I know what you are going through." He sounded not so much angry as tired. The ledger lines had migrated to rim the beard he sagely stroked. "But Judaism is not a ball of clay to be molded and stretched to circumstance. Whatever you or the gentiles do to your child, as yours he will still be a Jew, *farshteyn?*"

There seemed no point in prolonging the conversation.

The rabbi's hand gently brushed my sleeve. "I suppose you could give him the blessing on his head."

What such a blessing might require I had no way of knowing, but I sensed the rabbi was offering a gift and eagerly I seized it.

"You stand close and put your hands gently on his head, like this." The rabbi's fingers interlaced and haloed my pate like a fleshly crown. "You speak these words: *Ye'simcha Elohim ke-Ephraim ve'vhi-Menashe.* You are asking God to make your child like Ephraim and Menashe, men worthy of emulation. Jacob blessed his grandsons thus before he died, and Jewish parents the world over have continued to do so."

"May your child also be blessed."

"Whatever comes," he said with the absolute calm of a monolith, "*my* child will know where he belongs. A parent has no greater duty in times like these."

When, shortly before my due date, my husband arrived to

stand vigil, I told him to arrange the baptism. "The church, the holy water... whatever is customary. And make sure you get the certificate."

The satisfaction on the maestro's face could not have been plainer, but he had the delicacy to dissemble. "If you're doing this just to keep my family happy—they've been proselytizing to you, haven't they?"

"They don't need to. This is a Catholic country, like my own. The church has a long hand."

"It's nobody's business how we raise our own flesh and blood. You don't have to do this."

He was wrong. Soon there would be no mercy left on this Earth for a Jewish child.

"If it's a boy," I added, "make sure he's not circumcised."

No briss, no bar mitzvah. It would break my parents' hearts. The maestro cupped a hand to my belly and stood, satisfied, grinning down at me, never suspecting that by sparing a foreskin we had saved our son's life.

♪

When the maestro first saw the newborn, his words were, "*Grazie a Dio* he looks like you." But in truth the baby was blonde, fine-boned and rosy in the cheeks, a physical type associated with the Aryan ideal. We counted his fingers and toes and felt ourselves blessed beyond measure to have a normal child.

"Bixio has agreed to be *padrino*." Pasquale touched his son with a single finger, as one might probe the ripeness of a tomato. "Cesare Andrea Frustaci." The name did not fit somehow, but I agreed to it hoping that our Cesarino would grow up as successful as the high-flying music publisher.

"How long can you stay?"

"Bixio will come for the baptism and then it's back to the grind. We'll take our son home. It's all arranged."

"But your family has been so good to me."

"They should be, with everyone jockeying for hand-outs. You'd think I was a lemon the way they squeeze me."

"We can't take our son home, not yet. I'm having trouble nursing. The baby has been suckling at your sister Anna's breast."

He ran a hand over the slack vacancy of my belly and sighed.

"What's a few more weeks?"

"Don't ask me to go back to that apartment alone. I've got everything ready for the baby—a tiny chair, a big blue ball, his first books…"

Unable to indulge him, I resorted to diversion. "Do you know what your little brother said? Six more children and you'll qualify for the Duce's large family award. There's a woman in Naples with twenty-five! She must have enough milk to float a barge."

"Don't joke. Look at me: you've made me a different man. No one exists for me but you and my son."

The separation proved brief. I returned to Rome in early autumn, the heat having subsided and little Cesare loud with health. The apartment felt smaller, but my hands could only reach so far. Vittorio's wife had given birth only days before, and we would put the infants together in a padded crib and take coffee, remarking at their easy intimacy.

"I think they've fallen in love," my neighbor would say.

"They're already betrothed."

My Cesare could have done worse than marry De Sica's daughter, but when the time came it was a Hungarian he chose— a Hungarian model who had never seen an Italian sports car before and was as crazy to escape communism as the rest of us. But I get ahead of myself. My son was still in diapers. His cheeks had kept their baby fat, but the rest of him was so slender he seemed to weigh nothing at all. His father would race home from work each day to lift him in the air like a kite about to fly.

♪

When did we first notice the headlines, the sudden change of tone? Italy was in danger of becoming an empire of half-castes, the editorials warned, under threat by outsiders with foreign loyalties who would, if not held in check, defile the Italian race. People like me. Jews.

One newspaper after another spat its venom—for how long? Long enough to satisfy the Duce's friends in Berlin, one supposes. And then normality resumed, or what had come to pass for it. Was it not normal for Italy to conquer Ethiopia, indeed to redeem the Dark Continent stone by stone if that is what civilization demanded? Normal to ask women to surrender their wedding rings to the cause? Normal for every Italian from the age of five to don a uniform and march through the streets screaming, "*Duce! Duce! Duce!*"

"Pay no attention," the maestro would say each time I waved a newspaper under his nose or recounted a conversation. In his view, governments were like fireworks displays, a lot of noise that would soon be over.

"But we have a son now," I felt obliged to remind him.

"You worry too much, Manci. We're honest people. No one can touch you or our boy."

I chose to believe him. The Italians I knew were friendly to a fault, loved children. Fascism had not hardened them, it was a mere affectation, unnatural. People would soon tire of the hyperbole like some trinket bought on impulse.

"When the economy gets bad enough," the maestro declared, "the Duce's bootlickers will jump ship. An Italian can put up with a lot but not with a bad cup of coffee." By that time chicory had replaced, all or in part, the dark aromatic espresso so beloved of the populace. Milk had been diverted to the production of Lanital, which in turn had replaced wool. For leather we had cork, for coal lignite, for meat rabbit... the whole of our sensory world pervaded by alien smells, tastes, the chafe of synthetic fibers against our skin.

"We need to talk to Ferretti."

"Don't tell me that thug's got a friend in coffee?"

I kept my impatience in check. "My papers, Pasquale."

"Ferretti, eh?" My husband made no attempt to hide his

contempt. "It's not a good time to be talking to men like Ferretti."

"It's not a good time to be without papers."

He gave a sharp little nod, a wordless *touché*. "I don't know... they'll ask questions." The baby started to cry. Without consulting a clock, I knew it was midnight, time to change him and give him his bottle. The maestro could not hide his look of relief. "Let me go to him." By the time I rose from my seat, he was already halfway across the floor.

"What are you afraid of?" I said, but he had turned away. If he heard me, he pretended not to.

"Some set of lungs on our *bambino*," he called from the door of Cesare's room, "a regular Caruso!" The baby stopped crying and my husband stepped hurriedly inside, closing the door behind him.

♪

While I weaned my son, Cinecittá burst into operation, drawing actors and directors to Rome in droves. Most settled in Parioli and shuttled to and from the studio in official limousines. At another time, the maestro and I might have thrown ourselves into the social whirl engendered by such a rare migration, but smitten with our infant son we cocooned for a season, finding in his every gesture a cause for great expectations.

Having submitted to the dictates of pregnancy and lactation for the better part of two years, I began again to think of the stage. Italy had emerged victorious from the war with Ethiopia, but the lira had plummeted. People were not in a generous mood. Coupled with this was a further cooling toward foreigners, upon whom the blame was now cast for everything from low wages to housing shortages.

The maestro tried his stock response: "Pay no attention." We were in the kitchen, I remember, having put our son to bed only moments before. He never slept for long. With luck, Pasquale might finish his dinner before the next salvo of cries would send us both racing to the cradle.

"Perhaps if I changed my name..."

"What nonsense it is, everyone playing at good Roman. Look at Louis Armstrong. The public loves him, but Mussolini gets a bug up the *culo* and suddenly he's Luigi Braccioforte."

"I guess that makes me Margherita Lupo."

Pasquale's hands flew up in protest. The tines of his fork glinted in the beam of the electric light. "How many times do I have to tell you? Leave the worrying to me, eh? I'm bringing home a decent salary. We'll get by."

"With two salaries we could do more for our son."

The maestro couldn't dispute this. "Just let things blow over, eh? You want to get out, you can leave the bambino with his fiancée next door." A signature wink. "Matter of fact, I'll take you with me tomorrow to Cinecittá. Little errand for Bixio."

The next morning I dressed with more than the usual care, aligning the seams of my best silk stockings. The waistband of my tailored skirt fastened without undue strain. I examined myself in the mirror. If motherhood had changed me, the effect was of a softening, fewer angles, more curves and hollows.

We took a taxi to the film studio, which lay on the outskirts of the city just beyond the slums. Accustomed by then to such juxtapositions of squalor and modernity, I cannot say I was dazzled by my first sight of Cinecittá, which resembled nothing so much as a displaced fortress, but inside one entered a world within a world, a place luminous and sprawling. Setting the tone, a portrait of Mussolini posed behind a movie camera bore the caption, *"Film is the most powerful weapon."*

A receptionist looked up from a flickering switchboard. *"Momento,"* he said, frantically making connections.

Pasquale waved aloft his sheath of papers. "Don't bother, I know my way." He led me to a waiting area and settled me on a rubber-like sofa with spiky metal legs. "This shouldn't take long."

I watched his tidy back recede down a silvery corridor. Curious, I got up and strolled about the spacious foyer, through which passed a steady trickle of personnel, some suited, others costumed.

"Mr. Righelli!" I recognized the director by his monumental forehead and backswept hair. "We met at the Zingarellis' not long ago—Margit Wolf? My husband is just down the hall delivering some music."

He jarred to attention with a vague smile. "Welcome to the land of the *mille meraviglie.* We are all a little lost these first weeks. I need to return to the set for a minute—are you free to accompany me?"

"I would love to."

He strode ahead with a commanding gait. "The crew's on break." He spoke over his shoulder, more imperious in profile. "Watch your step, it can seem a chaos behind the scenes."

"Like backstage at a theater."

"Then you know."

"I don't presume to understand film, but I know about creating illusions."

He faced me fully for the first time. "That's right, you're a ballerina. And your husband—he's in music, you said?"

"Pasquale conducts, composes. What would a ballet be without music? Take away the score and the performance would be lifeless. Similarly with film, the talkies, an audience tires of unbroken dialogue."

"Cut! On to the next scene."

"But what of mood, magnetism, passion? What of the things that cannot be spoken?"

"For that we have images. Film has always been a visual medium."

"And the film of tomorrow?" He wasn't looking at me anymore but staring, returning audacity with intimidation. "Music has so much more to contribute," I went on, having hazarded too far for retreat. "The filmmaker who taps it, who marries the soundtrack to the images like fine art, will be declared a genius."

Again the enigmatic smile. "You are a very provocative woman, *signora*, but I am tone-deaf, I'm afraid. Congenital defect." Having found what he had come for, he pocketed his scribblings and motioned toward an exit. "What was your husband's name again?"

"Pasquale," I said. "Maestro Pasquale Frustaci."

"Frankly, I'm better with faces."

He gave a little bow and led me quickly along the corridor to our starting point. I glanced toward the waiting area and could see my husband pacing the aisle with undisguised pique.

"There he is. A man doesn't like to be left to cool his heels. Please, say a quick hello so he won't be angry with me?"

"With pleasure, *signora*." He strode up to the maestro and the two men clapped sides. "Waiting long? I've just been showing your wife around the set."

My husband put on his stage face, the handy mask of bonhomie. "Very kind of you, Signor Righelli. She's a great admirer of your films."

"And a great critic."

"If I spoke out of turn—"

"A nightingale could not have charmed me more," he hastened to assure me. "I will think about what you said." He turned to my husband with crossed arms, acting his part. "If she were my wife, maestro, I would keep her under lock and key."

Pasquale thanked him, ushered me out, and had barely reached the doorstep when he doubled over with laughter. "I won't even ask what you said to him—ah, *babuci*, I can't let you out of my sight! You're a danger to the whole male sex." I made to slink past him but he caught me in an embrace. "Not another step." His arms locked around my hips like a hoop skirt. "Okay, I can't stand it. What did you say to Righelli?"

"An earful. He's not likely to forget your name."

An elephant ambled past, its elegant trunk coiled like a serpent. Nothing would have seemed out of place at that moment, nothing overmuch.

"Imagine, you with your orchestra and me with my dancers. Frustaci and Lupo, stars of the talking pictures."

The maestro, grown younger in the space of a breath, balled his fists. "I'll make that screen sing."

"Of course, you will, maestro." And I would make it shimmer.

♪

We left Rome before the summer heat could set in and returned to Milan. Our son was a seasoned traveler by then, restless, if containable. The maestro sat up with him through the night. At the station, he shook me awake and we made our way home as the lamplights faded and the street-sweepers came out and every shutter seemed to open at once.

I put Cesare to bed, got Pasquale off to work, the rare unscheduled moment. A stack of glossy magazines had accumulated beside the sofa. Through the walls a woman's voice droned, "*Bevuto ancora, drunk... always drunk...*"

Into the room swept Ilona, dressed to slay dragons in a lacquer red crepe-de-chine cape. "Margit, you're back! I've come by a dozen times." Her arms sprang up to encircle my neck. "I would have visited you in Rome," she sighed, "but Ferretti arranged for me to attend the Olympic games. Berlin. City was jammed."

That my friend had gone to Germany on holiday bothered me less than her nonchalance in the face of it. "Did you notice anything—odd?"

"The Fuhrer was there, naturally." She glanced down at her hands and buffed the nails against her collarbone. "The fuss they make over him. *Odd?* You know how the Germans are, cold fish and so stuck on themselves."

"It's just, the things one hears..."

"About Hitler's being illegitimate? I wouldn't doubt it." Ilona untied her Chinese cape and slung it, billowing, onto a chair back. "But show me the little one," she demanded, already heading down the hallway. "Karola tells me he looks like that American actor, the one with the dimple on his chin?"

I followed her to the crib, where my son lay napping with his blonde curls pinwheeled across the pillow.

"What a little angel!" she exclaimed in a whisper. Hands clenched to her heart, she leaned down for a closer look. "How proud you must be, Manci, to have a husband, a son." Her voice thinned to a whine. "I confess I envy you. I thought with Ferretti maybe—marriage isn't out of the question, but time goes by. How long has it been?" She began to sob.

Not wanting to wake Cesare, I took Ilona by the shoulders and tugged gently toward the door. She might have been a length of voile, so lightly did she float behind me.

"Ferretti would be a fool not to marry you," I told her, "and you'd be a fool to have him."

She took a lace-edged hankie from her purse and daubed at her eyes. "I'm just being silly. Put a baby within reach and I turn to mush."

There was nothing wrong with my sister ballerina that steady work would not have cured. I sat her on the sofa and prepared a cup of tisane. By the time I brought it to her, she had composed her face and sat puckering to apply her lipstick.

"Your Ferretti—what do you know about him, about his politics?"

"Men don't talk to women about politics. He belongs to the party. They all do."

"Who are his friends?"

"He's not one to drop names."

"What *does* he talk about? He seems rather reserved."

"True, he's not much of a talker." She stretched and her breastbone pressed against the filmy bodice of her dress like a drawn bow.

"Ilonka, I need a favor. You know how much I miss my family. I'm overdue for a visit, but there's a problem with the passport. It will take a bit of finessing."

"Ferretti's speciality. Consider it done." She raised her cup as if to toast me.

From my son's room came a low familiar yowl, and excusing

myself I rose to prepare his bottle. "I'll have Pasquale talk to your beau. It's better that way, between men."

♪

It was September, late in the month, the Duce just back from Berlin, when I next ran into Herr Saunders. Were it not for the Austrian's height and Nordic pallor, I might have passed him by unrecognized, so greatly had he changed. A fraction of his former width, almost spindly, he inched along the pavement with a woman on his arm.

"Have I finally the honor of meeting your wife, Herr Saunders?" He had not greeted me in the customary way, indeed seemed embarrassed by our chance encounter. It occurred to me that the woman might be other than Frau Saunders but quickly banished the thought. The Austrian was every inch a family man, and the woman too faded and frail for a mistress.

"*Liebchen*," he addressed her, "this is Frau Wolf, the maestro's wife of whom I've spoken so often."

"Frau Wolf, the ballerina," she said warmly and shook my hand. "I too was a dancer, once." The disclosure seemed to knock her sideways. She hugged her ribs and began at once to cough.

"My wife has been ill," Herr Saunders hastened to say. "All summer, in fact. I wouldn't have brought her out, but our flat can be so stuffy." He wrapped a protective arm about her shoulders. "Time we get you back to bed."

"I can find my own way back, Gabe." She could barely wedge the words between the hacking of her chest. "You stay. Stay with your friend."

"Frau Wolf, you must forgive me."

"By all means, tend to your wife." I turned again to the poor woman, who in the hope of containing her coughs had cupped a hand over her mouth. "These chest colds can be so debilitating." It seemed kinder to evade than to acknowledge the obvious: Frau Saunders was wasting with consumption. "When we see each other next, you must let me invite you for coffee. We'll talk."

"I would like that," was all she managed to say.

Herr Saunders, never sparing in etiquette, jerked forward in a bow. "Next time, Frau Wolf, with pleasure. Only tell me, you have delivered the child?"

"A son."

"*Mazel tov.* Did you hear, *liebchen*? Frau Wolf has had a son. A fine boy he must be with such talented parents." He glanced into my eyes and a question passed between us, unspoken.

"What you suggested I have done."

I expected him to look pleased, but he only shook his head. "A loss, a sacrifice… what travesties of faith will be asked of us by the time this is over?"

♪

We spent the holidays in Rome, where the baby, prone to chest colds, could get sunshine. Vittorio invited us down the hall on Christmas Eve, a family affair. After we had finished supper, assorted uncles and cousins clustered in front of the nativity scene. Vittorio's wife tugged me gently forward with Cesare in my arms. She fondled his cheek and said, "Little Jesus needs to go beddy-bye. Tuck him in."

To place the Christ child in his manger was an honor bestowed each year on one guest only. With what solemnity my hostess took the wooden icon from its leather pouch. Chubby in its contours, the miniature gazed up at me—ivory white face, fuchsia lips, yellow hair. The manger lay ready. I had only to lay the icon atop its red satin lining, but Cesare grabbed hold.

"Give the baby to *mamma*, Cesarino."

The stubborn might of his grip thwarted any attempt at rescue. Vittorio's relatives looked on, more than willing to wait. I lightly spanked my son's hands, but he only blinked, gurgled, and thrust the Jesus into his mouth, digging in his sharp little teeth.

A stranger in a black shirt angled his chair for a closer look. "Jaws like a shark," he said approvingly.

"Listen to you," chided a matron in sackcloth. "He's got the Christ child in his mouth—in his *mouth*—and you call yourself a

Catholic."

"Open up, Cesarino," I softly scolded. The entire family had gathered at my back to murmur encouragement.

"The way he's chomping at that Jesus, you'd think the kid was a little *indigeno*." The man in black reached out and with one sausage-like finger tweaked my son's nose. "Either that or a Yid."

In a moment, the maestro had me by the arm. "Excuse us, we're late for a family engagement."

Vittorio shadowed us to the door. "It's like a plague," he stammered, "only you don't know who's got it and who doesn't."

"That old pansy," muttered Pasquale.

The two friends clapped backs. "Forget it, okay? The crank's had too much spiced wine."

"Vittorio's right," I said. "It's Christmas, no use making a fuss."

From inside the flat a voice urged, "Hurry, we'll be late for church." Vittorio kissed me on the cheek and gingerly closed the door.

Pasquale bundled Cesare into his arms. "*Dio mio*, the kisser on this kid! I thought we'd have to pry his jaws apart with a crowbar."

"You heard what they called him."

"Fascist talk." He strode ahead, avoiding my eyes. "Pay no attention."

I unlocked the door of our flat and switched on a lamp. My husband turned away, but not quickly enough to hide the flush of anger stretching from his cheeks to the backs of his hands. "It's time we pay attention. Face it."

He cursed under his breath.

"I'll make coffee."

"Don't," he said and drew me close. We huddled together on the daybed with our son between us, speaking of trifles, then whispering, and finally silent. I must have dozed, for when I again opened my eyes Pasquale, his head propped by pillows, lay smoking a cigarette.

"Why can't we spend Christmas just the three of us?" he sulked aloud. "Live just the three of us?"

"You're tired."

He exhaled, sending up a blue-gray tower of smoke. "I spoke to your friend Ferretti before we left Milan."

"Why didn't you tell me?"

"Not much to tell."

"He'll help us?"

"Look, I like Ferretti the way a cockroach likes the sole of a shoe. All brawn and no brain, but he gets things done." His voice had grown sharp as a needle. "The thug's out to fleece us good. It will take some time to put the money together."

"Don't worry," I assured him, "I'll earn it back with my dance troupe."

He mulled this only long enough to switch off the bedside lamp. "Just don't go putting my son in tights. My son's all boy."

♪

If it were possible to freeze time on a page of the calendar, to draw a line and say, civilized people do not do such things, 1938 might never have happened. But for two men, Hitler and Mussolini, it may not have happened. Had we refused to believe their lies, it could not have happened. But lies were what we fed on, all else having fallen scarce.

The Italian press spared the public anything that might disturb its sleep—unless the reader was a Jew, in which case the message lurked between the lines. When, in March, the Nazis seized Austria, Herr Saunders' prophecy merged with headline. The Germans interposed themselves between Italy and Hungary, blocking my path home.

Pasquale received the news coolly, a pose. "Give the Austrians six months and they'll laugh Hitler out of the country. He's an insult to their good taste."

"There's still Yugoslavia... the last I read, the border was open."

"This is no time to think of traveling."

"If not now, when? Things will get worse before they get better."

He looked scared. For a moment he let me see his undefended face, cheeks sallow, eyes too bright, and then he laughed, a mere release of nerves. "You read too many newspapers," he chided me.

With spring, allergy season, came Herr Hitler himself. It was the Fuhrer's second visit to Italy, a scant two years since the fiasco of his first, and the Duce was determined to impress as never before. From the Brenner Pass to Rome, from Rome to Naples, every inch of the Fuhrer's route was inspected. No unpainted façade, no trace of backwardness or want would be allowed to affront his gaze. Overnight, the Italian capital filled with swastikas, thousands of red Nazi flags having been draped over balconies, tacked to walls, flown from flagpoles.

"It's one more show," the maestro said.

"What will they do for an encore?"

He hung his head, but could not cache a flicker of dread. "We'll leave for Milan tomorrow. I'll tell Bixio."

"They've named a street after him, *Viale Adolfo Hitler*. He'll ride along it in a horse-drawn carriage like a conquering hero, and all the Duce's flunkies will cheer him."

"Lower your voice."

"Military exercises, parades, performances of Wagner... one endless spectacle. That's all there is anymore. You see it in the newsreels, Rome no less than Berlin, all the goose-stepping and shouting, and behind it nothing. *Niente*."

He touched a fingertip to my lips. "That's government. No use making yourself sick over it."

Back in Milan, no one took the least interest in the Fuhrer's joyride, except to gripe about its cost. The lira had lost value again. A drought was threatening the nation's wheat—and yet, when had the city seen so much sunshine? The weather was mild, the trees in bud. Bixio bought his godson a fine baby carriage, and Cesare would ride along in its cushioned interior sucking sugar-water through a rubber nipple. It was easy to stray too far, to lose oneself in progress' voids, the wrecking ball never far off.

I expected at any moment to cross paths with Herr Saunders, indeed wished to, but his long slouching figure did not appear. It occurred to me that he had fled the country, but how would he have traveled with a sick wife? I visited the piazzas where we had met in the past, lingered in the parks, watching, tracing circles, and still no sign.

Until the day the Austrian knocked at my door. "I hope I'm not intruding."

"Not at all."

"I wouldn't normally stop by this way..."

"Come in. Please. My son should be up from his nap any moment. I was just preparing lunch." I wasn't, actually, but how else to get nourishment into so stoic a man? I led him into the living room and settled him on the sofa, which, like everything else in the apartment, bore evidence of a baby's presence. "My son's at that age—toys, teething rings, whatever he can lay hands on."

"A house isn't a home without children."

"I must say, Herr Saunders, you're looking well." It was not form that prompted the compliment. The Austrian did, in fact, look the picture of health, trim and upright, ruddy in the cheeks.

He blushed with pleasure. "How kind of you to say so, Frau Wolf. I have just spent the week as a guest of the Italian government—in jail."

"No!"

"I assure you. The police conducted a sweep just before Herr Hitler's arrival. The company could not have been better. I shared a cell with a newspaper publisher, a cellist and a painter, gentlemen of the first order. Being pegged as subversives created a certain camaraderie, sharpened our wit—the lampooning that went on! I don't think I ever laughed so much. An absolute contagion of laughter! Not without its anxieties. What the authorities had in mind for us, we couldn't have known, and yet

I wouldn't have traded my captivity for a week on the Riviera."

"You can't be serious."

"But I am. It has banished my lethargy, you see. They will not catch me with my guard down again."

"It's outrageous the way people have behaved, and for what?"

"Open your eyes, Frau Wolf!" His own gaped so wide they might have leapt from their sockets. "The Fuhrer has guns, money and, most deadly of all, the will of a people messianic in their narcissism. All the things the Duce lacks."

From the back room, my son emptied his lungs in a broken whimper.

"The master calls. Come, we'll take him his bottle."

The Austrian followed willingly. Standing over my son's crib, his cheeks slackened into jowls. "Such a *punim*. How not to be love-struck by the face of a child?"

"You must miss your daughters."

He assented with a nod.

There fell between us an easy silence that needed no explaining. I bundled my son into my arms and carried him with us to the living room, which was sunny and made him squint. The Austrian fashioned an awning of his oversized hands. "It is becoming harder to visit my children. More borders are closing than are opening."

"I'm thinking of going home for a while."

"Hungary is in a bad way. Horthy would sell his own mother to recover Transylvania. I myself am looking farther afield—Palestine, America... whoever will have me. I'm willing to do any sort of work, to start at the bottom like the lowliest greenhorn. Anything beats this waiting, either for the worst or for a miracle. Either way we diminish."

"We are what we have always been."

"A man who can't feed his family, who can't protect them, feels himself nothing. I wouldn't say this to my own wife, Frau Wolf. These past months I can hardly bear her eyes on me, eyes brimming with questions: what will today bring, how will we go on...? I leave her in that furnished room and roam for hours, trying to puzzle it all out."

"Herr Saunders, if you'll allow me." I snatched up my purse from the armchair and drew out a fistful of bills.

"No, *danke*." He rose hastily to his feet. "I am glad we have seen each other, Frau Wolf. It may be some time before we meet again. In the short-term, prospects may be better elsewhere—Turkey, Portugal? One puts out feelers."

"Something will turn up. You'll get settled again, reunite your family."

"*Fun gottes gnaden.*" By the grace of God.

I had no choice but to walk him to the door. "But I haven't even made coffee—are you sure you won't stay? Join us for lunch."

"Thank you, really, but my wife is expecting me." Midway to the landing he turned, bowed, and said a muffled farewell. "To better times," he added, and was gone.

♪

The swastikas followed Hitler back to Germany, leaving no trace. Summer, honeyed as the skin of an orange, cast its glow.

My sister ballerinas spent much of their time in Milan, and although their circles had widened, we remained our own best audience. Ballet bound us more tightly than any clique or caste. "I've got an extra ticket for La Scala," one or another of them could always be counted upon to offer.

We would put on our best dresses, leave our men at home, and breeze into the theater looking, sounding, smelling like the women we had once admired in glossy magazines. That season, the ballerina Margarita Froman was a favorite in Italy—and for good reason. Bolshoi training produced technicians of the highest order. We watched her dance *The Hours* from *La Gioconda* and could not fault a single step. While my friends praised her line, her lightness, the seemingly spineless arch of her back, only one thought occupied my mind. If a ballerina with a Jewish surname could still dance at La Scala, what cause had I to doubt the Duce's designs?

The night was clear, moonless. There being few lit streetlamps, the stars remained visible. We might have gone to Savini's (compliments of Zingarelli), but feeling defiant we drifted down a side street and chose the commonest café.

"I miss these picturesque places," said Teréz, drawing her scalloped handkerchief across the chair before deigning to sit. "If my husband were to catch me here..."

Karola held out her gold cigarette case and the others helped themselves. "We've always done as we pleased—why change now?" The remark was mere puffery, and yet Teréz would not let it drop.

"But we *have* changed. Look at us. Karola's prima ballerina, Margit's a mother ... "

The waiter came and went, caddying unmatched glasses of all sizes.

Ilona downed a Campari in measured sips, her eyes everywhere at once. "And me, Teréz? How have I changed?"

"Ilonka. Dear, dear Ilonka."

"I ask because—I don't know sometimes, what I'm doing here, where my home is. Was Hungary ever a home? Is Italy? Ferretti says he can get me work in Germany. I might try my luck there."

"Why not? Look at that friend of Margit's, that Zarah Leander. Yesterday no one had heard of her, and today she's the best-loved film star of the Reich. It pays to move with the times."

Karola loosed one of her purring sighs. "To hell with the Reich! Anyone with talent has already fled the country. That should tell you something."

"To hell with politics!"

"To hell with men!"

Teréz spread her arms as if to shepherd a flock. "What's the matter with us tonight? We sound like—heck, what have we got to complain about? Margit's a mother, Karola's queen of the opera house..."

"I wish you'd stop saying that."

"I'm only saying—"

"What fun we used to have!"

Another round of drinks. It was not late, barely midnight, yet most of the surrounding tables had emptied. From somewhere nearby—a club, a brothel?—poured the familiar refrain, *"Bei mir bist du schon..."*

No one proposed a toast.

Karola shrugged and said, "It's getting late."

"I can remember when an early night meant three o'clock in the morning."

We broke off into pairs. Teréz and Karola hailed a taxicab and set off north, trailing silk scarves and the scent of gardenias. Ilona took my arm and we strolled back toward the Duomo, where the lamps stayed lit despite the shortages.

"Still thinking of going home?" my friend surprised me by asking.

"I must."

"Look, Ferretti has a fencing match in Budapest mid-October. We're going by car, his new four-seater. Come with us. Oh, I know Ferretti isn't everyone's cup of tea, but he loosens-up on the road and you'll have the back seat to yourself."

"Have you asked him?"

"Men are like wind-up toys," she said with inflated self-assurance. "I've learned how to work him."

How simple it suddenly all seemed: a car at our disposal, an alibi, and Ferretti's diplomatic passport to smooth our way.

"We'll stay for a week, maybe longer, depending on the opera house."

"You've secured a place?"

"Not yet, but Karola seems to think there are opportunities—for both of us, Margit. The *Pas de Deux*, remember?"

Borne along by anticipation, we encircled each other with our arms and pirouetted across the cobbles with more energy than grace. If the future had been a star, we could have seized it with our teeth and kept on dancing. "Why not?" And louder, "Why not!" Never had my legs felt so primed for flight.

♪

July 14, 1938. The day began like any other. I awoke beside my husband. We made love. I got up and fed the baby. Pasquale left for work. A fine enough morning until I went downstairs to the newsstand and bought *Il Popolo d'Italia*. Millions of Italians would read that day that the Jew, regardless of his origins or upbringing, was inferior, alien, and inassimilable.

The day remained sunny, passersby walked along the street whistling, dodging pigeons, the streetcar tooted its horn, but I did not venture out again. Through the walls other people called to their children, such thin walls, so many keyholes.

And then the maestro was back. "What, no *bacio* for your old husband?"

I motioned toward the coffee table, where the newspaper still lay.

One headline sufficed to bring the blood to his eyes. "Horseshit!" he spat, balling the pages. "Who could take such a crock of lies seriously? The gall."

"This is just a prelude. The Duce has a method: first propaganda then action."

"I don't know about method, but Mussolini's sounding more like Hitler every day." He raced down the hallway to our son's crib, as if the Nazis were already at the door. "My son's Italian. Italian, full stop." Cesarino began suddenly to bawl and to pummel the mattress with his hands and feet. "You show them, *bambino*. Inferior? What does some pear-shaped fairy who can't even grow a proper mustache know?" He turned away to swipe a tear from the corner of his eye. "Fairies, all of them. No one's going to tell me what my son is."

We hadn't long to rage. Within the month, a census was taken of foreign Jews, and soon after came the order giving us six months to leave Italy. It was written in the newspapers, broadcast on the wireless. The blow should not have surprised me, and yet for hours, while I waited for my husband to return from work, I suffered a sort of vertigo, clutching at the furniture, the walls, barely trusting myself to take the baby into my arms. I did not leave the apartment.

Pasquale arrived home whistling, tossed his fedora onto the sofa, and said, "Why's it so dark in here?"

The newspaper lay open on the coffee table. The baby had spilled milk on it—the milk had soured. My husband strode along the room's periphery, yanked open all the curtains, and only then doubled back to glance at the headlines.

"What's this?"

"It's all over," I said.

He did not react at once. For what seemed a long time, he hung over the newsprint, not deigning to take it in his hands. Only his lips moved. I remember thinking, this is what drives men to desperate acts, and still he said nothing, did nothing.

"Stand up straight."

He veered sharply, giving me his back. "Damn them! Damn them to hell! Who do they think they are with their big words and their big ideas?"

"This has gotten beyond words. This is law."

He turned to face me, his chin quivering. "Six months gives us time."

"To do what? Am I supposed to convert or hide or surgically remove my fingerprints? I'm a Jew. Don't ask me to deny my heritage."

"I'm not asking. Me, I'm fine with it. Hell, I married you, didn't I? It's our son we need to think about. If you're a Jew, what does that make him? And if he's a Jew... What kind of a father am I, if I can't defend my own son?"

The Duce had yet to fashion the legal definition of a Jew. Until he did, we could only grasp at straws.

"We'll go abroad."

"We're not going anywhere," the maestro said. "You're an Italian mother. You're my wife. No one's throwing you out."

The moment was wrong, too charged, our nerves frayed, but I could put off the argument no longer. "My papers are ready. Ferretti's holding onto them until—"

"I don't want to hear this."

"Until Cesarino and I leave for Hungary."

"Don't! Don't even think of it. Ferretti—what does Ferretti know? Tripe for brains. It's a minefield out there."

The door to Cesare's room stood open. I closed it, and then the windows. Pasquale reached on reflex for his collar button.

"My parents haven't seen their own grandson. I haven't been home in years. Once the war starts, there will be no crossing the borders."

"Who said anything about a war? Chamberlain's kissing Hitler's ass, Roosevelt's twiddling his thumbs, and anyway, Italy's not ready for another war. We haven't got the arms."

"Wake up! Horthy and Mussolini are both in Hitler's pocket. It's just a matter of time."

He faced me squarely. "If what you say is true, I'd be mad to let you go."

"I'm not asking permission."

"Not asking permission?" He seemed to shrink where he stood. The anger drained from his voice, leaving it small, a child's measly whine. "*Not* asking?"

"We leave next week."

"Some wife I married. Some wife."

"But you did marry me. You knew I was headstrong."

"How to resist you? How to resist a woman who dances like an angel and fights like a heavyweight? If anything were to happen to you—" Arms outstretched I went to him, but he held himself steely, separate.

"Ten years we've had together. Ten happy years."

"And what of your dance troupe?"

"I'll scout for dancers in Hungary."

He seemed to mull this. "*Porco mondo*, if anyone can do it, you can. Go now, if you're going. Go and come back quickly.

Our bed will be coals and daggers until you're home."

♪

The departure was a simple affair. Having made our peace, the rest was a matter of logistics: a suitcase each for my son and me, another with gifts for my family. My few pieces of jewelry I stored in a strongbox, locked the bolt, and handed my husband the key.

"Collateral."

Ferretti's car horn blasted and we made our way down the stairwell, the maestro holding tightly to his son and I managing the provisions and stuffed toys.

"*Buon viaggio!*" cried the concierge, holding open the street level door.

Outside, passersby cast curious glances at the sleekly new Alfa Romeo. Ilona, her hair pinned back for the road, stepped onto the curb to kiss cheeks. "Ferretti's in one of his moods," she whispered.

We set about arranging the luggage.

"Did you pack Cesarino's bib?" the maestro said. "Will he be warm enough in that suit? Where's his little pillow?"

Ferretti, inscrutable behind a pair of tinted goggles, supervised from the driver's seat. "Just the essentials. This is a four-seater, not a warehouse."

"Where's his bear? He can't sleep without his bear."

"He'll sleep fine, Pasquale. He'll sleep better than you or I."

"Write to me. Write the moment you arrive in Budapest. Tell me everything. Tell me when I can expect you, and don't dally, eh?"

"We'll be back before you know it," I tried to reassure him.

"*Baciami*, Cesarino, and be a good boy. Listen to your *mamma*. Speak to him in Italian, only in Italian. He's Italian, my son."

"Ferretti's waiting."

When we could delay no longer, the maestro clasped his son to his breast and clung. "Careful at the wheel, Ferretti," he said, "this is precious cargo you're carrying."

"Relax, Frustaci, you're talking to an ace."

Ilona gave me a pleading look, and I took Cesarino from his father's arms and bundled him into my lap. "Say goodbye to your *papi*."

The maestro looked stricken. "Not goodbye, *a presto*."

On an impulse, I took the gold wedding band from my finger and thrust it into his palm. "Hold onto this for me. It's safer with you."

"If I thought I could convince you to stay... hell, you'll never change." He kissed me with a sudden urgency, squeezed me roughly, and broke away. He stood on the curb forcing himself to smile, but it looked all wrong, the sort of smile a mortician fixes on the lips of a cadaver.

I took my son's tiny hand and waved it stupidly. He put up no resistance until the car began to move, and then he pitched forward, willfully, as if to throw himself from the window.

"Hold onto him!" were the last words I heard my husband cry out as the distance between us grew. I watched him though the rear window until his dead smile and his waving arm blurred, and the whole of his figure dwindled to a speck. Within moments I had lost all sight of him.

♪

"A tiskit, a tasket... *ta-da-da-da* basket..."

"Stop singing that stupid song!"

Ilona and Ferretti were not getting along.

"Was I singing?" my friend said drowsily, half turning in her seat to enlist my support. "I must be deaf. It's always the silliest songs one finds oneself repeating, *eh*?"

The Alfa Romeo took an angry lurch. "Why we put up with this primitive American music I'll never understand. I say, ban it and that's that."

Cars did not have radios in those days. There was either banter or silence. Of the scenery I remember little, except for fields of polenta with their fallen stalks and glinting silos and the occasional steam engine passing, puffing black clouds into the unbroken blueness.

"Tired, *caro*? You took that turn a little wide."

"Don't tell me how to drive. Light me a cigarette. Damned roads, nothing is properly maintained in this country. Driving should be a pleasure, life should be a pleasure, but no, the ground is full of holes, people herd their goats across the *superstrada*. There's always something in the way."

"A tisket, a tasket…"

"Again! How many times must I tell you?"

Ilona threw up her hands with an artless grace. "Who notices, *caro*? It's like breathing—do you stop and think, the air is passing in and out of my nostrils? No, you just breathe." Then to me, "It's the silliest song, really. I don't even know what it means."

"The words sound African," said Ferretti. "It's all the rage in America, these native ditties." He slowed the car. In the distance loomed a long wooden trestle and to either side a pair of soldiers—not the tailored sort one would see marching in formation, but boys with cowlicks and trousers that bagged in the knees. Almost without our noticing, we had passed Trieste and reached the Yugoslav border. "Quiet!" the fencer ordered. "Not a word. This won't take long."

Passport in hand, he slid to the pavement and began to speak to the boys, who seemed more interested in the Italian's imported cigarettes than in his papers. A flurry of hand gestures and he was back. "Useless country. Government's dissolved the parliament. Croats are on the warpath. For all we know, it's the start of a civil war." He re-started the car engine and executed a full turn. "Damned waste of time."

"But where will we go?" I had to ask.

Ferretti eyed me in the rearview mirror. "Austria, where else?"

"But the Germans—"

"You'd better get used to them. They won't stop with Austria."

He applied his foot to the accelerator with deliberate ferocity and the car sped down the same forgettable road. Still in Italy, we put up for the night at an inn. My son, cutting his teeth, cried until he wrung himself hoarse and dropped off to sleep.

The next day, we got off to a late start, which may or may not have had something to do with the love bites on Ilona's neck. However they had spent the morning, the lovers were soon quarreling again.

"Looks like rain."

"It always looks like rain to you."

"I don't make the weather, *caro*. Do you look at a cloud and see sunshine?"

We continued north toward Klagenfurt, the terrain turning alpine and the air crisp, if unnaturally still. Cesare wriggled out from my lap to shimmy the door handles. Along the roadsides, a flock of sheep, shorn bare, foraged the last dandelions.

And then another checkpoint. From a distance no more daunting than the last: the same wooden trestle, the same paired soldiers.

"Nazis," pronounced Ferretti on closer inspection and thumped the steering wheel with his fist. Cursing their mothers, he navigated steadily toward them. "Let me do the talking. You girls adjust your garters or something."

Ilona swiveled in her seat and giggled.

"What did I just tell you? Not a sound!"

The car jarred to a standstill. Before Ferretti could step out, the brawniest of the soldiers thrust a hand through the open window.

"*Dokumenten.*"

"With pleasure, *amico*." The Italian proffered the passport with a flourish followed by his monogrammed cigarette case. "Help yourselves, don't be shy."

There were no takers. The soldiers, loosely huddling, conferred among themselves.

Ferretti sidled from the car and gave his trousers a dusting.

He crossed his arms. "Look, I'm in a hurry. *Capisci*? Who's in charge here?"

The beefy one detached from the huddle, half saluting, half shooing the Italian back where he had come from. Stepping up to the car, the soldier poked his head in and studied each of us in turn. "*Dokumenten,*" he said evenly.

"Kid's a broken record," grumbled the fencer, tapping a toe on the running board. "Doesn't know what a diplomat is, doesn't know how to treat people. I eat at the same table as the Duce, as the Fuhrer, and this snot-nosed kid thinks he can toy with me..."

Ilona, in the meantime, had surrendered her passport.

As the soldier thumbed its pages, I touched his sleeve and said in German, "Please don't mind our friend. You know how toffee-nosed diplomats can be."

His lips faintly upturned.

"I know you're busy, but—" My son grabbed hold of the Nazi's buttons and began to tug. "Forgive me. He gets like this when he's thirsty. I was about to ask you for water."

He stood to attention, turned on his heels, and came back moments later with a jerry can. "It's not spring water, but it's purified," he said in a tone of apology. "Tell your friend to keep to the main roads. Graz is quiet. You should have no trouble crossing the border from there."

"You've been very kind. Are you sure we can't offer you and your men a cigarette?"

He pocketed a few and leaned in closer to tousle my son's hair. "By the way, how is it you know German?" Hardly a casual question.

"Convent school. My family sent me to the nuns in Bolzano."

Ferretti made a show of consulting his pocket watch. "*Allora?*"

Without another word, the soldier handed back the passports and waved us on.

The fencer got back into the touring car, started the engine, and sped away with his shoulders tensed and his knuckles blue against the wheel. For several minutes no one spoke.

Ilona snapped open her compact. "*Dokumenten*," she mimicked, composing her face in the mirror. "*Dokumenten. Dokumenten...*"

"You find it funny?" The fencer kept his eyes straight ahead. "If they had asked for your friend's passport... It's got 'Hebrew' marked on it clear as day. Go on and laugh. Laugh! Next time she won't be so lucky."

We rode along in silence with the windows closed tight and giant sheaves of fog trundling down the mountains. My son slept. I could see only far enough ahead to count the mile markers. The road narrowed, ascended, seemed for miles at a stretch to disappear altogether.

At a railway crossing, we stopped while a brightly painted string of freight cars crept by.

Ferretti tilted onto the window, leaving it shiny with hair tonic. He cleared his throat. "A tisket, a tasket..."

"You're singing it now," said Ilona.

"Singing what?"

She turned in my direction and rolled her eyes. "Never mind, *caro*."

♪

We crossed into Hungary at Körmend along the River Rába.

"How does it feel to be home?" asked Ferretti at his most civil, baring his fishmonger teeth.

Growing up, I had ventured out of Budapest only as far as the Gypsy camps along the Györ Road, never losing sight of the city skyline. Provincial Hungary was as foreign to me as China.

"I'm not home yet."

As we wound through the Bakony hills, memory too traced spirals. *Sylvia*, 1927. The oceanic red curtain rising. Out from the wings floats a chorus of dancers, tutus fluttering, faces slick with greasepaint, circling *en pointe* until they form a halo about me. The music swells to a crescendo. The conductor turns to the string section, lifts his white gloves, and stabs at the air igniting a piercing pizzicato.

I have memorized this moment a thousand times: the spotlight pans across the stage to bathe me in light, such golden light, and I raise my eyes to the boxes and find there, not the dignitaries and courtesans of other nights, but my father, still wearing the same frayed collar I'd seen him in that morning at his machine. Feeling his tender gaze upon me, I leap, the stage a pale shadow, the stars so close I graze them with my open palms. *Look, apa, how high I reach! Look how the audience clamors to its feet ...*

There were few cars on the road, few distractions from the gray hills and dormant fields and bald sheep. As the sun began to set, Ilona took Cesare from my arms and I flopped like a sack of barley onto the car seat.

"What's wrong with her?" I could hear Ferretti grumble.

"Nothing, *caro*. You make it sound like a crime. She's just tired—can't a woman be tired?"

"If I were her, I'd stay alert. Countryside's a hotbed of Nazi agitation, not to mention the German officers taking their recreation in the capital. I can't be responsible."

"Relax, we're almost there."

"I'll relax when she and her brat are out of my car."

At Székesfehérvár Ilona shook me gently awake and we walked in the dark to a pension and stopped for the night. I washed diapers. My son found a crater in the straw mattress and drifted off to sleep. Through the walls came the sound of coupling, a slow inarticulate crescendo cut short by "I'm being eaten alive!" The day dawned colorless, smelling of tar. We piled into the car again and waited while Ferretti did calisthenics beside the road.

"Nothing like fresh air," he said, finally taking his place at the wheel.

It was not far to Budapest, but the road was in poor repair, rutted, its white line worn to powder. Ferretti compared it to the Appian Way. The Alfa Romeo lost speed. At every turning, the fencer blasted the car horn for sheer malice.

"This keeps up, I'll be late for my match," he said.

"You can see the Buda Hills from here."

"That manure heap? We're still miles away, and where am I going to find petrol?"

As we neared the city's outskirts, there were more roads to choose from, more railway crossings and smokestacks. Piles of gut-red bricks rose like monuments to the god of industry.

"Which way, which way?" Ferretti thumped the steering wheel.

We entered Buda near Castle Hill. The city flag had changed a stripe, green for blue, but at first glance the city itself had not changed, had only aged, its patina finer, its landmarks under siege by pigeons. I felt little fondness for the place, only a yearning to step into my parents' parlor, set down my luggage, and deposit my son pink and perfect in their arms. Beyond that I did not allow myself to think.

"Christ, what's this—a revolution? We'll never get to the other side of this bridge."

He was referring to the Chain Bridge, across which lay Pest and the road that would take me home.

"Oh, *caro*," Ilona said brightly, "don't you know a revolution from a religious procession? It's our dear St. Stephen. Drive up close. Perhaps we'll see the Holy Right."

"The Holy Right?"

"St. Stephen's right hand." She had opened the window and leaned out, craning for a glimpse of the relic. "Cross yourself." The Italian did so, nervously kissing his fingers. "They don't often let it out of the basilica, but it's his anniversary. He died nine hundred years ago."

"A severed hand—can you imagine the rot on that thing?" The Italian's nostrils pinched. "By the time traffic budges, we'll be as old as your saint. Look, can't your friend take a tram?"

"With the baby? How will she manage?"

"*Allora?* Drive this mob into the Danube and we'll be on our way."

"We told Margit we'd take her home," my friend insisted. "A promise is a promise."

I had had enough of Ferretti's hospitality. "Not to worry, Ilonka, I'll take the metro. There should be a station not far from here."

Ilona turned to the fencer with her eyes two molten slits. "You'll take Margit to the station and find her a porter, *capisci*? You'll put her on the train. There's a proper way to do things."

I boarded at the Deli station, taking with me a well-scrubbed boy with holes in the toes of his rustic boots. He carried two suitcases and I the third. Staying together, we changed trains and headed north to the Nyugati hub from which my destination lay but a short taxicab ride away. Cesare grew heavy in my arms.

We were on our way to the taxi stand, when a pair of gendarmes stepped to either side of us and blocked the way. "Coming from abroad?"

I might have said no, but the sheer bulk of the luggage gave me away. "Please, I'll just pay the boy."

They studied our two passports, mine and my son's, and taking a suitcase each led us to a glass booth alongside which stood a man similarly uniformed and armed with a polished saber. "She's come from abroad," said the original pair, handing me over like a smuggled side of beef.

The armed man paged through our papers, glancing up only long enough to observe, "You've been in Italy for some time."

"My husband—the boy's father—is Italian. My son is Italian. We're here for a brief visit."

The paired gendarmes listened intently but did not react. Jurisdiction had passed to their colleague, and yet they lingered.

"We'll just hold onto these," said the one with the sword. He stepped inside the booth with both passports and emerged moments later with a scrap of paper. "Your receipt," he said and gave a clipped bow.

"But I'll need the passports for my return passage. As I said, I won't be staying long."

"Then we'll be seeing you again soon, Mrs.—or is it Miss? You said you were married, Miss Wolf?"

I was not unduly alarmed. When had a petty official ever lifted a rubber stamp without *grateful money*? "Please, isn't there someone with whom I could speak? My husband is a man of some importance." I slid my hand into my purse, where a rolled bundle of bills lay ready.

A fourth uniformed man sprouted from the platform like fungus after a rainstorm. "Is there some problem?" he asked in a thick Teutonic accent.

The three gendarmes exchanged a look and swiftly separated, leaving the armed clerk to deal with the meddlesome officer.

"Nothing we can't handle."

I forced myself to smile at the Nazi, and he blinked and relaxed his vigil.

The remaining gendarme hovered close enough for me to chance a second parley. "We Hungarians know the value of a favor."

He snapped to attention, his saber thwacking the heavy canvas of his creased trousers. "Stop back in a fortnight, Miss Wolf." His eyes fixed on my son with just enough candor to suggest a smile. "In the meantime, you might want to take the little one to the zoo. They've acquired quite a few exotic specimens since you were last here. Good day, madam."

"Over our lives a black shadow gathers
Threatening our days so serene, so gay
Please, interrupted melody, begin again!"

"Melodia Interrotta"
Interrupted Melody

♪ Three

Another letter from Pasquale.

My mother took an envelope from her apron pocket, glanced with a sort of awe at the foreign postmark, and hovered near, pretending to dust the spinet piano. Never had the piano been tended and polished with such zeal, as if she expected the maestro to walk through the door at any moment and take his place before the keyboard.

"Aren't you going to open it?"

My father's sewing machine wheezed to a halt. "Has he sent anything for the boy?"

Sheet music.

The machine started in again, and I walked to the window and rubbed an opening in the frost. January already and still the authorities had not returned my son's passport.

Ilona, having found no suitable role at the opera house, left her mother a stack of lire and followed Ferretti back to Italy months ago. Pasquale's letters, two or three per week, arrived from Torino, from Rome, from Ravenna... wherever there was a train station and a theater. *My adorable wife, my dear Manci,*

119

Mancikám... Dated according to the fascist year, they made the world seem younger.

"*Nu*, a song he sends you?"

"'*Tu Solamente Tu*', it's called." I walked absently to the piano and tapped out the first notes. "*Again this year spring returned with arms full of flowers and the bells ringing all around...*"

It was Pasquale's first published composition since parting ways with Bixio back in November, a melody so stung with heartache it could only have been written in the weeks following my departure. My husband had never learned to be alone. Strapped for cash, he had let go the flat in Milan, pawned my valuables, and taken to the road on an eight-city tour, sending me his schedule so that I might write ahead.

"*...Only you don't return.*"

Already the song had claimed me. It was silken on the ear, what the Italians would call *orecchiabile*.

"Pretty tune, but didn't he say last time he'd be coming to Budapest? Does he give you a date?"

I perched on the piano bench and skimmed the letter. "No date, *anyám*."

The calendar hung on the wall blank of even the most casual appointment. I had arrived determined to assemble my dancers, an even dozen, ready to leave for Italy on short notice. But the climate was wrong, my contacts suddenly inaccessible. The Jewish laws, in force since the previous May, had begun to make of even the most assimilated a new subspecies to be counted and gradually isolated. I felt it in the way people looked at me, in the distance they kept.

"*Where are you? Don't you hear my voice full of love?*" The lyricist had done his job well, melding the words to the melody like flesh to spirit. Did he know it was our story he was writing? "*All the dreams we had return to tell me you, only you, won't come back any more.*"

"*Mamma?*"

Cesarino, wobble-walking in his one pair of hard shoes,

appeared in the doorway trailing the same downy pillow his father had tucked into our luggage. In an instant, Mano was on his feet. "The boy looks feverish, don't you think? Szidi, come feel his forehead."

My mother gazed at her grandson with the wistful look that would become her second skin. "The poor child's not sick, he's outgrown his shoes. Look at him, limping like a cripple."

"I'll find him a pair."

"They've become dear as pearls. There's an old pair of József's in the closet, five sizes too big. You could stuff the toes with cotton wool."

"In Italy there are plenty of shoes. I'll have the maestro send a pair."

Her lips tautened until all the little creases ironed-out. "Love songs he sends—what does he know from love? Love is putting food on the table, sitting by your child's bed when he's sick."

"It can't be easy for him either."

"Don't ask me to feel sorry for him. Don't ask me to feel for him, too. It's the boy I pity."

"I'll find shoes."

"What's a growing boy to do with sheet music? Songs he doesn't know how to sing, words he can't read ... "

Mano cupped hands to his grandson's ears.

I refolded the letter and replaced it in its envelope. "One day he will, one day these compositions will send him to university." My fingers gravitated once more to the keyboard. "*Tu Solamente Tu*" was more than a "pretty song." In the solitude of our empty flat, in the shadow of events my husband didn't understand and couldn't change, he had written an anthem to longing.

♪

"*My Dear Husband,*" I wrote on my best stationery, "*It is late, our son sleeping, and I am tired.*" Tired of doors closing, tired of unkept promises. "*What seemed possible in Italy here becomes a fathomless maze. Circumstance does not permit me to form a troupe. The Magyars brace for war, but for Hungary's Jews the war has already begun.*" A war fought not with guns but lies. "*Of Budapest, what remains to be said? Redeem herself the city does not.*" One winter sufficed to remind me why I had left in the first place: Jewish publications shut down, Jewish businesses looted, our own home-bred Nazis parading under the banner of the Arrow Cross through the streets.

My family and I rarely went out. We would sit in the kitchen—my mother and father, my brother József, his wife Ibolya (like Pasquale a Catholic)—repeating old stories, honoring the absent and the dead, whose memories we invoked to fill the gathering silence.

My sister's aura lingered in the flat like the must of bread taken too soon from the oven. Her empty bed still wore the coverlet she had embroidered with her deft, unerring hands. She had been so young—how does someone so young drift off like that?

"It was her constitution," explained József, citing no particular illness.

Szidonia had her own diagnosis: "It was the violin."

My sister had dreamed of studying at conservatory, impossible under the *numerus clausus.* Jewish aspirants always exceeded the small number of places allotted them. Had times been better we might have sent her to Vienna, not that she asked. She simply stopped playing.

"She could have been a *virtuosa,*" my father said, his cheeks sunken and his eyes gleaming from the hollows like wet moss.

But only one daughter could be chosen, only one lavished with advantage. My lessons and tutus had been bought at the cost of my sister's pent-up passion, bought stitch by killing stitch.

"She was never strong."

"If only we hadn't given her that instrument."

"Where would I have found the *gelt* to send her to Vienna?"

A family wounded is no less a family. By matching tradition with common sense, faith with elbow grease, mine had endured millennia.

"How long will you stay in Budapest?"

"Hard to say—the Germans, the border... "

Then in whispers, "The Nazis are everywhere. Soldiers come to sit in the cafes and make loose with local women. They swagger around the train stations—there's no getting on a train anymore without passing under their noses."

"This is still Hungary," my father interjected without conviction. "A relic Horthy may be, but he's an honorable man."

József drew in his breath. "Since when has Magyar honor spared us?"

I watched his wife stiffen in her seat.

"Did Horthy stop Parliament from taking away our livelihoods?"

Ibi pulled on her sheepskin coat. "I'd like to go home now, József."

"Why, aren't you well?"

She said nothing, only waited at the door with her hands tightly knit.

"Come, Ibi," I said, taking her arm, "we'll look in on the little prince." My sister-in-law, brassy in appearance, proved rather simple, easily led. "My son's father doesn't like me to leave him alone. He issues orders in all his letters: keep him company in the night, show gentleness, don't raise your voice to him..."

"József wants children."

"Don't you?"

She shrugged her shoulders. "There's the shop to mind."

I opened the door to Cesare's room. "Fast asleep." My sister-in-law peered over her shoulder at her husband and frowned. "Ibi, you mustn't mind the things József says."

A look of umbrage overspread her broad cheeks. "I'm not the enemy, but I'm no traitor either. I believe in Hungary." She jutted her chin. "Who is József to question Regent Horthy?"

Had her chin not reminded me of a dentist's mallet, I might have tried to soothe her. "If you love my brother, put aside your differences. He's going to need you in the days ahead."

She assented in silence, pulled close her bulky coat, and walked out of the flat.

József, still seated at the kitchen table, stifled a sigh. "How about another cup? I'm pouring." My brother half-filled our cups with coffee and sat back to warm his palms over the steam.

"Your aunt Sadie—may she rest in peace—used to make the best mandel bread. The kind you could dunk and it wouldn't fall to mush."

"Sadie and her mandel bread..."

József, having nothing to dunk, kept the spoon in his cup as he sipped. "So, when do I meet my brother-in-law, the famous composer? What's he waiting for anyway? For Mussolini to install his mistress at the Gellért?"

My mother scolded him with a glance.

"Easier for him to travel than Margit."

"They returned Cesare's passport, did I tell you?"

If my brother heard the optimism in my voice, he was quick to dispel it. "Now just try to get an exit visa—you'd think they'd be happy to see us leave, but a person could go to the grave waiting for a rubberstamp."

"Uncle Bernie used to say Sadie's mandel bread tasted like a sponge."

We lingered over our empty cups as if to read the grounds.

"If your maestro comes in May, we'll loan you the holiday house and the two of you can steal some time alone."

"If he comes in June, we'll go to Margit Island—"

"Enough! Please. Can't we speak of something else?" In truth there was little else. Each day our world contracted a bit more. Rationing hope, we sat at our kitchen table and waited—for a rescuer to appear, for Hitler to fall on his sword, for Europe to pull back from the abyss... "József, didn't you have a friend at *cheder* who joined the opera house?"

"Gyula, you mean? Haven't spoken to him in a dog's age. Far as I know, he's some sort of administrator. Gets his name in the papers, the old *pisher*. I would need to make inquiries."

"Leave that to me."

"I'd hardly call him a friend, but who else do we know? My one acquaintance at the Ministry has started quoting Goebbels." My brother's lips drew taut. "I'd better get home." He began to gather cups and saucers and to walk them to the sink.

Szidonia snatched up the cutlery.

"Ibi shouldn't have pranced out like that," József said to no one in particular. "It isn't right."

My mother opened her mouth to speak, but contrary to custom it was my father who had the last word. "These are matters beyond your wife's understanding. Be patient with her."

♪

The opera house looked smaller than I remembered it but no less imperial. Its paired marble sphinxes had lost none of their hauteur. Having dressed well for the occasion, I entered the frescoed lobby unimpeded, passed through the smoking corridor, and located Gyula's office without calling undue attention to myself. I recognized no one, only the elongated necks and regal postures. The halls still smelled of the same floor wax.

A secretary sat posted outside Gyula's door. My brother's "friend" had done well for himself, judging by the size of his quarters and the officious ill nature of their gatekeeper. Seeing no way around her, I introduced myself.

"Mr. Radnai knows you?" the girl asked without looking up from her typewriter.

"Yes, I used to dance here."

She glanced at me only long enough to throw the carriage-return. "I took you for foreign."

Gyula, prematurely stout, stepped into the reception area. "Well, well," he said, inclining over my hand without kissing it. "How's the family?"

"József sends regards."

"Haven't seem him since spats—or you, for that matter."

"I've been abroad making a career for myself, seeing the world."

"So I've heard."

"And you, Gyula? News travels in both directions. I've heard about your rise through the ranks."

He waved the compliment away. Cufflinks peeked out from his jacket sleeves, minotaurs in gold plate. "Small world the ballet."

I took a few steps in the direction of his half-shut door, which left him little choice but to follow.

At my back, he murmured, "It's not a good time."

"Would tomorrow be better?"

He lowered his voice. "What I mean is... oh hell, come inside." He motioned me ahead of him and closed the door behind us. His office was orderly, the papers atop his desk set out in arrow-straight rows. He didn't offer me a seat. "You've been gone—how long? The situation has changed. Don't you read the newspapers?"

I dipped at the knee to admire a framed portrait. "Your wife?"

"I married not long after you left. Hannah is also an artist: she paints. Her work hung at the Fine Arts—until recently."

"It's that bad?"

"Open your eyes, woman! We're all hanging on by a thread. Just this past week they started Aryanizing the theatre. Our turn will come."

"But there are so many non-Aryans at the opera house."

"Fifty three, to be exact."

"How can they let you go? You're their lifeblood."

"That won't stop them. They're out to break us this time." He circled his desk with clipped steps, straightening things that were already straight, the inkwell, a pair of gilt cherubs. "If you want my advice—"

"I didn't come for advice."

"This is not the moment for pride, Margit."

"If I were proud, would I be throwing myself on your mercy? I need to provide for my son. Ballet is all I know. I can dance, choreograph, teach."

"Why did you come back? Why now? Ever since Hitler, the noose has been tightening around our throats and you step right into it. There's a Nazi in every box, and you want to dance? No stage will have you."

I turned to leave, and he trailed me to the threshold, huffing like an asthmatic.

"What do you want from me? Who am I? You think because I sit at this desk that I'm exempt from this madness?"

I might have walked out, left him to rage at his cherubs and silk-lined walls, but history held me. "Four years old I was when I first walked through these doors. I had so little to offer, yet they took me. Now I have something to give back, a love of the art so deep it's imprinted in my bones, a vision of what it can become."

"Art has little to do with it, and love less."

"My life has not been a lie."

He grabbed hold of the door handle but did not turn it. He had stopped wheezing, seemed indeed to have stopped breathing. I could hear steam waft through the radiators. "The lie was that we had a place—a voice—a chance. I believed it the same as you."

"But my son—"

"What were we thinking, bringing children into such a world?" He glanced up as if expecting an answer from on high. "History will damn us for it. There's not a thing I can do, not for your son and not for my own. It will be bad this time."

♪

"Margit, about the boy..." My father sat hunched over that morning's *Magyar Hirlap*, reading the fine print through a magnifying glass. "Parliament has changed the laws again."

That would have been May of '39, the spring I took up dressmaking to buy my son a pair of shoes.

"Look, here." Mano pointed with his chin. "The definition of who's a Jew. Under the old law, anyone with an Aryan parent and baptized before a certain year would be considered Christian. Now, the law has taken the racial line as in Germany. Jewishness is determined by the blood of the grandparents. Your mother and

I, by our origins, doom your son. He's not safe under our roof."

"Don't talk that way, *apa*. We're a family."

"It's as family that I tell you this."

The newsprint sheets fell from his hands and lay on the parquet like a soiled garment.

"But Cesare is a foreigner. Surely a Hungarian law can't be applied to an Italian citizen."

"The only law that matters anymore is German. Hitler decides what we are." My father, narrow as a child in his bulky robe, rubbed his arthritic knuckles. "It wouldn't hurt to introduce yourself to the priest. See that the boy goes to church. For now."

The following Sunday, I dressed my son in his one suit, tucked an ironed handkerchief in his pocket, and walked him to the Church of Saint Teresa, which was not far from the opera house and drew a respectable crowd. "Sit in the front pew. Watch what others do and do the same. Take this." I emptied my change purse into his hand. "Put it in the box they carry up the aisles. I'll be back to get you after Mass. Wait for me here."

He had learned a bit of Hungarian by then, but his gestures, the very expression on his face, were his father's. "*Aspetta*, eh?" he made me promise.

I watched him weave through the clustered families and enter the chapel's gaping gray mouth. An hour and a half later, he came out again, walking alongside a man in black robes.

"Your son, madam?" The clergyman spoke in a monotone, head bowed and his long black beard flush against his chest.

"Thank you, yes. I hope he has caused you no trouble?"

"Not at all, but one does not often see a child so young alone at Mass." He paused and studied my face.

"I am not of your faith, but my son is a Catholic—like his father—and properly baptized. I brought him here to learn what is expected of him as a member of your church."

He placed a hand on my son's shoulder. "A child cannot be held to account for his parents' actions. I shall expect him next ɔut fail, your excellency."

gh the dark plugs of beard, his boyish cheeks pinkened. "I am not yet a priest, let alone someone worthy of honorifics. Address me as you would a friend. And your son, what do you call him?"

"Cesare. Cesare Frustaci."

"We may have need of an altar boy soon. If your son's Hungarian should improve, I don't see why he wouldn't be suitable."

Cover was what he offered, a gift more precious than prayers. "You have only to say when," I told him.

He glanced dubiously at Cesare, half nodded, and strode off. The last of the congregants filed out into the light, well dressed for the most part, their fur collars turned up. No one I knew.

"Did you take the wafer?" I asked my son.

"I tried," he said, as if to defend himself. "They told me I wasn't ready."

"But you crossed yourself?"

"Wasn't I supposed to?"

"You're to do as the others do. Precisely."

My father was at his machine when Cesare and I returned to my parents' flat. My mother had baked *knadlach*, and the sweet scent of cinnamon permeated every corner of the living room. A Viennese cut-glass vase adorned the dining room table. On the mahogany buffet, a pair of Sabbath candlesticks. Everything about that place spoke of who we were and from where we had come.

My father half rose from his seat. "Are you all right?"

"Why, don't I look all right?"

"Just pale," he said, absently testing a seam. "My beautiful daughter so pale."

♪

While we waited for the maestro, I worked most days at my cousin Zili Silberman's dressmaking business, which attracted a select clientele of actresses, courtesans and politician's wives, the only women in Hungary who could still afford the luxury of fine custom-tailored clothing. My cousin was single, roughly my age, and a redhead with a redhead's temperament. We'd talk as we worked or listen to the wireless. It made the endless repetition bearable. By noon, my head would start to ache and I'd take half of an aspirin, not wanting to exhaust our supply.

"Can you turn it down?"

My cousin liked her music loud, her food heavily spiced, and her perfume flowery. "Delicate ears," she ribbed me. "Just let me finish this zipper."

"Never mind. Where did you put the second pair of pinking shears?"

"I bartered them for face cream. French."

"And the gray satin for lining?"

"Bubble bath."

"My father may have something suitable, not the best quality."

"That always happens in a war. Everything goes short."

"But we're not in a war."

Zili clacked her tongue. "We will be soon. Herr Hitler will drag us in."

The aspirin was not working.

"He won't even need to drag us," my cousin went on, peddling her machine with a gathering fury, "we'll march in goose-stepping."

I could only rub my temples. "There's enough of this talk in the streets, why bring it home?"

We resumed a steady pace, seldom raising our heads from the needle. As the bobbin emptied, I heard my cousin tramp to the closet for a fresh bolt of fabric.

"That's a lovely voile, isn't it?"

"For La Gitane, the count's mistress. He'll shell out for it."

"Aren't the Gábor sisters due for a fitting?"

"Éva will be by this evening, with ZsaZsa there's no telling."

My cousin curled forward in gossip posture, her cheeks an

unwholesome shade of mauve. "I hear she's seeing a Turk, someone from the embassy. That's the sort of friend to have these days, a diplomat. I wouldn't expect the Gábors to go on acting much longer—you don't see Lili Darvas on a marquee anymore. Same with Ferenc Molnár. If the Magyars have their way, we Jews will be sweeping streets and shining shoes." The shears glinted in her hands. She wielded them like a weapon, severing the length of fabric with a single lunge. "And you so serene, Margit, so uncomplaining. I wake in the night suffocating, wanting to scream—and you? You float above it all. You take pleasure in a bolt of voile."

"Rest, Zili. Let me get you something."

She sat slumped over a pair of half-sewn lounging pajamas. "The things women wear! You'd think we had never left the harem." Exhaling, she thrust down hard on the peddle. "If you should see any pearl buttons ... "

Handicapped we may have been but hardly helpless. "Leave the buttons to me."

♪

And still the maestro didn't come, only his letters—from Naples, from Brescia, from Reggio Emilia... Behind the many-colored postmarks unfolded a litany of missed connections and red tape. Without a stamped declaration my husband could send no money to his son; without a work contract he could not secure a passport. *"I beg you, Mancikám, to be a little patient. I am finding my way and soon we won't want for anything. Beautiful days lie ahead of us."*

"Anything for the boy?"

A picture of a horse, hurriedly sketched in pencil.

"Does he give a date?"

"No date." My parents studied my face with an anxious *nu?* I skimmed the letter for good news. "Vittorio—Vittorio De Sica, the actor—recorded '*Tu Solamente Tu*.' It's all the rage in Italy. And Righelli—Alberto Righelli, the filmmaker—has put the song in a soundtrack. In a *movie*. And, when the credits roll, Pasquale's name flashes across the screen a meter high." My husband, I knew, had a tendency to exaggerate, but I quoted him verbatim, hoping to lift my parents' spirits.

Szidonia worried the hem of her apron. "You'd think he'd have sent the shoes."

Separation had taught me not to second-guess my husband, over whose actions I seemed to have lost all influence. I pictured him riding alone on a train, composing with that fixed look he would get, plotting the melody along an imaginary keyboard, and the countryside streaming by green and gray and waiting for war. *Beautiful days lie ahead for us.* If he believed, why then were his songs so sad?

♪

The opera house was packed to capacity the night Karola danced *The Wooden Prince*. She had sent me two tickets, but at the last moment my mother, needing to call on a sick relative, excused herself. I sat alone with an empty seat beside me, scanning the audience for a familiar face. The houselights dimmed. The overture struck up: early Bartok, by turns folksy and ethereal. Within months the composer would flee the country, but what did we know then? Only what was before our eyes, charmed figures dancing across a stage, tunes we had known from the cradle. Karola took center stage, molded to the role of princess in life as in art. She gave a more than competent performance, earning her ovation and the copious bouquets of roses in which she stood wreathed as the curtain came down.

I hurried backstage. Swarms of admirers had already penetrated her dressing room to pay homage. Corks popped, fans fluttered, and at a vanity table, still in her filmy tutu, the prima ballerina extended her hand to be kissed. For a moment I caught her eye, and she smiled and shrugged an apology.

The next day she sent a note to the flat, and later her driver. She received me in her suite at the Gellért, still wearing her satin nightdress and a white mask of cold cream.

"Darling, don't tell me it's five already! But come in. Let me look at you: elegant as always. I hardly knew what to expect."

"Budapest isn't Siberia."

"Is what Ilonka says true? Are you working as a seamstress?"
She clamped hands to her hips, as if daring me to deny it.

"Shouldn't you get that cream off your face?"

"Then it *is* true! Oh darling, it's dreadful, wasting your talent
that way. I'll speak to someone at the opera house."

"I already did."

"Then we'll just have to go above his head. This is not
acceptable." She pouted becomingly, motioned me into the sitting
room, and began to daub the cream from her face with a silk
handkerchief.

"You gave a wonderful performance last night."

She waved the compliment off. "Not much one can do with
The Wooden Prince." She melted onto a chaise. "Did I get all of
it?" she asked, holding out the hankie.

I removed the last remnants.

"Shall we go down or ring for room service?"

"Let's stay in. I want to hear all about Italy."

"As you like, darling, but one meets some interesting people
at the Gellért, men with titles, men with companies, men who
give away diamond bracelets as if they were small change."

"You seem to have forgotten: I'm a married woman."

"So am I, darling, so am I." She laughed, accentuating her
dimples. "A person learns to keep her options open."

"But your husband has always been so attentive."

"Zingarelli's okay, but when a man feels too sure of a
woman... better to keep him a bit off-balance, if you see my
point."

"Have you run into Pasquale?"

"Oh *him*." She got to her feet and stretched, arching her
supple back like a pedigreed cat. "What shall we order? I'm
starved."

"What did the two of you talk about? How did he look?"

"Goulash, stuffed mushrooms, goose liver..."

"Was he in good health?"

"Stewed mutton, ragout of pork... impossible to diet in this country."

"Karola, is there something you're keeping from me?"

She crouched and encircled my knees with a weightless arm. "Manci, it hurts to see you this way, you who deserve only good. You don't need to put up a brave front for me. What sort of life is this for you?"

"It's not Pasquale's fault."

She sighed and pulled away, landing on her haunches. "It's no use saying anything, you'll only defend him. But, from what I hear, he's back to his old ways. A woman. A dancer, naturally."

"Have you seen them—together?"

"No, and I'd better not."

My friend might seethe, but I felt no anger, only a bottomless sinking of the heart.

"Don't you want to know who she is?"

It hardly mattered. Those sort of women (if women they could be called) were interchangeable.

"Don't you want to strangle them both? Couldn't you wring their necks and toss their filthy bodies into the gutter? Couldn't you mince their genitalia? It makes me so fighting mad. For godsake, say something!"

"Weren't we about to order dinner? Whatever you're having will be fine—and a shot of brandy, please."

"As you like, darling." Karola sprang to her feet and pressed a silver buzzer. "I'd best get a wrap, the bellboy can be so excitable." She disappeared into the next room and returned wearing a fringed shawl and Lana Turner slippers with fur pompoms. Her lips were painted the color of snapdragons. "Let's spoil ourselves tonight, let's be gay. Tomorrow belongs to madmen, have no illusions about it."

The bellboy appeared, took our order, and left, promising to return with a magnum of champagne.

"What are we celebrating?" I asked my friend.

134

"Ourselves," she said, preening her bodice, draping her sculpted legs across the chaise like an exotic bit of contraband.

♪

"*My Dear Maestro,*" my hands quaked as I wrote, "*This morning I walked down Andrássy út, passed a newsstand, and chanced to notice a headline: Pact of Steel Binds Axis.*" This is how history happens to ordinary people, out the corner of an eye. "*Fearing the worst, I checked the expiration date on my passport: May 22, 1939. Today. As of this writing, I can no longer cross a border.*"

It was the sort of day that marked a change of season, disorienting in its perfection. I had been on my way to my cousin's flat but changed course and strode north toward the Italian Embassy. A doorman stood at the threshold. Having tipped him on a previous occasion, he recognized me and doffed his cap.

"Come to see the consul, madam? He's in his office. Don't let the secretary tell you otherwise."

Inside, there were the usual queues. Off to one side, a sympathetic-looking clerk lolled beside the water fountain. Needing to rivet him instantly or risk being sent to the back of the line, I blurted, "My husband in Italy is at death's door. His son is crying for him, endlessly, all night and all day. What shall I tell the boy? Would you deny a child a last visit with his dying father?"

"*Tranquilla, signora.* You have been here before, no? I can't promise anything, but in such cases we are sometimes able to issue a temporary permit."

"I knew you were a kind man."

He took a pair of wire-rimmed spectacles from his breast pocket and put them on. "Of course, the consul will require documents."

"What sort of documents?"

"Medical documents to begin with and then the usual: birth certificates, affidavits, marriage license…"

"But there's no time. I might lose my husband at any moment."

"Our lives, *signora*, are in God's hands."

I have never known an Italian indifferent to a child's suffering. "Is that what you'd have me tell my son? When he wakes in the night screaming *papi! papi! papi!* shall I say, the Duce cannot be bothered to issue a visa, he leaves it to God?"

"*Tranquilla*," the clerk pleaded, clumsily patting my elbow. "Give me what you have and I'll see what I can do."

I would return every day for the next two weeks. The clerk, having nothing substantive to report, merely repeated that he had left a note for his superior detailing my predicament and hoped to receive clearance soon.

"And your husband?" he asked for the sake of form.

"Hanging-on by a thread."

"Truly life is a vale of tears, *signora*. Come back next Monday."

They could not have done other than refuse my request, and yet I clung to hope like a drowning woman to the tail of a shark. Until I succeeded in reuniting my son with his father, there would be no safe harbor.

Once a fortnight had passed, the clerk could no longer put off the inevitable. "If your husband has survived this long, *signora*, with the Lord's grace he will live to a ripe old age. The consul has asked me to convey his good wishes, but he cannot issue a visa at this time. *Arrivederci*." He began immediately to shuffle papers. To look me in the eye could only have shamed him.

I did not budge.

He continued to fidget and then began to whistle. I recognized the tune, "*Si Tenesse na Cumpagna*," one of the maestro's early compositions in dialect.

"That's my husband's song," I said.

He didn't look up, only paused his whistling.

"My husband wrote that tune and many others. You must be from Napoli."

His index finger sprang on reflex to his lips. "I'm Roman," he said. "If your husband wants a favor of the consul, he had better be Roman, too." He winked and went back to his papers. When I still did not remove myself, he exhaled and eyed me over the rims of his spectacles. "Is there anything else we might help you with?"

"The embassy runs a school, does it not? I would like to enroll my son."

"Certainly, *signora*." He reached into a file drawer and drew out a stack of papers. "Need I say we will require documentation?" He lowered his voice. "When you're ready, bring me what you have. Depending upon what you're missing, I may be able to wangle something."

My son entered the Italian kindergarten that autumn. He learned proper Italian grammar and to revere the Duce alongside Christ and all the saints. He dressed for school in the uniform of the *Balilla*—black shirt, tassel hat, white cross-strap and a glaring "M" for Mussolini. No one could mistake him for a Hungarian child, let alone a Jewish one. Each day he reminded me more of his father.

♪

"When will they install elevators in these old tenements?" ZsaZsa Gábor arrived for a fitting at summer's peak. "It's uncivilized. A lady shouldn't have to climb stairs in heat like this."

ZsaZsa may not have had a sterling reputation, but my cousin knew the value of a client in the public eye. The Gábor sisters, having wooed a certain Viennese film producer, were fast gaining popularity on the screen. It was Éva who had the talent, but the younger Gábor served herself to the camera like a five-course meal.

Zili brought out the shirtwaist dress she had made for the actress, low-cut and tight across the hips. Sucking in her rounded belly, ZsaZsa wriggled into the garment and held her breath while my cousin fastened the buttons. "Shall I let out the seam perhaps?"

"But darling, a woman mustn't hide her assets." She admired herself in the three-way mirror, assuming a dance posture as if to waltz. "I'll just have to watch my figure."

"Not much food in the shops lately."

"Who relies on the shops? The embassies are stocked to the rafters with caviar."

She remained glued to the mirror, turning this way and that.

"How is your mother? Well, I hope."

ZsaZsa checked the alignment of the darts. "You know Jolie, always on top of things."

"Excellent taste, your mother has. Everyone remarks on it."

"You'd think people would have plenty more important to talk about, with our neighbors to the west up to their old tricks..." She rested a hip on my sewing cabinet and leaned in close. "You seem like a smart person. Hungary is no place for—a smart person."

That the Gábors were Jewish everyone knew, but to acknowledge the fact in their presence would have been indelicate. "One puts out feelers," I said, borrowing a phrase from my old friend Herr Saunders.

"Better sooner than later, darling. Anyone with gumption already has a ticket out."

Zili gave her handiwork a final inspection. "The dress suits you beautifully. Will you wear it or shall I wrap it for you?"

"I'm too lazy to change," ZsaZsa said with a sort of pride. "Keep my other dress as a gift. I may be away for a while."

My cousin swept up the imported sheath, barely worn, and slung it over a shoulder. "I'll save it for a special occasion—your next film, perhaps?"

The actress sidled up as if to whisper, but did not lower her voice. "Hungarians are becoming very popular in Hollywood, have you noticed? America appreciates what we have to offer." She stole a last look in the mirror, adjusted her cleavage, and pressed a bill into Zili's hand. "Goodbye, my darlings. Mind what I said."

♪

"*Dearest Pasquale,*" I wrote, watching the sun rise over the Buda hills, "*What we most dreaded has come to pass.*" Was anyone surprised, that September, when Molotov gave Ribbentrop the nod? Overnight, German armies flooded into Poland, leaving England and France no choice but to declare war. And then a baffling paralysis. "*Hungary turns in its hour of need to Italy—just as I, your devoted wife, must now rely on you. Your son prays for you every night. Please hurry.*"

The High Holy Days found Budapest's Jews at once piqued and muzzled. I had not been to the Great Synagogue on *Dohány utca* since childhood. Orthodoxy rubbed against my temperament. It irked me that the women sat passively in a gallery with the children, while the men clustered before the ark. I balked at parroting prayers in a language I didn't understand. But in the autumn of 1939, with Hitler on our border and the Arrow Cross gaining muscle at the polls, such things seemed trifles. It was a comfort to sit in the immensity of the prayer hall and count our numbers.

"Look over there, that's your cousin Bella." Szidonia gestured with her lower lip toward a dark woman of indeterminate age seated alone in a far corner. "You have to give her credit. All her family has converted, and yet she comes to shul. The only one."

I caught Bella's eye, and she raised her net veil and faintly smiled. "She must be lonely."

"I wouldn't worry about her," Szidonia whispered. "They say she has a lover in the Treasury."

"And that woman over there?" A bird-like matron with prominent hands, long-fingered and tapering. "She looks familiar."

"You've probably seen her at the opera house. She plays harp—or did. Like all the other Jewish musicians, she got notice in July."

"She had to have been with the opera from the time I was a child. What will she do now?"

"There are still weddings. The greatest virtuosos are falling over one another for a chance to play 'My Yiddishe Mama.'"

Below, amid the horde of bodies, I could see my father bob and rock as he prayed. Could a single surge of piety suffice until he next put aside the pork meat that he loved, dug out his yellowed *tallis*, and presented himself in shul? Mano would not have expected it to. He prayed because it was in his genes to pray, to utter the sounds and let them resonate inside like a second heartbeat.

"He hasn't been himself," my mother, following my gaze, whispered. "Not since Rosa."

"Has he seen a doctor?"

"There's no doctor for what he has."

I left the synagogue before services ended, needing to collect my son from a neighbor, Nora Mátrai, who had children of a similar age. We had met in the courtyard, where the little ones would gather to play marbles and hopscotch. She seemed a decent sort, literate enough to see that her children did their homework, a meticulous housekeeper, and, unlike other women in the building, not given to gossip. Cesare liked her little daughter Bebe, a tomboy with arresting violet-blue eyes and a sixth finger on her left hand.

"Did he behave himself?" My son raced ahead of me down the open corridor to my parents' flat.

She shrugged her workhorse shoulders. "You know how boys can be."

I let Cesare into the flat and he ran to our room for the pop-up book his father had recently sent from Italy, a juvenile version of the *Mille e Una Notte*, lavishly illustrated in the finest inks. My son was mesmerized by the volume, seldom putting it away.

"Wash your hands before you open it!" I called after him. "Come and sit with me. We'll read together."

The book was an extravagance, but so finely crafted I could not fault the purchase.

"I know the story," my son boasted. "The prince, being a

capo, has many women, lots and lots of women. So many women he can chop off their heads and still never run short."

"Put the book away," I said more sharply than I had intended. "The bathwater is warming. Bring the soap."

He stamped off and returned in his underclothes. "I want to go to Arabia."

"You might not find it as in the book. You might not like it."

He puffed out his mulish little chest. "I'll like it just fine, eh? There are no kikes there."

"What did you say?"

"Mr. Mátrai says there are too many in Budapest."

I grabbed the bar of soap from beside the tub. "Will you force me to wash your mouth out? Must you repeat every filthy slur you hear? I never want to hear you say that word again."

"Kike?"

I hunched over the cauldron of hot water and my reflection stared back, tired eyes swimming atop a quavering chin. "You don't even know what it means, do you?"

My son shook his head.

"Come, take off the rest of your things." I drew water from the spigot and filled the tub halfway. Mustering what remained of my strength, I hefted the pot from the wood stove and emptied it. Whatever grime the world deposited on my son, I would scrub clean. I would scrub him clean as a china teacup.

♪

My husband's burgeoning success only seemed to fuel his despair. "*Mancikám, I can barely stand this life longer. I live badly and my heart is broken.*"

With Germany at war, he no longer spoke of coming to Budapest. For reasons I never quite grasped, he didn't send the shoes for Cesare, the train tickets for our return journey, or money for our upkeep. We began to spar by post, I reminding him of his obligations, and he reproaching me for doubting. "*You will be compensated for all your sacrifices and together we will enjoy a peaceful old age.*" Had he still not learned to hold onto his wallet?

My last pair of silk stockings thinned and ran, and I took them to Mrs. Bajcsi, Ilona's mother, who had a business in her home selling needles and thread and mending hosiery. A mousey woman as unlike her daughter as water is to fire, she had no one in her life but Ilona and nothing but worry with which to fill the long months between letters.

"Still in Budapest? My daughter always asks for you."

"My last letter came back unopened."

"She's been moving about—Milan, Munich, Berlin... I have stationery from all the hotels where she stays, such strange names." She held my stockings up to the light and chalk-marked the holes. "Good quality. I can make a pair of stockings like this last a lifetime."

"What does Ilonka say? Is she working?"

"On and off. That demon, the one who lured her to Italy, caught up with her again."

"You mean Buffarino?

"The very same. Put her in some sort of circus between a contortionist and a family of pygmies."

"And her beau?" It was a wonder that the fencer hadn't run the "impresario" through by then. "He's usually so good at keeping an eye on her."

"So you haven't heard?" Mrs. Bajcsi unrolled a length of thread and wet the end with her tongue. "Mr. Ferretti fell out with the Duce—something to do with foreign bank accounts. Before Ilona knew what was happening, he had dropped from sight. She made inquiries, searched for him—the prisons, the hospitals... Finally, she gets a postcard from Buenos Aires. Could she send him his favorite foil, it says."

"She's better off without the rogue."

"You're probably right," said Mrs. Bajcsi in a choked voice, "but I don't like to think of my little girl all alone."

The poor woman needn't have fretted. After the war Ilona would return to Budapest, still single, and go into business with her, the two sitting side-by-side mending stockings. Daughter and mother would become the *pas de deux* she and I never quite managed to be.

♪

Once Italy entered the war, it was only a matter of time before Hungary followed suit. Mail delivery, never a model of efficiency, slowed while letters passed through a censor. A subtle stiffness entered the maestro's script, our words no longer ours alone. Somewhere in a smoke-filled cubicle, a man in uniform, red pencil in hand, pored over our endearments and rebukes.

However murky those years may have been, they were my husband's making. His melodies won favor with the celebrities of his day. Wanda Osiris opened shows with "*Sentimental,*" Macario with "*Camminando Sotto La Pioggia.*" I have photographs: the maestro hamming it up at the keyboard with Vittorio, the maestro raising his wine glass in a toast to Totó, the maestro flanked by Clely Fiamma, Bernardo DeMuro, a pubescent Renata Tebaldi... He has put on weight. He smiles for the camera, would never be caught on camera without a smile, yet he looks (to my eye) more clownish than happy.

I can barely stand this life any longer.

If only we had had a code, an inviolable wavelength. I dreamed of sitting with my husband in a sealed room where we might speak the secrets of our unequal exile, but no such place existed. Our hearts were on display like cuts of meat in the window of a butcher shop.

My reluctant abettor, the Italian clerk, took lunch at the same café where my mother often stopped for a tisane. I made of point of introducing them. When Szidonia baked strudel or *flodni,* I would wrap a serving in muslin and take it to him to have with his coffee. It was not long before etiquette obliged him to offer me a cup. His name was—Sergio? Stefano? He had a fiancée back in Naples who cared for an elderly father.

"Are you homesick?" I asked him.

"I'd go back home tomorrow for 50 lire a day and a pension."

"How I miss Italy!" The Italy of my innocence, rolling past the fogged window of a train. "I'd do anything to go back."

He looked at once irritated and pitying. "You're wasting your time at the embassy. Italy has closed its borders to certain—classifications." He blushed at the term, whose meaning was only too clear. "We are not unique in this under the current circumstances."

"How do you like the pastry?"

"*Dolce*," he said and took another bite. "Of course, no border is impenetrable. Visa or no visa, people desirous of entry will find a way in."

"I would imagine that certain points of entry might be more vulnerable than others."

"Lugano," he said point-blank.

"Mountainous country, isn't it?"

He let down his façade of nonchalance and faced me squarely. "A person would need to be fit. It is a not a crossing suited to old people. *Pasatori*—guides, you might call them—operate in the area, simple farmers most of them. Luck plays a part, as in any game of chance."

"And once inside?"

"You'll need papers—there's quite a traffic in these right now. Common names work best." He stood and emptied a pocketful of coins onto the tabletop. "Please thank your mother for me."

"You must try her noodle pudding."

Hat in hand, he dipped at the knee to whisper, "Forget you know me, *signora*. We haven't had this conversation."

♪

The opening bars of Beethoven's *Fifth Symphony* signaled the start of the BBC service. Zili tossed aside her sewing, daubed blood from a pricked finger, and turned up the volume.

"*There is no need to tell you of my personal anguish and that of many others over the news announced a few hours ago.*" The familiar Anglicized Hungarian of Professor McCartney battled a blitz of static. "*This is the second time in our generation that the ominous power of Germany and its agents has swept Hungary into war against us…"*

"As if I didn't smell it coming?" muttered Zili. "We rush in hoping for a share of the spoils—not that there will be any." She reached on reflex for the aspirin bottle. "We always pick losers."

"We offer you freedom," McCartney droned on, *"the Nazis offer you captivity. It is up to the Hungarian people to decide."*

"Drown every last politician in the Danube and be done with it!"

"Calm yourself, Zili. Wars end. After the last one we all got on with our lives well enough."

My cousin hurled the unfinished garment onto a chair back. "I want to live *now*. I want my happiness *now*. All the men will be drafted. We women will be left alone to prowl and scavenge like alley cats."

"We have family. We earn our livelihood. We are not animals."

She drew her chair flush up against mine. "Take away their bread and people are whatever circumstance makes them. This is a war of everyone against everyone, down to the last crumb. Already they look at us like prey."

"Zili, Zili… no one is looking at us. People are out of sorts, that's all. Things will be better once winter passes." I went back to my work, hoping she would do the same.

"I'm going out," she said, bolting to her feet and grabbing a herringbone topcoat from the rack. It was a frigid day. Anyone with sense would have stayed indoors. "There's bound to be a stir on the streets."

"La Gitane is coming tomorrow, don't forget."

"That pink satin ball gown—where would the creature wear such a thing?" She flattened a woolen cloche onto her flame red hair. "Don't wait for me," she said and dashed off as if to catch the last street car that would ever cross a track.

♪

József had begun to come for Shabbat dinner alone, bringing

a few flowers or a jar of marmalade. He would arrive after sundown (no one would have thought to rebuke him for it), having stopped home to change into a clean shirt. Cesare would be getting ready for bed.

"So, big man, how are you getting on at school?"

My son proudly displayed a tin likeness of the Duce, a useless *tchotchke* over which he had doted all that week.

"They gave it to him at the kindergarten," I explained, "for Christmas."

Cesare scampered off and returned with the three or four primers he would take to and from school. These were little more than picture books with a few stock prescriptions. Cesare fumbled over the Italian phrases, which I then translated: *The Italian land is blessed by God; A book and a rifle, the perfect fascist; The Duce is always right...*

"Don't look so stricken," I said, closing the jacket cover. "Cesarino is his father's son. No one can tell him anything."

My brother sat back in his chair and stroked his chin stubble. "I don't suppose a Hungarian school would be much better, and soon they'll dismiss the rest of the Jewish teachers, as they've done elsewhere in *greater Germany*."

We took dinner in the kitchen, where it was warm and the smell of honey cake induced a short-lived euphoria. There was still enough to eat back then if a person wasn't fussy. The meat in the beef barley soup had an odd stringiness about it, but we all pretended not to notice.

"Who was it this week?" my father would ask.

By which he meant, who had been called to the labor battalions, the freshly legislated martyrdom of Hungary's Jewish males. The young and unmarried were the first to be called, marching off with nothing but a shovel in their hands en route to the Russian front. We pooled names and silently prayed. Each week that my brother escaped the list gave us hope the war might end before his turn came.

"Why don't they just let us fight like everyone else?" József said, appealing to reason. "I have nothing against the Russians, but if I'm going to get sent into battle let me defend myself. Give me a gun."

Szidonia clamped the lid on the cast-iron casserole. "Better they shouldn't call you."

Mano lumbered to his feet, leaving the food on his plate untouched. "Isn't it time the boy went to sleep?"

"I'll take him, *apa*. Sit."

By the time I put my son down and returned to the kitchen, coffee was brewing. My mother stood with her back to the door, slicing the cake into generous portions. My father had lit his pipe.

"If things get bad," József was saying, "Ibi has relatives in the country outside Tatabánya."

Down came my mother's knife, thudding against the wooden cutting board. "I would never impose on your wife's relatives."

"Szidonia, József was just suggesting—"

"I heard what he's suggesting, that we go crawling to the gentiles." We sat in silence while my mother poured the coffee into her best cups. "I'd sweeten it, but the stores have run low on sugar."

The cake tasted sweeter for the coffee's bitterness.

"Look," József started in again, "if they should take me, I would feel better knowing you have someplace to go. We've all heard the rumors. The Nazis are waging two wars: a war among nations, and a second war—the one we know only through hearsay—against us Jews."

My father hunched so low to the table that his chin nearly grazed it. "The bad smell will blow over. It always does."

"There's Italy. The maestro will get us all papers." I knew even as I said this that my father would not undertake the journey, and that my mother would never desert him. Duty bound her to him like a third arm.

"You go, Margit." Szidonia positioned herself behind Mano, her bosom seeming to crown his head. Never had I seen her stand so straight and wide. "At the first opportunity, take the boy and go. I'll never forgive you if you don't."

♪

The summer of '42 brought Horthy down from his white horse. His eldest son, Stephan, was dead. The Germans called it an accident, but airplanes don't just drop from the sky.

Arrangements for a state funeral began at once. Long black streamers hung from the balconies, thrusting the city into a premature chill. Count Galeazzo Ciano, the Duce's son-in-law, arrived at the Western Station, where a crowd had been mustered to greet him and the red carpet rolled-out. Along one side stood arrayed the whole of the Italian diplomatic core, and along the other a coterie of Hungarian politicians. Because of the Regent's mourning, no anthem was played.

As the train ground to a halt, the consul placed a bounteous bouquet of rare blooms—wild orchids, white muscari—into the arms of a small, well-groomed boy, an Italian student hand-picked for the occasion. My son.

I stood in the dense heart of the crowd, camouflaged in black, not wanting Cesare to see me. Szidonia had pressed his suit that morning. She had shined his shoes to a high gloss and tamed his hair with tonic. At a signal from the consul he started down the red carpet, just as Ciano, affecting the fascist stare, alighted from his carriage. Step by measured step, the distance between them narrowed.

It is one of those memories time seems only to sharpen. I have a newspaper photograph somewhere. My son sprawls forward on the long carpet, having tripped over his own feet; the flowers lie scattered. And kneeling, taking the crying child into his arms, is Ciano, not the studied demagogue of a moment before but a man fully human, a father moved by the sight of a child's shame.

"*Non piangere, piccolino.*" Don't cry, little one.

He must coo the words rather than speak them, for he puckers. One after another the camera shutters click.

I never spoke of the incident to my son. Some months later,

the clipping arrived from Italy, sent by the maestro's sister Maria, who had seen it on the newsstand. Before the image could pale, Ciano too would be dead, executed by a firing squad for betraying the Duce. I only know what I saw that day: a man stooping to comfort a little boy. For years I kept the photograph in the same tin box as Pasquale's letters, never suspecting the service it would one day render.

♪

Within weeks of the funeral, the Allies bombed Budapest for the first time. Thirty or forty planes streaked overhead (even the boldest of us lost count), randomly tearing pieces from the cityscape. It grew difficult to find one's way. Night after night, the landmarks by which we had navigated all our lives toppled: the Museum of Fine Arts, the Museum of the Capital, the Millennial Monument... Anti-aircraft guns were installed in the Buda hills. Powerful search-beams began to scour the night sky. We blacked-out our windows, but still the light penetrated, robbing us of sleep.

My father refused to leave the flat, even during air-raids, when the rest of the building's inhabitants would race for the cellar. Mornings, he would sit down to sew and barely take a stitch, his gaze lost in the warp and woof of the fabric, in the questions for which he had no answers. It was the same at table. The contents of his plate seemed suddenly to hold some metaphysical puzzle.

"Stop staring at your food and eat it," my mother would plead.

"Save it for the boy. He's got some appetite, *taka*."

He stopped reading the newspapers, complaining of vertigo. The whirligig of his mind, the free-fall into which a wrong word might plunge him, we could only imagine. He rarely spoke except to ask for József, whose visits had become more frequent.

I continued to spend days at my cousin's, grateful to find the building still standing each time I arrived. Zili would be pacing in front of the wireless, sometimes dancing, too restless to take her place at the machine.

"Fabric has gotten so scarce," she said once, "soon we'll all go naked." The notion had seemed funny at the time.

How many thousands of uniforms were sewn during those years, the ugly khakis, the drab browns? Bolt upon bolt of canvas and duck, twill and gabardine... and later the shrouds—bleached muslin, white gauze. The Hungarian army lost half its men in a single battle outside Stalingrad, the cold so bitter they could not have felt the bullets tear through their flesh.

I remember arriving home one evening, the blackout already begun, searchlights streaming across a steely sky. A single candle burned in my mother's parlor.

"Where's the little prince?" I asked.

My mother took my coat and hung it in the closet. "At the Mátrai's."

"Where's Papa?"

Szidonia moved about the room with a feather duster, flicking beneath the curtains, along the sills. Her face held no expression, but her breath came in heaves as if someone had clamped a hand to her mouth.

"Your father didn't get out of bed this morning." *Flick, flick.* "It's Joseph..." *Flick, flick.* "His letter came. They're taking him day after tomorrow."

I snatched the duster from her hand, took the hand, chapped, wrinkled, and tried to soothe it.

"But surely he doesn't intend to go?"

"He'll go. They all go."

"But he has a family. Let them take someone else."

"They all have families."

"This is madness! They march us off in all directions, and have you noticed? No one comes back."

"Madness it may be, but if we didn't go they'd say we were unpatriotic, and then the mobs again."

"What is the Axis if not a mob?"

She covered her own lips as if my words had been hers, as if by silencing them she might protect me. "Go see your father, maybe you can get him to eat something."

The door to my parents' bedroom stood ajar. With the curtains drawn, I could not see Mano, but his smallest movement set the old bedsprings creaking.

"*Apa*? Are you asleep?"

"Just resting my eyes," he said softly. "I want to be awake when József comes."

"Can I get you anything—broth?'

"What do I need it for? Keep the food for the boy, he's growing."

"Please. A cup of broth. You must get your strength back."

"I was never strong." His hand reached out in the darkness and lightly brushed my sleeve. "Your mother's the strong one. You take after her. The house painter (by which he meant Hitler) is no match for the two of you."

"If that were true, I wouldn't let József be taken. There must be somewhere he can go, a hiding place. Talk to him, *apa*. He's afraid if he runs away, they'll come for us, that we'll be made to suffer."

"Who's to say he's wrong? My son is a mensch."

"Yes, a mensch." To debate would only have augmented my father's grief.

"Sit by me." I could hear him make space, pulling his brittle frame from the edge of the bed. "There are things bigger than us. There are things beyond our understanding. I don't know why, I only know it's so."

We sat in silence, in darkness, rationing breath lest we rile the bedsprings.

"Forgive me, *apa*. Forgive me for all the years I stayed away. If I'd have known—"

"There's nothing to forgive."

"I wanted to come sooner, I should have, and then Rosa—"

"Hush, *shayna maydela*. What is there to regret? How sweet our lives have been! To see you dance gave me the most exquisite

151

pleasure I have ever known. I can still see you dance, my precious ballerina, so high on your toes, so high..."

He drifted off. We thought he was sleeping. After dinner Szidonia put on her flannel nightgown, and not wanting to wake him, slept on a chair beside their bed. Only at dawn did the slackness of his features make her reach for his shoulder and give a shake. I went for József, and we rushed Mano to hospital, but our father didn't want to be saved. By evening we were back, carrying his nappy bathrobe and worn leather slippers, and telling anyone who asked, "He went gently. No pain. No fear."

♪

There are stories we tell ourselves in order to go on. While my father's corpse lay in its casket waiting to return to the soil, we allowed ourselves to believe that József might be granted at least a deferment—a month, a week, long enough to sit *shiva* with his family. Was he not, after all, an only son?

"It's the wrong time to ask favors." József tapped cemetery soil from his polished, if worn-down, shoes. "The war is going badly. And besides, it's Sunday—who can I ask on a Sunday?"

He was due to report to the sports stadium at nine a.m. the next morning. We sat up with Szidonia through the night, brewing cups of tea she did not drink, beginning conversations only to have her doze off, bobbling like aspic atop her mourning stool.

"I hate to leave her at a time like this."

"We'll request an exemption. I have a gold wristwatch I won't miss."

"Keep your things," my brother muttered, "cash works just as well."

He left before first light, taking with him our father's generations-old *sidher* and the brass carriage clock he had kept on his sewing table. Szidonia, ashen, her swelled lids closing, would not get into bed.

"József will be back soon, what's the use?"

I lay down beside Cesare and tossed in and out of sleep for

what seemed no time at all. When I awoke, the bed was empty. My mother stood framed in the doorway, combing her coarse black hair.

"Eight o'clock," she said and glanced over her shoulder. "Your father would be at his machine by now. I'll never get used to this quiet."

József arrived a half hour later, looking older than the evening before. He wore a clean, ironed white shirt and stout brown boots. His wife had stuffed his knapsack with boiled potatoes and tubes of liniment until the seams strained. He put on a brave front, set his jaw, but his shoulders sagged under the weight.

"I won't say goodbye, *anyám*." His voice held steady. "I'll be back."

She stood bunching her apron front. "Do you have enough to eat?"

"More than I can carry."

They embraced quickly, seemed almost to thrust each other away. "I'll always be proud of you."

I set out with my brother for the stadium, the two of us striding briskly through a gray drizzle. With rubble strewn to all sides, it was impossible to walk a straight line. We wove from pavement to pavement, keeping to the narrow side streets where military trucks couldn't go.

"My wife may be with child," he said, expressionless. "It's not certain, but we can't take chances. She'll leave the city immediately."

"You've always wanted to be a father."

He winced, angled away. "What kind of father can I be from the front?"

"Women are stronger than you think. You'll have a family to come home to."

We entered the seventh district, a maze of fear, its streets emptied of peddlers. The shops stood shuttered. A fat gendarme stood watch on a corner, kicking the alley cats each time they crept toward the gutter to drink.

"Do you remember when you left for Italy in that stinking Fiat? I could have punched the guy, that—what was his name? Macaroni?"

"We had worse names for him."

"Some impresario! Had con-artist written all over him."

"Things didn't turn out that badly."

"No," he conceded after a moment's reflection, "I suppose they haven't."

Too soon, we crossed Rottenbiller utca and turned right. The stadium came into view. Men with knapsacks began to appear everywhere, stepping out from doorways, down from streetcars. They carried themselves with a certain posture, back-leaning and poised to flee.

My brother's tired eyes cast about. "Isn't that Gyula across the street? Gyula Radnai, from the opera house."

None other, though I barely recognized him in his coarse shirt and clunky shoes. Hardly an athletic man, he might have been out netting butterflies.

József called out, "Gyula, over here!"

His old schoolmate hesitated and then raised a hand in mock salute. "*Et tu*, József?"

"Come here, you old *pisher*. This is no time to be alone."

Grunting under the weight of his knapsack, Gyula shambled toward us.

My brother clasped him in an awkward embrace. "Just like a high school reunion, no? But where have you been keeping yourself?"

"In a broom closet. But pardon my manners—how are you, Margit?"

"Fine, thank you. And your wife?"

"Low, I'd say. Every canvas looks more and more like the destruction of Valhalla."

"When we get back," my brother said, "bring her to our chalet in Hüvösvölgy. Change of air."

From every corner the recruits converged, hundreds and then

thousands of gray figures trudging toward an open gate. Where they would be sent, no one seemed to know. In the absence of supervision, the men clustered loosely in groups. The dozen or so uniformed watchers—some soldiers, others ordinary policemen—served no other function than to shout, "*To the left! To the right!*"

"Wait," I said, grabbing my brother by the sleeve, "we'll speak to someone in authority."

"*To the left! To the right!*" A man in brown waved his Billy club in our direction. "Kiss your sweetheart goodbye and send her home, Jew boy."

What happened next I saw only in flashes: my brother lunging toward the cop with the cords of his neck twitching, a bystander sandwiched between, the blow ricocheting as club met bone...

"Hell, did he break it?" Gyula clapped a hand to his chin. There wasn't much blood, but the angles of his face had rearranged themselves in the manner of a Cubist painting.

My brother slung a protective arm about the injured man's shoulders. "There's bound to be a doctor inside."

"But you can't go inside!" Desperate to stop them, I lunged into their path. "If this is what they do to you on the street, in broad daylight—"

The bone-breaker, not yet satisfied, drew up beside me, poking at my ribs with the black wooden phallis. "Time's up, sister. Scat! Now."

I grabbed for my brother's arm, but a pair of soldiers had wedged themselves between us. The line of recruits inched forward. Gyula, gazing back, clutched his crooked chin. "Didn't I tell you, Margit?"

József took the injured man's knapsack and added it to his own load. "Go home and tell mother that it isn't so bad," my brother's voice drifted back, "tell her I'm with friends."

♪

The men marched off, the Danube froze, and still the maestro did not come. Fewer letters arrived from Italy. Those that did painted a picture of mayhem: Mussolini deposed and reinstated, a sickly puppet of the Reich; Pasquale's little brother Emilio languishing in a prison camp somewhere in British India; the rest of the Frustacies moving from flat to flat, bombed-out before they could so much as light a fire in the hearth. Voids opened into which our dreams vanished without a trace.

And through it all, my husband continued to make music, having joined forces with Macario, a comedian with whom neither side could find fault and whose shows brought laughter back to a people sapped by daily privations. Pasquale's tunes found their way abroad, translated into German and English even while the war raged. Once, while sewing, I heard a familiar melody, *"Du immer wieder du..."* The song my husband had composed for me, crooned with a Bavarian robustness suggestive of a beer fest.

"What's the matter," said my cousin, "you want I should change the station?"

"Leave it. We might hear some news."

"Where are the British, the Americans? *That* would be news." She stopped pedaling and swiveled to face me. "I know someone, someone connected. He says terrible things about—" She muffled her voice with a cupped hand. "About gas. About how they use gas to kill us."

"Who is he?"

"I can't say. There are people working underground, the less you know the better."

I turned up the volume on the music, swept aside my cousin's riotous mane, and put my lips to her ear. "I wish I could disbelieve it. I wish I could tell you your friend is mad. *Gas*? Find out everything you can, but be careful. You have a family, remember."

♪

Regent Horthy was in his box at the opera house when Hitler's summons found him. He was to go to Schloss Klesheim near Salzburg, where the Fuhrer would be waiting. No sooner had the gullible patriarch crossed the border, than hordes of armed German troops began to advance on Budapest. They occupied the city without firing a shot—who dared to oppose them? Before we could get our bearings, Hungary's own Nazis emerged from the shadows, donned the uniform of the Arrow Cross, and rampaged through the streets.

Overnight came the government orders, a veritable barrage posted one after the other: Jewish-owned stores must close; Jews may not travel or change residence or listen to foreign radio broadcasts; Jews must wear the yellow star...

"If they could siphon the air from our lungs, they would!" raged my cousin Zili, rifling the remnant drawer for the proper color cloth. Piss-yellow, she called it, though in truth it was closer to canary.

I took a length of the fabric home to Szidonia, who in silence traced the stars, measured them from point to point, and carefully hemmed the edges.

"No one will notice the patch," I said, unconvinced myself but hoping to ease her mind.

She did not look up from her work.

"We have nothing to feel ashamed of."

Still my mother, her stitches taut and even, kept silent.

I chose two dresses from my wardrobe, practical garments, and handed them to her. "Just these, please."

Cesare entered the room at a trot, carrying the black shirt from his *Balilla* uniform. He went to his grandmother, and with juvenile bluster flung the shirt onto her lap. "Sew a star on mine. I want a star, too."

Szidonia stabbed her needle into the yellow fabric. "That's not for you."

My son, pouting, hung on her knee. "Why not? Why can't I have a star like you?"

"Because... because you come from Italy. You're special. You already have your uniform." She did not look up again until her work was finished.

The next day, I left the flat wearing the patch for the first time, on my coat, the morning being unseasonably cold, and walked down the stairs to the courtyard thinking, from this day forward I have no country. Not a single neighbor greeted me. In the foyer, a place of perpetual twilight, I crossed paths with Mr. Mátrai.

"Good morning," I said. "Please give my regards to Nora."

"Who are you to speak my wife's name? Who are *you*?" The front door opened and a ray of light fell upon his torso. He too displayed an emblem: the intersecting barbs of the Arrow Cross. "You stay away from my family and tell your filthy brat to do the same."

I walked past him and out of the building. In the street I saw others like me, marked and uncertain, and others like Mr. Mátrai, the new master race that would set the world right. We were all marked, all strangers, and the distance between us gaped wider than the Danube.

♪

"Twenty-five kilos per person."

Szidonia had to have repeated the edict a hundred times as she walked through the rooms studying our belongings, weighing them in her mind. There was no question of taking the mahogany wardrobe that had belonged to my grandmother, or my parents' nuptial bed with its claw feet, or the hand-cut crystal vase given to them by a rich uncle on some long-ago wedding anniversary. My father's sewing machine had already been carried to my cousin's, but there was still the settee, the curio cabinet, the Chinese screen...

"Twenty-five kilos. It would take a mule to carry that much. We're only allowed one load."

I watched my mother gather together the last of the flour, the dried beans, the jar of *schmaltz* and place them in a makeshift knapsack sewn from a pillowcase, watched her stack the folded sheets and pillowcases, the handkerchiefs and towels.

"At least we haven't far to go." Up the street to 9 Andrássy út, one of several dozen buildings designated for Jews and marked with a garish yellow star over its entrance. "I've found a small carriage for Cesare. He can push his things in it." The contraption was a gift from Zili's mysterious friend—that it smelled of burnt gunpowder, no one seemed to notice.

"We're supposed to turn in the Sabbath candlesticks." For the first time since receiving the edict, my mother stopped her calculating and tallying and braced against the table edge.

"Give them to me. Give me anything you can't bear to lose." I had already scouted out a hiding place and secured the metal box that held the maestro's letters. She handed me the candlesticks and slipped the thin gold wedding band from her ring finger.

Cesare traipsed into the room, pushing the rickety little carriage, into which he had piled his *Balilla* uniform, his father's pop-up book, and the shiny Mussolini.

"Must you take that thing?"

Szidonia compressed her lips. "How much can it weigh? It's only made of tin."

When the time came to vacate the flat, we gathered up what we could carry and dragged it onto the landing. A Jewish neighbor we had barely known—suitcase strapped across his back, a crying child in his arms—nodded from across the courtyard. Mr. Mátrai relieved the man of his house key as he trudged past. "Have you turned in your valuables?"

"Yes, see for yourself."

"Don't wise-mouth me, Jew. It's bad enough I've had to live in the same building with you—for how many years?"

"Thirty," the man said with a dignity lost on the diehard. "We've been neighbors for thirty years."

My mother silently pulled closed the door and handed me the key. "*You* give it to him. I don't want him speaking to me."

And then we heard the barking. Outside, on Andrássy út, waited armed escorts barely restraining the attack dogs they led on thick leather leashes, dogs brawny as boars, baring their spiky fangs. A policeman blew a whistle. Braying conflicting orders, his cronies formed the growing throng into columns and began to herd us to our assigned living quarters.

Cesare, having been trained to march in formation at the Italian school, fell readily into step. "A parade!"

We adults made our way up the boulevard mustering the last of our strength, shifting our load every few meters. We were many and varied: professional people in smart suits, old women in housecoats, the newly poor and those who had known nothing but want. The yellow star, still enough of a novelty to make us shy from one anther, branded us like cattle.

The building to which we were assigned was not unlike the one we had just left. We walked through a foyer into a courtyard and found ourselves in the midst of bedlam, hundreds of people dragging luggage, balancing children on their hips, searching for a door—

"It really isn't that bad, is it?" A woman in a well-tailored dress and high-heels paused beside me, appearing almost to smile. "If it weren't quite so crowded…"

She was Klára Kemény, wife of Oszkár, once a prosperous textile merchant, and mother to Éva and Ádám, well-behaved young people denied the right to an education. We would live together in the yellow star house, two families crammed into a cubicle measuring eight feet from end to end with no beds, no closet, and from seven o'clock each evening no light. We would become the best of friends.

♪

When did we first hear the name Eichmann? Zili's friend in the resistance warned that a German official had been sent to Hungary on a special mission: to remove us.

"What does he mean, *remove?*"

Zili pinced my forearm. "Look it up in the dictionary. What does anything mean anymore?" She had developed the habit of chewing her lower lip; it looked like raw liver. "They say the German stays in the background while his Hungarian flunkies do the dirty work. At night. No witnesses, no reprisals. Damn, I miss the radio!"

The cattle cars were already carrying the Jews of the provinces to places like Auschwitz and Dachau, but we in the capital, blind to their passage, subsisted from curfew to curfew, scavenging the fistful of barley or blackened potatoes that would be our next meal. Some days we were not allowed out at all. We would sit on our folded quilt with our backs against the wall and tell stories or sing songs, anything to distract ourselves from the gnawing hunger.

One day, Ádám Kemény brought out a camera he kept hidden in the building's furnace room.

"Put that away!" Klára scolded in a whisper. "If the Arrow Cross were to catch you taking pictures..."

"Someone has to. Someone must show the world."

Klára turned to me, her gaze soft and direct. "Young people and their ideals. Ádám thinks the West cares what happens to us. He sends the photographs abroad—who knows where they end up?"

The young photographer, undeterred, cleaned the camera lens. "They can take away our homes, our businesses, but not our faces."

I smoothed back my hair. "Snap my picture, Ádám."

He cleared a sunlit patch of ground, improvised a backdrop, and posed me with a surprising deftness. "Relax your jaw, Margit. Pretend you're receiving Madam Horthy for tea."

I heard the shutter click.

Several days later, he presented me with the portrait. The woman who stared back at me—dark, gaunt, hard-bitten—was no one I would have chosen to become. I turned the snapshot over and wrote in red ink, *The Butcher of Children is here. Save our son.*

My face, the ruin of it, spoke to my husband in a way words never could. Within the fortnight, I had my reply: "*Carissima, a man named Marchetti will contact you. Do as he says. Tell no one. P.*"

♪

My son was not safe. Without the shelter of the Italian school, without proper meals or laundered clothes, he roamed the city's streets, freer than we who wore the yellow star but no less in peril. Through these same streets sauntered fresh Arrow Cross recruits, many in plain clothes, the poorest and most fanatical spoiling for a fight.

"They're shooting people into the Danube," Cesare told us one shut-in afternoon. His voice held no fear, no revulsion. He might have been recounting a fairytale. "They take them to the river and tie them together with wire, two or three of them together, and then they shoot one of them and the rest fall into the water."

I watched the color drain from my mother's cheeks. "Doesn't anyone stop them—the police? The oarsmen?"

He only shook his head.

"They shoot people and no one does anything?"

There were no private conversations in the yellow star house. Klára reached out a hand and patted Szidonia's unbending shoulder. "Why don't we just lose already? Once the war is over these ruffians won't have a leg to stand on."

"It will be Trianon all over again," muttered someone in the next room.

Ádám, bright-eyed and calm, looked up from his book. "Have you seen the lines in front of the foreign embassies? A Jew has only to ask and some of them—the Swiss, the Swedes, the Spanish—issue protection papers."

Szidonia heaved a breath so hot and full it could be felt across the room. "I do nothing but stand on lines."

That evening at curfew, I took my son's pillow and stuffed the last piece of bread into the case. "Come with me," I told him. Asking no questions, he followed me down the stairs to the front entrance. "This is not your home. Find someplace to spend the night, a stairwell or a basement. If someone asks what you're doing there, tell them your house was bombed and your father is a soldier on the Eastern front." I expected him to argue or to cry, but instead he took the bread from the pillowcase and began, intently, to nibble.

"I know how to defend myself," he said.

Where had the child learned such bravado? He was not yet eight years old.

"Stay away from anyone in a uniform. And here, take this." I handed him his baptismal certificate, neatly folded in a manila envelope.

It was a mild night, for which I was grateful. The air raid siren had not sounded in two days. Cesare clutched the pillow to his measly chest and stepped onto the pavement. "I'll be back for breakfast, eh?" he said, already steering for the shadows.

♪

Marchetti turned-up in early June, asking for me at the yellow star house and leaving behind his calling card with the scribbled assignation, *Café Gerbaud—Saturday—11 a.m.*

I felt conspicuous in such an elegant venue, not only for my yellow patch but the threadbare state of my clothing and unstyled hair. Marchetti, on the other hand, could not have looked more at home. He was seated at a window table when Cesare and I arrived, holding a copy of Goethe's *Faust* (as he'd said he would) and smoking a plump, fruity cigar. He rose at my approach and pulled out a chair. "You had no difficulty finding me, I hope?"

"Everyone knows the Gerbaud."

He looked pleased with himself. "What will you and your son have? My treat."

We ordered and made chit-chat. To the casual observer we might have been friends, stealing time between work and the next air raid. Nothing about Marchetti drew attention. He kept his voice low and his gestures close to the body.

"Nice weather. Good for traveling, eh *signora*?"

"I suppose it's hot in Naples?"

"I'm not the person to ask."

"But I thought you knew my husband?"

Marchetti fanned himself with a crème-colored fedora. "We

have operatives on both sides of the border. You take me for Italian? Italian heart. Swiss passport."

"A person is what's in his heart."

"Then you're right, *signora*, I *am* Italian." He laughed, but not loudly or long enough for anyone to notice.

Cesare looked up from his chestnut puree. "So, is he going to take us to *papi* or not?"

"Patience, *signorino*. Your mother and I have things we must discuss." He took a last puff from his stomach-turning cigar and snuffed it out. "You and your son have landed on the wrong side of the border. You think it's bad here *now*? The sooner we get you across, the better."

"Then it's true, what we hear?"

"If I were you I wouldn't wait around to find out—*capisci*?"

"How soon do we leave?"

"Depends. Our people in the field keep us informed as conditions change. Cat and mouse."

A pair of German officers stepped through the doors, their gait brisk and uniforms freshly starched. Instinctively curling my right shoulder, I turned away.

Marchetti subtly clenched from his jaw down to his fists. "Why don't we plan on meeting again in three days? At your place, say. I'll arrive just before evening curfew. You can pay me then."

"Pay you?" What had I left to give him? "I thought my husband took care of it."

"That was a down-payment, *signora*." He scribbled a sum on another of his business cards and slid it toward me across the white tablecloth. "Once I have the balance, the wheels start turning. Your son could be back on his native soil in a matter of days."

I nodded, scanned the room, and rose to go. The officers had invited two young women to their table. An earthquake could not have pried their eyes from the nubile bosoms.

Cesare jabbed a finger at Marchetti's ribs. "No funny

business. I know how to defend myself, eh?"

The smuggler, forcing a smile, straightened the lapels of his well-cut jacket. I could see the outline of a pistol neatly etched against his hip. "Friends?" he said and handed my son a chocolate mint wrapped in gold foil. Then turning to me, "What's left us, *signora*, but our pitiful pleasures? *A presto.*"

Szidonia, her face slack from hunger, was waiting for us on the landing of the yellow star house. "*Nu?* Will he take you across?"

"He wants more money."

My mother bunched the fabric of her apron. "How much?"

"More than I have."

Cesare thrust his hands into his pockets and extracted three or four coins.

"Where did you get those?" my mother asked sternly.

He hooked thumbs in the waistband of his trousers. "Chasing balls at the tennis court. I run so fast they don't have time to hit the ground. People pay me."

"There are worse ways to earn a livelihood," Szidonia conceded. "Turn around, *boychik.*" She reached into her brassiere and retrieved a wad of bills. "Take them quickly," she ordered in a whisper. "Who knows what they're worth now? If you need more, sell the candlesticks." The value of things seemed to diminish by the moment. "The wedding ring, too."

"Three people can't cost much more than two. Come with us. I won't sleep knowing you're still in this city."

"I have to be here for József when he comes home." We hadn't had a letter from him in months. "And who will tend your father's grave?" She was seventy-two, yet I knew I was no match for her. Each loss, each thwarted hope, only seemed to make her mightier.

"If you should change your mind—"

"Come back after the war and see us. We'll be here."

It was dark on the landing. If either of us cried, we were spared the sight of it.

♪

I told no one of the escape plan—why compromise them? What was the point of saying goodbye? Uttered at the edge of an abyss, words are trivial things. There would be time enough for words once my son was safely out of Hungary.

On the day Marchetti was due to return to the yellow star house, the Arrow Cross held a book-burning, dozens of pyres set alight and the ashes left to blow along the gutters. The streets echoed with ecstatic singing. A daylong curfew kept us indoors, straining to hear when the music turned to gunfire.

"Stay clear of the windows," Klára cautioned her children.

An old man in the next room whimpered, "Radnoti, Buber, Singer, Proust, Spinoza…"

And then my savior was at the door, accompanied by a woman too old to be his wife. "My associate," he introduced her, to which she added with maternal warmth, "Call me Ilus."

"Ilus is an old hand. She has made the crossing dozens of times. Of course, it's getting more difficult by the day."

"And more costly," added the matron.

"*Certo*. When operatives are risking their skin, there's no haggling. I myself barely cover expenses. I'm not in this line of work to get rich, but to help the innocent."

"The innocent have everything to fear." The smuggler's associate was beginning to sound like a Greek chorus.

Marchetti concurred with a fraction of a nod. "Trust me, *signora*, I'll have you and your son out of this hellhole before you can say Frank-a-lin Delano Roosevelt. The latest intelligence from my people at the border isn't bad—which is good, considering. Can you and your son be ready to leave in three days?"

"We'll be ready."

"Take only the bare essentials. There are no porters on this circuit. Leave any identity papers at home—the last thing we need is for some overly efficient Swiss official to mark your passport with a "J." We need to get an early start. The moment curfew ends, go to the metro station at Andrássy and Villmos Császár.

We will meet you there."

He was waiting to be paid, I knew. "Half now and the rest at departure?"

"All or nothing, *signora*." He looked at me as if I had laid an egg. "This is not some pleasure trip along Lake Balaton. I pay my people upfront. It's a point of honor."

"Of course," I said and handed him all I had. "I'm short only a few pengö."

"We trust you. Just bring it with you next week." He pocketed the cash without deigning to count it. "As a special favor to your husband, the maestro, let me look into recovering the possessions from your flat—28 Andrássy, wasn't it? Chances are there's not much left by now, but whatever your neighbors have spared I'll put under lock and key until the war ends. Free of charge."

"That's kind of you."

"My pleasure. I'm a great aficionado of Neapolitan music. Whatever I can do for Maestro Frustaci."

Ilus patted my arm reassuringly. "You can rest easy. Our storeroom is guarded around the clock."

Marchetti smiled for the first time, baring a row of gold fillings. "You've kept a duplicate key?"

"Of course. I'll give it to you when we meet."

He tapped a finger to his head. "I knew I was dealing with an intelligent woman. *Bene*, we're all set."

Ilus unlatched the door and poked her head out, glancing first in one direction and then the other. "Rejoice, *signora,* in a fortnight you'll be snug in your husband's arms. You'll forget any of this ever happened." She kissed my cheek, and the pair of them slipped hurriedly away.

♪

The waiting I could bear, the overcrowding, the tetchiness of an empty stomach. I had tamed my appetites long ago, but the scent of my unwashed body still shamed me. More than food, it was a bath I craved, a bath with lavender-scented soap and apricot kernel oil and steam so thick I could lose myself in it—

"Have you heard a thing I've said?" My cousin tossed her sewing onto the unwashed floor. By then anything might drive her to the edge, a loose button, a sour kitchen smell. "Human beings aren't meant to live like this, strangers thrown together like cubes of beef in a goulash. The Germans won't have to kill us; we'll kill ourselves. Half the Jews in Budapest are walking around with cyanide capsules."

"Don't talk like that."

"We're short a half meter on the crepe-de-chine. Someone had to have cut it from the bolt during the night."

"Perhaps I miscalculated."

"You don't miscalculate, Margit. Someone stole it." She said this loudly, baitingly, turning her gaze on a woman in polka dots (also a redhead), loafing at the far end of the room.

I pulled my chair flush against my cousin's and gripped her by both shoulders. "Lower your voice. We have enemies enough *out there*"—indeed, it seemed that anyone might suddenly turn on us. "Can't you see the poor woman's struggling just as we are?"

Zili curled forward, butting me softly on the collarbone. "How clever these Germans are. They turn us against each other, against ourselves. By the time they finally pull the trigger or flick the switch, we won't even be worth saving."

"Can't your friend, the connected one, help you get out, hide you, whatever it is they do?"

She began to sob. "He disappeared. Ten days ago. We used to meet in a secret place. We'd leave messages for each other there. All those double features I used to tell you about—I made them up. For once I didn't need Johnny Weissmuller swinging from a vine."

"Zili, Zili... when the war ends you'll start your own family. The Germans are not as clever as you think. They'll lose this war. They'll lose, and we will be left." I reached into my pocket and took out the slender bar of soap for which, that very morning, I had bartered my mended silk stockings. "Here, cousin, take this. Smell how lovely it is."

She closed her red-rimmed eyes and inhaled. "Like a garden, jasmine, roses... like springtime used to be."

♪

My mother and I awoke before dawn the day I was to leave Budapest, awoke in a feathery darkness while the Kemény family slept. We felt our way around the familiar bodies and left the bedroom, each of us carrying a small bundle prepared the night before.

"And the boy's pillow?" asked Szidonia.

"He has it with him."

My mother hastened to the kitchen spigot and opened it. A trickle of water spattered onto her cupped hand. "Bring the towel. I'll wash your hair."

"I have no soap."

She took a sliver from her pocket, positioned my head under the tap, and began to work up a lather. Her touch had remained firm and sure.

"Up so early?" Klára, always a light sleeper, stood in the doorway.

I straightened, and my mother set about towel-drying my hair.

"It's nothing," I said. "Go back to bed."

"As long as you're well, my dear." She had to have suspected something, but Klára was too sensitive a soul, too excruciatingly tactful, ever to question me. "I'll see you later then." Her gaze lingering, she slowly turned and padded back into the bedroom.

Once the door had closed behind her, my mother whispered, "I'll say goodbye for you. She'll understand."

I sponged myself clean and put on the least threadbare of my dresses.

My mother, smoothing the bodice, murmured, "In Italy you won't wear the yellow star. You'll be *Signora Frustaci*."

"I'll still be your daughter. I know who I am, *mamala*."

We gathered up the bundles and stepped out onto the landing to savor a few moments' solitude. There was too much to say, so we said nothing at all. Side-by-side, we descended the stairs. Having sold my last wristwatch, I listened for the church bells.

"It's not too late," I couldn't stop myself from saying, "you could still come with us." But I knew she wouldn't. Had József been my son, I would have done the same, wait for him, wait until the last Nazi had bled into the earth.

And then the bells sounded, more bells than I could ever remember hearing, and Szidonia, maintaining an outward calm (at, God knows, what cost), walked me to the exit.

"We won't say goodbye."

"Don't let the soldiers touch you," my mother whispered. "Tell them you have something."

"I'll write as soon as I arrive. I'll send whatever I can."

She embraced me tightly and then thrust me out the door. "Go. Go! Don't let my grandson forget me."

I shouldered my load and walked briskly ahead. When, midway, I turned back, the door of #9 was closed, my mother nowhere to be found. Up the street I could see Cesare, pacing circles in front of the metro station with his pillow tucked beneath an arm. I scanned the pavements for Marchetti and Ilus, but there were only the street-cleaners with their broad, lazy brooms. I willed myself forward thinking, Szidonia will be watching from the window; József will be come home soon; the bad smell will blow over...

"Did you bring bread?" Cesare, his trousers crumpled, eyed the bundles.

"We'll eat later, once we're on our way."

Before my son could protest, I caught sight of Marchetti racing up the metro stairs with Ilus several paces behind him. Spotting us, they stopped short of the light and waited.

"The rest of your money," I said and handed the smuggler a handkerchief tied with coins.

He sighed nasally. "It's not enough."

I felt my stomach clench. "Not enough? How do you know if you haven't counted it?"

"Because, my dear *signora*, costs have risen since last time and the pengö is worth nothing. Like I told you, conditions change. I lost two operatives this past week, *two* in one week, snagged by the Gestapo."

"But we had a deal."

Ilus, taking me by the arm, cozied up. "We're doing the best we can for you. We're not making a cent on this, but our operatives must be paid. Surely you've kept a little back?"

Cesare hugged the pillow to his chest.

"Give it to me," I said.

My son turned on Marchetti, pressing into service the fascist stare he knew so well. "We had a deal, eh? I don't like this funny business."

"Excuse him. It's just that he's desperate to see his father."

Marchetti glanced at his wristwatch. "I don't have time to play children's games. Either we go now or the crossing is off. If you think it's tough to get across today, just wait a few weeks."

I wrenched the pillow from my son's arms and emptied nearly its entire contents, silver dollars (a black market bonanza), into Ilus' outstretched palm.

"Not enough," said Marchetti.

Ilus, pocketing the coins, goaded her boss, "Look at this boy, are you going to leave him stranded here? Can't we do something for him? For them both? They're honest people."

"*Santo Padre*, I'm not a charity. I've got a dozen operatives shitting their pants at the border."

I felt inside the pillow for the last of the coins.

"Please, can't we get started? We'll call attention to ourselves if we stay here any longer."

"You win, *signora*," said the smuggler finally. "We'll take the boy right now. You, be here next week—same time, same place. The family will meet-up in Bolzano. We'll send word to your husband."

"But why must we go separately?"

"Logistics, *signora*. You want to cross the border? Then let me do my job."

The ever-compassionate Ilus patted my hand. "Don't worry, I'll take good care of your boy. I'll treat him like my own son."

Marquetti started down the stairwell. "We're behind schedule. We'll miss our connections."

"Hurry," urged the matron, "and don't forget the key."

I surrendered it without hesitation. "Please, if you could recover my parents' wedding portrait..."

"Whatever you ask."

I looked at my son, who seemed in that moment a copy of his father, princely and smug and radiating mischief. My hands gravitated to his head, rested there as I recited from memory, "*Ye'simcha Elohim ke-Ephraim ve'vhi-Menashe.* May God make you like Ephraim and Menashe." I planted a single kiss on his brow. "Go with auntie Ilus. I'll catch up later."

The woman took the smaller of the two bundles from my arms, grabbed hold of Cesare's hand, and trailed off after Marchetti.

My son half-turned and his eyes met mine. I expected to see fear or sadness there, but the gaze was clear, a window on the future. "See you in Italy, *mamma!*"

♪

When, at the appointed time, I returned to the metro station, a blind beggar occupied the space where I had last seen the smugglers. Having no pencils to sell, she sang, "*Minden vágyam visszaszáll...* All my dreams go back where my sweet country lies."

I held my bundle in front of me—it could not have weighed more than a head of cabbage—and stood on the top step, watching for Marchetti and Ilus.

"You're casting a shadow," said the beggar woman, angling her gaze in my direction. "It chills me."

I excused myself and walked to the opposite end of the

stairwell. People streamed past me, their eyes darting to the yellow patch and the muscles around their mouths growing hard with scorn. I descended further into the metro's gray mouth. The beggar had changed her tune and was singing, "*Ösz van és peregnek a sárgult levelek* … It's autumn and the leaves are falling."

The bells rang eight and then nine. Slow to surrender hope but afraid to linger, I walked the hundred meters back to the yellow star house, and not for the last time buried my bundle among the bedding.

"I'll keep an eye on it for you," whispered Klára with so much sympathy I wondered if I had spoken in my sleep.

"You needn't feel badly for me. My son is safe—his father has seen to that—and as for Szidonia and me, things could be worse."

"I don't know how I could bear it without you, these four walls and never knowing."

"After the war you'll visit us in Italy, and I'll take you to the grandest theaters you've ever seen. We'll stroll along the *Via Veneto* like two ladies of leisure—" My friend's gaze dropped to her worn-flat pumps. "We'll strut, Klári. We won't always be down at heel."

I returned to the metro station the next day and again a week later, but saw no sign of my hired saviors. The beggar must have picked up my scent, for she turned to me and muttered, "You again, always in my light." Having tired of singing, she lounged against the wall with one hand open upon her knee and her eyes loping after me. "You'd do better in the Castle District, plenty of johns there."

♪

Naples went silent in '44, the dockyards in ruins, a smallpox epidemic raging, Vesuvius disgorging its ire in a storm of molten ash. Hell in black and white, the color of news back then.

At the worst of times, I'd think of my husband and son, picture them together, Pasquale stout in his newfound success, Cesare lean and street-wise. Nourished by a father's love, my son's childhood would begin again. He would learn to play the piano. In daydreams I would hear the maestro say, "*What a prodigy we've produced, Mancikám, a regular Mozart!*"

If my husband wrote, his letters never reached me. They had nested in fallen trees, burned with the cathedrals, moldered in the trenches.

♪

With our savings depleted, Szidonia and I ate less well and less often. Most of the grocery stores in our neighborhood had closed. How far my mother trekked each day in search of food I didn't stop to think about at the time. "If you'd have seen the wild mushrooms for sale at the *Nagycsarnok*," she would recall aloud. Or the goose livers, or the grain-fed chickens... luxuries she would devour with her eyes while purchasing the beans and tubers that kept us alive.

I had either to provide or perish.

As the days lost their bright edges and the first frost reached the plains, we braced for the biting hunger cold was sure to bring. To stay alive a person needed friends, but guests were few at the yellow star house. Those that pulled the string buzzer were announced with shouts and ushered inside like visiting royalty.

"A lady to see Margit Wolf."

Ilus, I thought. But even from a distance the woman waiting in the foyer bore no resemblance.

"At last I've found you!" cried the young blonde, throwing open her plump arms. I barely recognized my sister-in-law. Country living had tempered her brassiness, brought a becoming glow to her broad-cheeked face. "My uncle's waiting on the outskirts with his cart, the trains have gotten impossible. Have you heard from József?"

"Not since last autumn. And you?'

She shook her head.

Hoping for a bit of privacy, I led her onto the first-floor landing. "Sit down, Ibi. Catch your breath."

"I can't stay. We must make it home before dark. The air

raids…"

"What can I offer you, a cup of chicory?"

"I nearly forgot." She thrust forward a rustic wicker basket. "A few things from the farm: the last of the apricots, my aunt's elderberry preserves, sugar—beet sugar, that is—a bit of meat. Sorry, I could only get pork. Damn this war! Why doesn't József write? Maybe we weren't getting along toward the end, but still…"

"And the baby?"

"There is no baby. No baby, no József, just this stupid war." She buried her face in the crook of my shoulder and wept in silent heaves. "I'll be a better wife. I'll take care of him. I'll be a daughter to Szidonia—oh, I know she doesn't approve of me, but for József's sake. It's József we need to think about."

Whenever I'd see the yellow armband that marked the labor conscripts or read of new troop movements east, I pictured my brother marching off with his lopsided knapsack. Nothing offered the least clue as to his whereabouts.

I made inquiries of Gyula Radnai's family, but he too had stopped writing. His wife, the artist, had burst her eardrum during an air raid and could hear little but ringing. "Speak louder," she urged me, but looked so pained each time I shouted into her ear that I swallowed my questions and just held her.

"Gyula isn't cut out for physical labor." She had a child's voice, melodic and small, a child's undefended openness. "He's never used his hands for anything except signing papers and playing the violin—your sister played, didn't she?"

"You knew Rosa?"

"I'd sometimes run into her at the library. We both liked German literature, admired its moderation." She, too earnest a soul for ironies, gestured toward a bookcase at the room's far corner. And then a train whistle sounded, sending her into a paroxysm of grimacing. "This ringing in my ears—I feel as if I'm in a tunnel and will never find my way out."

I would have liked to tell her we're all in our own little

tunnels, but the words would only have driven her deeper inside. Cupping hands to her ears, she shadowed me to the door. "If you should hear from József..."

"I'll come back."

She studied my lips and nodded. "I think Gyula was in love with you once. You danced, didn't you? You must have been very beautiful."

I kissed her goodbye, feeling as if I had made a friend only to lose her to a consuming resonance. Child-women like that did not survive the war.

♪

Winter hit like a hail of shards. The starving fed on frozen horses, hacking the carcasses bare. Finding nothing with which to fill our plates, we dined on rumors of coups and secret negotiations.

"The yellow star has come down," cried Zili, racing into the sewing room with her coat flapping open and cheeks flushed the color of late radishes. "Horthy has announced an armistice. The Allies are on their way. To hell with this patch!" She dug her fingernails under the stitches and ripped it clean off. "I've stayed cooped-up in this sardine can long enough. Dance with me, Manci! Let's go down to the street and dance."

"Praise the day only at sunset." It was something my mother would have said, the cautionary note age brings to impulse.

"I won't wait another moment," declared my cousin, twirling out of reach. "No more yellow star, no more curfew, we're Hungarians again."

The euphoria lasted a matter of hours. By afternoon, it was the Arrow Cross that had control of the airwaves: "*My Hungarian brothers, Horthy thought he could abdicate his patriotic duty to love and defend our sainted motherland...*" By evening, the yellow stars were back in place and the Jews of Budapest braced for the reprisals they had learned to expect.

I hurried back to #9 Andrássy to be with my mother and found the flat barricaded.

"Quick, get inside," ordered Szidonia as Oszkár and Ádám Kemény wrestled a massive oak wardrobe from against the door. No sooner had I crossed the threshold than they rammed it back again.

"They say the Germans kidnapped Horthy's son," reported Ádám, "that's what made him back down." He shook his head, his youth spent in the course of a day. "The Hungarians had been making overtures to the Allies for months. I don't understand it. Why didn't they take us on board?"

Klára, her face paste pale, curled onto her husband's chest. "What's to stop the Arrow Cross now?"

Three days later, Oszkár was taken, marched off with legions of other Jewish men too old or infirm to be anything but a liability to the Hungarian army. The malice of it was as clear as the blood spilling down the Danube in the heart of Budapest. Then it was Ádám's turn, snatched in the night and made to stand on the pavement with his hands in the air until an armored truck carried him away.

"Your men will come back, Klári," I tried to comfort my friend, who barely rose from bed except to ask her adolescent daughter, "Any sign of them?"

Once the curfew ended, Szidonia put on her kerchief and her star and went out to scour the city for food. She returned home hours later with a few limp carrots and a vacancy in her eyes that made me shudder.

"What's the matter, *anyám?*" I asked her.

"They're all gone," she said with a tremor in her voice, "all the men. We're only women and children now."

And finally it was our turn, Klára's and mine. We were summoned to the sports stadium on November 11, 1944, a date lodged in memory like a bullet in bone, my mother's birthday.

I bartered a length of merino wool for a square of the dark chocolate she liked so much and gave it to her at breakfast as she queued for the wood stove.

"It's a trifle, but I couldn't ignore your day."

"Take it with you," she pleaded, "one day is like another now."

When the time came to leave, Klára braided her daughter's hair, tied it with ribbons, and held fast to the coils. "It's inhuman. How can they ask a mother to abandon her child?"

Éva, helpless in the face of her mother's immobility, searched for my eyes.

"We have no choice but to report, we're on a list. We'll go, we'll pretend to cooperate, and then..." I was thinking aloud. Truth was, I could not have imagined what lay ahead, but I vowed to myself I would not go meekly.

"The dogs! The guns!"

"The Nazis are greedy. They'll take too many of us. They won't be able to control us all."

Klára thumped a wilted hand against her chest. "Look at me, Manci. *Look* at me. I've barely budged from this room in six months. Without my husband, without my son, I can't face that mob down there."

I tied the bundle onto her back and buttoned her coat. "Don't make the soldiers come looking for us. Think of Éva." Shoulders squared, I made for the door and she followed, quaking like a cull lamb.

♪

Bricks. Bricks, oxblood red and stretching in all directions. Their iron stain bled onto limbs and faces, clothing and blankets. Slivers pierced my skin, sliced through the soles of my shoes, tore to shreds the scratchy woolen stockings my mother had tucked into my knapsack.

"Why would they bring us to a brick factory?" whispered Klára, wedging herself between two towering stacks with elbows pinned. "Why not to the train station?"

"They'll assemble us first, count heads—if these slum boys they've recruited know their arithmetic. Most of them don't even have uniforms, did you notice? They look like the ragamuffins who toss coins in some alley."

"Margit! Margit Wolf?" Two sturdily built young women pushed toward me through the crowd, stepping over bricks and bodies with nimble care. The first I recognized, Sári Braun, a former neighbor. "It *would* have to rain," she murmured, swiping the water from her eyes with a squarish hand. We introduced our companions. Hers was Ágnes Láng, a junior colleague from the high school at which she had taught before the Jewish laws. "Why don't we form a foursome?" Sári proposed. "We can look out for one another that way."

An oddly matched *pas de quatre* we made, Klára still smelling of French perfume, the two schoolteachers plain and level-headed. But ours was a choreography of survival in which grace and symmetry played no part.

Sári lowered her voice. "They say there are no trains, that we'll be marched across the Austrian border on foot."

"Impossible," I rejoined, clinging to logic, "Austria is more than two hundred kilometers from here."

Within hours we were trudging in columns along the Vienna road in a driving sleet. The makeshift soldiers bullied us forward, faster, faster... butting us with their rifles. To them we were nothing but Jews, dirty Jews, the only kind.

Gradually, the rain washed the red dust from my hands and legs, and my shoes filled with mud. I glanced sideways at Klára. She was already hobbling, her face contorted in pain.

"A stone's come through my instep."

"Keep up," I urged her. "Don't give the soldiers an excuse to hurt you."

And then the first woman dropped, dropped to her knees in the mud with a low *glug*. I nearly trod on her. When I tried to raise her up, she whinnied and clasped her belly with both hands.

"Leave me be," she pleaded, curling onto her side.

My companions threaded their arms through mine and kept walking.

"Can't you see she's pregnant?" I whispered. The woman,

stick-thin except for her bulbous belly, might have given birth at any moment. Breaking ranks, I freed my arms and turned to go to her aid.

"Don't! You'll only call attention."

A bullet finished her.

"Don't look back," said Ágnes and began to pray the mourner's kaddish in a choked whisper. "*Yitgaddal veyitqaddash shmeh rabba...*" Glorified and sanctified be God's great name throughout the world which He has created.

Kilometer after sodden kilometer we marched, our hunger and thirst, our frozen limbs, our panting mouths, on display for all to see. Shopkeepers, farmers and schoolchildren lined the road to stare after us, sometimes in pity, as often jeering. I scanned the column for soldiers, noting their positions. I counted the attack dogs, calculated the distance to cover.

More shots.

"*Yitgaddal veyitqaddash shmeh rabba...*"

Ágnes' prayers were no comfort to me. If God hovered within earshot, why didn't he jam the rifles, smite our captors? Why did he allow our helplessness to be paraded before a world that didn't care enough even to hold out a dipper of water?

Beside me Klára softly moaned.

"Try to keep up," I urged, taking her frail, chapped hand. "Here, put your arm around me."

"I don't want to be a burden. If I should fall behind..."

"You won't."

She fixed me with a look at once firm and replete with affection. "If I should fall behind, go on without me. Just go on. I won't have it any other way."

We walked all that day and into the evening. An unending succession of church steeples and barley fields, the dogs lusting after hares, the women dropping. Darkness fell and still they drove us. It seemed we would never stop. At last someone gave an order, and drenched and exhausted we were led onto a soccer pitch and left to rest for the night. There were few stars and those were red, a reminder, perhaps an omen.

"Tomorrow will be easier," I said, knowing it wasn't true but taking heart from the oddly persuasive timbre of my own voice.

♪

At sunrise we were back on the road, having eaten nothing but a cup of thin soup. Our captors' dispositions had not improved. Indeed, they drove us harder, insulted us with greater impunity than the day before. Klára limped from her first step.

"Remember what I told you," she said gravely.

I bound her foot in a handkerchief and kept silent, knowing I could never do what she asked of me.

"Look," said Sári, brightening, "they're letting those pregnant mothers ride in a cart." The women, most with young children, rode a short distance ahead, bracing against the wind.

Ágnes gazed after them. "It's only fair."

The cart jarred to a halt, commandeered by an officer of higher rank. "The ladies will kindly disembark," he said with mock gallantry, jerking the nearest to the ground. "Line up along that ditch. Take the kiddies with you. That's right." His colleagues looked on in apparent amusement, as if watching a play. The march did not stop, but for a few moments the pace slowed, just enough to allow us a glimpse of the women's faces, blue with cold, white with horror. "My dear ladies, I trust you will have no more difficulties." He raised his automatic rifle and opened fire, killing them all, saving for last the one little girl who dared to run away.

"*Yitgaddal veyitqaddash shmeh rabba…*"

"Prayers won't save us," I whispered to my companions. "Those women lying slaughtered in the dirt believed in the same God we do."

Ágnes raised the collar of her bulky coat. "What makes you think we can save ourselves?"

The column kept moving, thousands of souls pressing through the mud and ice toward a black horizon. "Save ourselves? I didn't say we could. But if we don't try, we might as well lie down and die right here."

On the third day—or was it the fourth?—a dense snow began to fall, through which we moved like weevils in cotton. The soldiers would pause to tip the flakes from their caps and then bring up the pace. We moved as one mass, one body, dragging forward with diminishing volition.

"Klára can't go on like this," I told Sári.

The schoolteacher, still hale if less hardy, sidestepped to buoy my friend's other flank. "Give us your weight," she instructed, but Klára resisted.

"You mustn't sacrifice yourselves for me. I won't let you."

The soldiers, having gotten their hands on a keg of Tokaji, called a rest break and the marchers drifted to the roadside, some to sit on the ground, others to relieve themselves in clear view. We were between towns, somewhere near Dorog. Farmers heading for Budapest inched along the road in horse-drawn carts laden with cash cargo—potatoes, wood, charcoal. In an instant I saw my chance.

"Get in that wagon," I told Klára. Then to the schoolteachers, "That one, there. Help me lift her."

The chosen conveyance looked solid and had a low-slung hold. Its driver sat with benign indifference on the wooden seat, lighting a corncob pipe. Sári and Ágnes sprang to my aid. Heaving and shoving with our frozen hands, we maneuvered the failing Klára onto a bed of coal.

"Lie still and let me cover you. Once the cart enters Budapest, you slip away, no one the wiser."

"Bless you," she whispered, blinking the snow from her lashes.

I heaped the coal onto her with both hands, and the cart began, squeaky-hinged, to creep away. There wasn't time for doubt. Already our captors were tossing their empty keg into the scrub, shouldering their rifles. I wiped my hands down the front of my coat, adjusted my load, and resumed my place in the column.

With luck Klára would be home before dark. A thought miraculous to ponder: that a road so fraught with dread might lead to life.

♪

How many women fell on that march? Too tired, too cold to go on, or prescient, preferring the bullet to what lay ahead. The dead went quietly, their open eyes trained on the clouds.

"*Yitgaddal veyitqaddash shmeh rabba...*"

"Ágnes, we must get you a new pair of shoes." Hers were losing their soles, opening and closing like clamshells at every step.

"What would you have me do, hop a tram for the *Piac*?"

"The dead have become our market," muttered Sári, an unsuspected dark side eclipsing the sunny disposition for which she had been known. "We take their shoes, plunder their knapsacks. Soon we'll be stripping them bare and cannibalizing them."

Ágnes shook her by a coat sleeve. "You're not yourself. You don't know what you're saying."

"You need shoes," I repeated.

"I'll crawl before I steal a dead woman's shoes. Leave me alone. Leave me alone, both of you."

We walked on in silence, the horizon flattening to a gray-blue jot. Sári raised a hand to her eyes.

"Isn't that a Red Cross truck in the distance?" she said in a tone of wonder.

The boxy vehicle drew closer, its emblem unmistakable.

Ágnes cavorted forward on her clamshells. "They've come to stop the march! The Swiss will put an end to it. They'll take us home."

The attack dogs began to bark, lunging forward on their leashes as if to sever their own heads. The march paused as a commanding officer met with the Red Cross delegation.

"Of course, this is only the advance guard. Next will come the field kitchen, the ambulances, a fleet of trucks."

"They'll look after us until the war ends, in a refugee camp, perhaps, or a hospital."

As we speculated, the proud red emblem swelled to the size of providence. We forgot our aches and exhaustion and began to compose menus: guinea hens in paprikash, mushroom soup, glacéed cherries...

And suddenly the column was moving again.

"What's wrong?" Ágnes rasped. "Can't they see we're doomed?" Her hands jerked to her head, and for a moment I feared she might tear out her hair.

Trudging forward on frozen limbs, we watched the truck execute a U-turn and drive back the way it had come. We watched it fade until it seemed nothing but a pinprick of blood.

"I want to run." Ágnes began to pound her temples. "I want to run. I want to run. I want to run." Sári and I had no choice but to clamp hands on her wrists. "I want to run. I want to run..."

Rationing breath, I pressed my blue lips to her red ear. "First, the shoes."

♪

The guards grew lax. They drank and vomited on the flea-powdered coats of their dogs. Midday they drowsed. Even the dogs gradually seemed to lose discipline, mounting one another in a fruitless heat. Our numbers had diminished, theirs not, and yet gaps opened in the column through which, at the right moment, a person with the will to survive might scramble for her life.

"Keep down and head for the woods!"

I ran bent at the waist, camouflaged by the dirt clinging to my clothes and the tall grasses through which we fled. My lungs burned. The frigid air whipped my face as if to skin it.

"The dogs," Ágnes jabbered, "blood-thirsty curs like their masters, teeth tearing us limb from limb ... Can't you feel their breath at our backs?"

"Keep down," I urged, "keep moving."

"A neighbor had a dog when I was growing up, ugly thing, fanged. They said it ate babies…"

We entered a landscape of trees and shadows and moss peeking out from mounds of snow. I could hear storks overhead, squirrels underfoot. We went deeper. Sári's heel caught on a root and she tumbled forward.

"Don't stop," she whispered, already back on her feet and scrabbling toward us with her hands bloodied and covered with leaves.

"The dogs, they train them to kill. Can't you smell their sickening musk?"

We went deeper, where the trees towered and larks streaked among the branches. Snow everywhere. Lurching from trunk to trunk, we sought the heart of the forest, the invisibility of solitude. No longer afraid, we tumbled onto a log to rest. Sári pressed close to Ágnes whispering, "The march has moved on. It's so still. So still."

The briefest silence returns me to that white world. In memory I am light-headed—from hunger, from freedom—and the snowflakes dance in intricate patterns I have never noticed before. I catch them on my tongue. And then decisions must be made: where to spend the night, how to get food, who to trust. City-dwellers to the tender soles of our feet, we knew nothing of survival in the wild.

"If we could find a tavern."

"A farmhouse."

"A barn—I once read that peasants sleep with their animals for warmth."

From rumor we knew the Arrow Cross had adherents in the towns, but how numerous or fervid they might be we could only guess. Instinct tugged us east, back toward Budapest, where we had families, if not shelter, and knew danger's face.

"There's my brother's wife near Tatabánya," I volunteered, thinking of Ibi and her cornucopic wicker basket.

Sári cradled my arm. "Don't get your hopes up. The whole

community may have been taken by now."

"This woman is Catholic, a person of confidence. We mustn't place her family at risk, but she'll give us food for the journey. She'll know the back roads."

We set out at once before the cold could paralyze us.

"Take off your yellow patches," I instructed, making quick work of my own and burying it in the snow like a malignant seed.

Watching for chimney smoke, we scrabbled through the undergrowth in failing light. On the edge of darkness, still miles from Tatabánya (though we could not have known it then), I thought I heard a violin.

No longer feeling our hands, we made a bed of branches and lay down overlapping bodies. Sleep came, and with it, dreams. Nicola Guerra, dwarfed by his long black pointer: *You didn't reach high enough, little mouse. Not a single star, not a sliver of moon have you brought me.* And suddenly I am onstage, trailing the night sky behind me as if it were a veil. I am Sylvia, and the maestro gazes up from the orchestra pit, tracing the constellations with his suave white gloves...

"Papers!"

Morning had broken, the brightest we had seen since leaving Budapest. Beside me I could hear Ágnes and Sári labor to their feet. And then I saw him: a gangly boy soldier in a too-large uniform.

"Show me your papers," he ordered again, nudging me in the ribs with the toe of his boot. Still young enough to suffer from acne, he carried a rifle from the last war.

"We lost our papers in an air raid," I hastened to say. "Lost everything we had."

He paced circles around us, inspecting his quarry. "Where did you come from anyway?"

"Budapest. We're visiting relatives nearby."

"What relatives, where?"

"Komárom," I said randomly, having little knowledge of the environs. "I have an uncle there who farms."

"What's wrong with your companions, are they mute?" He stepped up to Ágnes and lifted her chin with his rifle butt. "Why should I believe you? I'll tell you what I think. I think you're from that march. Escapees."

Ágnes closed her eyes and swallowed. "No, *uram*, I swear. We're going to a farm to get food. From relatives."

"You city folk, look down your noses at us until you're hungry." He lowered his rifle and Ágnes' head dropped to her chest. He seemed about to walk away, but instead reached out and kneaded her breasts. "Flat-chested," he said in disgust. "Useless. I could kill you, you know. Those are the orders with Jews, shoot to kill—and why shouldn't I?" He stepped up to Sári and worked a hand under her coat. "No ass. Not my type at all." Sulking, he leaned against a tree and trained his rifle on us. "Somebody light me a cigarette."

Having brought along a handful for barter, I fished one out and quickly lit it.

Snatching it from between my fingers, he took a drag and his eyes loitered on my face. "You—you're pretty. Come here." I stayed where I was. Up shot his rifle. "I said come closer. Don't make me use this, okay?" I took a scant step forward, and he reached out a hand and caressed my throat. "What's your name?"

I said the first that came to mind: "ZsaZsa."

"Like the actress? Regular whore, that one." Carefully, he snuffed out the cigarette and put the remainder in his jacket pocket. "Do you like me?"

I forced a nod.

"Because maybe I don't need to kill you. If you like me. Say it, that you like me."

"I like you."

"But you're whispering. What's the matter, ZsaZsa, shy? And these friends of yours, pair of sphinxes. Tell them not to run away, understand?" Without warning he backhanded Ágnes across the jaw. "Turn around, Jew bitch. Turn around both of you and lie on the ground. Face-down. One chirp out of you and

I'll shoot." He took me by the sleeve and walked me to the base of a dying sycamore. "You do like me, ZsaZsa, don't you?" he said almost tenderly. "I don't want to have to kill you and your friends. If you'll just be nice."

"Promise you'll let them go," I began, but he clapped a fist to my mouth and worked in the knuckles.

"What kind of talk is that?" He guided my hand to the fly of his pants. "See what you do to me? See? Now just be nice and I'll let you go back wherever you came from. The sphinxes, too." He shifted the rifle to his left hand and with the right tore loose the buttons from my coat.

"Don't do this."

"But I thought you liked me, ZsaZsa?" The barrel of his rifle pressed hard against my nipple. "Now get down. Get down before I break all your bones." Yielding under the pressure of gunmetal, I sank to my back. "No, not like that," snapped my assailant and widened his stance. "On your knees."

"I live with you in my dream
I do not want to wake up
In my dream we are happy
Wrapped in each other's embrace…"

"Vivo Nel Sogno"
I Live in My Dream

♪ *Four*

Looking for someone?" asked a smudge-faced girl in a tattered dress.

"Aren't you…?" Nora's little daughter. "Is my mother here? Szidonia Wolf?"

"First floor," she said curtly and started to skip away. "If your son asks, I don't play with boys anymore."

Whether an hour or a lifetime had passed since I last communed with Budapest's ghosts, let history decide. Does time exist in hell? Does memory? The calendar read August 3, 1945, a homecoming of sorts. Dressed in handout clothing and sweating onto a rolled 500-pengő note snug within my brassiere, I zigzagged through the broken city to stand before 28 Andrássy út—or rather, what remained of it. The top floors had collapsed to rubble. The front wall was gone. Uninhabitable, I judged it and nearly walked away. And then Bebe Matrai had appeared (Bebe of the witchy eyes and sixth finger).

"You're dressed funny."

She stuck out her tongue and skipped off to play among the toppled buildings and decomposing corpses.

I picked my way along a narrow trench snaking through the debris. In the courtyard lay heaps of scrap iron and shattered glass, amid which patches of grass strained toward the light. The sturdy old staircase had been patched, and I climbed it, warily testing each step. The doorframe to my mother's flat held fast, along with much of the door, but the windows had shattered.

"*Mamala?*" I remember calling, and again, "*mamala?*" the word suddenly a lifeline.

A gaunt, yellow face appeared in the opening where the casement had once been. There was an expression every Jewish face held in those days, bereft, the bones laid bare, more a question than an expression: *what is left?*

"I'm looking for my mother," I said.

The old skeleton backed off and stared at me.

Not wanting to frighten her, I stayed where I was. "I'm looking for Szidonia Wolf. This is her flat."

She brought the apron to her eyes and peered out from behind it. "Manci? Don't you know me?"

A moment's uncertainty.

"Don't you know your own mother? Wait, I'll get the door." I heard her drag something across the floor and then the door opened. "*Shayna maydala?*" She cupped her withered hands to my cheeks. "Look at you."

"Look at us."

The room stood empty except for a mended chair and a pair of milk crates. I tossed my bundle onto the floor and drew my mother, by mass a fraction of herself, through the pillaged rooms.

"Have you heard from Cesare?"

She shook her head.

"From József?"

"Nothing."

"Was it bad, the siege?"

She shrugged with her lips. "I hid in a cellar. I thought about my children. When it was safe, I came out." There was so little left of her, but her hair had remained black and her posture erect. My father had been right: the "house painter" could not break her. "The gentiles abandoned the flat, so I moved back in before someone else could." How had she managed alone? As if reading my thoughts, she murmured, "*Zug nischt.* What's to be gained by speaking of it?"

"I would have come back sooner, but—"

Her gaze locked on the number tattooed on my arm. "They didn't? You didn't? Not that it matters now."

Everyone had heard about the camps by then. Half Europe wandered displaced, millions of scarred souls drifting back to homes that would not be again. Millions more would never return.

Watching my mother pour a thimbleful of schnapps into a chipped glass, I promised myself she would never again know hunger or want. There would be no more questions. "We'll just patch things up. I'm here now."

♪

Imagine a mammoth salvage operation—that was the Budapest I returned to after the war. People digging up their hidden treasures, bartering, mending... to sit still was to remember, and to remember (heaven forbid!), that we would never be ready to do.

At twilight, on my hands and knees, I scratched through the rubble until I had unearthed my precious tin of letters, dented. No one had thought it valuable enough to steal, but gone were the former contents of our flat, down to the last spoon. The sum of our possessions would not have filled a bucket.

And somehow my mother carried on, not speaking of the past except to say, "I sometimes think I hear our piano somewhere across the courtyard, that flat note it had."

"I haven't seen Nora."

"Gone to work for the Russians, something to do with the people's courts. That battle-axe of a mother-in-law moved in to mind the children."

Few of our Jewish neighbors had returned. The other tenants kept to themselves, barely looking us in the eye. Relatives stopped by. My brother's absence lived among us as palpably as his presence once had, only lightless, silent. Other conscripts had already returned from the labor battalions—why not he?

When, soon after my arrival, Ibi appeared at our door, we were relieved to find her wearing a rose-colored dress and matching rouge, hardly the outward show of a widow.

"You don't look half bad," she said, sizing us up like goods at market, "compared to some."

We invited her inside, insisting she sit in the one armchair. Plumper than I had last seen her, she filled it from side to side.

"Still staying in the country?" I asked.

"No reason to come back here." She gestured vaguely about her. "Our flat isn't in much better shape than yours. There's the holiday house, but… too many memories."

"Then you haven't—"

"Heard from József? Not a word."

"We'd offer you something, but—"

"I've brought a few things." She nudged a sack across the bare floor with the toe of her rustic shoe. "I know what you're thinking, how easy we've had it away from the fighting, always a little something in the larder." To her usual bluntness was added anger, shrill and raw. "What's the use of measuring my suffering against yours? I've been without a husband for three years, and the shop hasn't fetched but a pittance."

"You've sold my brother's shop?"

"What did you expect me to do? I couldn't ask my family to go on supporting me forever. You know what it's like, a woman on her own."

My mother rose from her crate, and without excusing herself, left the room.

"It figures," said Ibi. "Szidonia never approved of me. Maybe if I had given her a grandchild…" She shrugged the thought off.

"Well, I don't expect we'll be seeing much of each another."

"Please, if you should hear from József—"

She veered on me, her blue eyes narrowed to slits. "I don't expect to. Why go on fooling ourselves?"

♪

My first visit was to the Kemény family, whose address I had memorized back when we lived together in the yellow star house. Their building boasted glass panes, which made it seem a pleasure palace alongside its harder-hit neighbors. Inside, the elevator did not run. The doors had no numbers, but a cleaner looked up from scrubbing the floor to point me toward my friends' flat.

"Manci!" Klára cried, throwing open the door before I could knock. "I was so afraid I'd never see you again, so afraid of... what came after." Coiffed and perfumed, she clasped me to her silk bodice. "Was it terrible?"

Noticing the scrubwoman, she drew me inside and bolted the door. "We've all seen the photographs: the living look worse than the dead, and the dead you can't begin to count. The stories people tell..."

"*Zug nischt,*" I heard myself say and knew I would never speak of what happened, not to my best friend, not to my own husband. It lay outside comprehension, unutterable, a stench.

She searched my eyes. "I thought so," she whispered and limply shook her head.

"And your family?"

"Alive, thank God. Those protection papers Ádám insisted on getting us—Éva, Oszkár and I spent the worst of the fighting in a Swedish safe house under the protection of Wallenberg." A name much whispered in the days following the siege. "Only Ádám they took, to a place called Mauthausen. We just got a letter. The Americans are seeing to his care. Typhus."

"I'm sorry."

"Others were not so lucky. We've got a relative from Eger staying with us. Lost everyone."

"What do you make of the Russians?"

She inclined toward my ear. "Rapists," she whispered. "Rapists and thieves. They help themselves to whatever they want. They took my husband's Jaeger." Her eyes gravitated first to my legs, which, infected, had swelled to thrice their normal size, and then to the lump on my head, compliments of the hellcat of kapos and her weapon of choice, a rusty soup ladle. "But you need a doctor."

"There's too much to do."

"You must let me help you." She opened a drawer and spread its meager contents across the sideboard. "Have they left you any knives and forks? Coat hangers? Matches?"

"It can't be easy for you either."

Not easy, but having stayed behind in Budapest she had already recouped a semblance of comfort. Her seasoned leather pumps had new heels. Every inch a lady, she led me to an upholstered sofa. "You've heard the joke. A Jew is talking to a Christian friend, 'How are you,' says the Christian. 'Don't even ask,' says the Jew. 'I have dragged myself home from the camps and have nothing now, except for the clothes on your back.'"

"And the authorities?"

"Biggest thieves of all—but we really must get you seen to." She could not keep her eyes from my legs. "My cousin is a doctor. Across the river, unfortunately."

"I hardly know Budapest without its bridges."

Her eyes brimmed. "It's only now that I know this place. Have you seen the American luxury cars the rich have imported? But try and buy a morsel of meat, a loaf of white bread." My friend rose suddenly and headed at a trot for the kitchen. "Let me fix you a plate. Éva paid a visit on a friend who keeps a kitchen garden."

"Please don't trouble yourself."

She detoured to the closet. "Come choose a bolt of fabric— does that cousin of yours still sew?"

"Zili?" My mother had gotten a letter from Sweden. "Zili met a widower at a transit camp. She won't be back."

"Better for her," Klára said and at last dissolved in tears. "You'll leave too, Manci. Anyone with any dignity will leave after what's happened."

It seemed pointless to sit half-starved and contemplate a future as opaque as dried blood. "I will have a quick bite to eat, Klári, and then I must go."

"Of course," she said, collecting herself, "I'll make a plate for Szidonia, too."

Later that day, the Keménies would return the visit, bringing with them a water-bloated chicken. Oszkár, apologizing for his directness, asked, "Have you thought about how you will earn a livelihood?"

It was agreed that, until the maestro made other provision for me, I would enter the Kemény textile firm as a buyer.

"Margit knows from fabric," my mother assured all present. Flouting our guests' polite protests, she brought out unmatched glasses and a bottle of plum brandy, scavenged from God-knows-where. "A toast!" she cried, coming to the end of the bottle before her own glass could be filled.

Yet again, I found myself the tailor's daughter, caught in the warp and woof of necessity.

♪

Made presentable by borrowed clothes and a bit of innocent artifice, I set forth, a changed woman in a changed city. The Italian embassy (downgraded after the war to a consulate) had endured the bombing. The familiar doorman, snatched away for "common work" by a uniformed Russian, acknowledged me from a distance with a clipped bow. I let myself in and passed through the lobby to the reception area, looking for the Neapolitan clerk whose favor I had once bought with strudel and cream puffs. Not a familiar face in sight.

I stepped up to a window behind which hunched a clerk with a conspicuous bald spot, not unlike a monk's. The clerk, chewing a toothpick, did not look up from his crossword puzzle. "*Scusi,*" I said and tapped lightly at the glass partition.

"A five-letter word for unmilled grain…"

"Has my husband left a message for me?"

"Your name?" he asked mechanically. I gave it, adding Frustaci as a second surname. The clerk consulted an oversized ledger. "Not on the list," he said and looked at me for the first time. "Have you tried the central post office?"

"I've been away." The phrase meant nothing to him. He did not ask, away *where*? Away *why*? "My son is an Italian citizen," I launched in again, hoping to hold his attention long enough to state my case. "My son's father is Italian. They are together in Italy. I wish to join them."

His lips tautened. "The Russians would rather not have people moving about right now. Well, I suppose it wouldn't hurt to get started on the paperwork. Your marriage license?"

"Lost. Somewhere in the rubble."

"Your son's birth certificate?"

"This is all I have." I held out the newspaper clipping of my son clasped in the arms of the once-mighty Count Ciano. "Surely someone on your staff must remember my Cesarino."

He leaned nearer the partition and lowered his voice. "The old guard has decamped. The most senior officer arrived only weeks ago. Between you and me, you will make no friends flaunting such a photo. There are no fascists in the new Italy."

Just as there were no southerners in the old.

"Can you get an urgent message to my husband?"

"Is he a diplomat?"

I had to admit he wasn't. "But he's a person of some fame, a composer for the cinema. He works with Macario."

"Good, then you should have no trouble getting a message to him by some other means." Again he inclined toward me and said in a whisper, "The Russians take a great interest in the diplomatic pouch. Better not to call attention to yourself." Straightening, he handed back the clipping. "Anything else we might help you with, Signora Frustaci?"

"I'm very fond of puzzles myself. The word you're looking for is grist."

"Of course. So many distractions on this job. We shall look forward to seeing you again, Signora Frustaci." Then barely above a breath, "There's no way around Ivan quite yet. Give it time."

What did we know about these Bolsheviks with their fist-first manners and evangelical disdain of the very things they stole? Too much to like them, too little to fear them. But a person good with puzzles pieces things together. "*A presto*," I told the clerk, in whose bald pate my future had come to nest.

Even while the populace grumbled about civic chaos and the enigma of the Cyrillic alphabet, routine crept back into quotidian life. Trains came and went on an approximate schedule; letters trickled in from abroad. After long silence I heard from the maestro's sister, Maria, a few lines scribbled in haste months earlier, legible only in part. "*We have lost our dear old father Salvatore. Pasquale came home for the funeral. Everyone asked for you...*"

My mother read over my shoulder, though she could not have understood a word of the slapdash script. "How is the boy?"

I read and reread the lines. "She doesn't mention Cesare."

"Maybe he hadn't arrived yet?" suggested Szidonia, bunching the hem of her apron in hands now bony.

I scanned the letter for a postmark: March of '45. My son should have been in Italy long before then, reunited with his father, beyond harm.

"I don't understand." A trace of panic had entered my mother's voice, a juddering unlike anything I had ever heard before. "A child. It wasn't even his war."

"I'll find him."

"What could they want with a child?"

"Don't worry, I'll find him."

Her malnourished figure might have been a monument to doubt.

"I *will* find him," I repeated, more hell-bent than certain.

Until I did, I would never stop searching.

♪

That same day I paid a call at the Swiss consulate, an oasis of calm amid the frenetic activity that reigned in the streets. I owned no wristwatch, no jewelry, carried no wallet—why make it easy for the Russians, whose appetite for booty we knew too well? It was the hottest day of the summer, humid, the air stagnant. The bureaucrats at their matching gray desks sat buttoned to the collar, faces shiny with sweat.

Mustering optimism, I approached the least damp man at the biggest desk. "I'm looking for a Swiss gentleman resident in Budapest. The name is Marchetti."

"Marchetti?" Pronounced with evident distaste and dismissed just as quickly. "I've never heard of such a person—have you tried the Italians?"

"He's Swiss. During the German occupation he took my son across the border."

"And?"

"I want him back."

"Marchetti?"

"No, my son. He was seven years old when he left Budapest, a bit older than in this photograph."

The man roused from his stupor long enough to study the newsprint image. "Why, isn't that Mussolini's son-in-law? As I said, madam, this does seem a matter for the Italians." He looked me full in the face and frowned. "You might try the Red Cross. They processed a great many orphans at the end of the war."

"My son is not an orphan."

"Most fortunate, madam. Good luck."

I lost no time in leaving the building. What did these well-fed men behind their bulwarks of paper know about maternal longing? Their elegant evasions would not bring my Cesarino back to me. With the sun overhead, the rubble burned like cinders. The shade trees stood like amputees, thrusting out their stubs for loose change. I walked back toward the Italian consulate, weaving to dodge the Russian soldiers in their threadbare uniforms.

"Looking for your son, madam?" The doorman, back at his post.

"Yes, how did you know?"

He tapped an index finger to his temple and waited.

"I have nothing to give you today," I said in apology.

"But I, madam, have something to give you." He sidled closer and whispered, "Visegrád."

A town north of Budapest on the Danube Bend.

"Visegrád," he repeated gravely, as if gifting me with the meaning of life.

"What's in Visegrád?"

He caught a bead of sweat on his tongue. "See for yourself, madam. You'll be glad you did."

I thanked him, and he tipped his cap and began to whistle. The pavement burned through the soles of my shoes. A crone in rags brushed past me chiding, "Watch where you're going!"

Getting to Visegrád—getting anywhere at that juncture—proved no small task. With patience one might succeed in boarding a train, but the cars seldom went far before being halted, commandeered. Tracks would dead-end. I would sooner trust the roads, though they swarmed with soldiers. As a precaution I dressed in the least attractive clothing I owned at the time, a pair of canvas overalls scavenged from a Jewish charity. I set off walking, hitched a ride in a peddler's cart, walked some more, and with just enough daylight left by which to read the road signs arrived. The town, sleepy piece of nowhere, had survived intact. Uncertain of what I was looking for, I stopped the first local who passed and held out my precious newspaper clipping. "I'm looking for my son."

The man squinted. "Lots of boys came though here during the war. The Jesuits saw to them."

"Where? Was there an orphanage?"

"You could call it that." He pointed me toward a step-path

ascending a steep black hill. "Proceed at your peril, missus. Boys have all gone and the Jesuits too. You might find a caretaker."

Taking off at a trot, I climbed the rickety rungs, dozens upon dozens of them... Apricot and plum trees lined the path (I filled my pockets) and finally a building came into view, rambling and abandoned.

"Anyone here?" My voice echoed. I tried the nearest entrance, unlocked, and stepped into what might once have been a dormitory, room after empty room. At the end of a corridor stood a communal bath, its floor littered with empty bottles of bleach. Off in a corner hung a fraying towel, and doubled beneath it a pair of summer shorts such as a child might wear. I knew these shorts, having sewn them myself and packed them into my son's small knapsack. Beginning to tremble, I retraced my steps through the bare and neglected rooms, calling, "Cesare? Cesarino? *Boychikal?*"

No one.

I tucked the shorts into my purse and left the building. On the grounds, surrounded by unpruned almond trees, stood a small chapel. It was there, I would learn years later, that my son had made his first communion, and there I sat with my back against the granite wall and waited for morning.

♪

Back in Budapest, the Keménies had leased a small storefront and managed through the usual bribes and cajolery to install a telephone.

"We've rejoined the human race," declared Oszkár, dusting the ungainly black instrument with a monogrammed handkerchief, listening in ecstasy to its dial tone. "There's fine cotton to be had in Cairo, silk in Bangkok, cashmere from the looms of Dublin..."

That these privileged few telephones would be tapped, we didn't stop to think.

"I heard Ádám's voice," Klára said, clutching excitedly at my arm. "The Americans put through the call."

"How did he sound?"

"Recognizable. Not much changed." She smoothed away a worry line. "Of course, there was static, but you wouldn't expect someone that young to be much altered, would you? He's just a bit weak at present."

I thought it best to skirt the question. Klára would see soon enough what the war had done to her son.

"Our Ádám," she insisted, "plainly."

Oszkár folded the handkerchief and replaced it in the pocket of his linen jacket. "Once the Russians clear out," he assured her, "we'll see about getting him back into university. You know Ádám and his big ideas."

In my next letter to Maria, I included the Keménies' telephone number. Wishful, considering the king's ransom it would cost to place the call. For years we kept an ear to that ugly black box, waiting for the world to reclaim us. It never did.

♪

My next stop was the Red Cross office, a drab antiseptic-smelling suite of cubicles no amount of sunshine could brighten. Only the familiar red emblem lent any color at all. A pale woman with a pencil tucked neatly behind her ear stood behind the front counter, pointing visitors toward a hub of corridors.

"I'm looking for my son," I told her.

"Missing persons. Second door on the left."

Tired-looking seekers in clothes unsuited to the weather lined the walls, eyes trained on one or another door. A man with a harelip called out names—"Kovàcs, Wellmann, Szabo…"

I raised a hand. "Wolf."

Blinking, he consulted a clipboard. "Wolf? Did I say Wolf?"

"Missing persons. I've been waiting all morning."

"This heat must be getting to me. Wolf, you said? Come with me." I followed him into another room, identical to the others except for the towering numbered cabinets. "Vitamins, penicillin," murmured my escort in explanation. Arriving at last at a glassed-in cubbyhole, he addressed a powdered woman in widow's weeds, "Mrs. Wolf to see you."

With the image of a receding Red Cross truck lodged forever in memory, I strode forward and extended my hand. "I have reason to believe that my son entered your care during the war."

She deflected my handshake with a genteel little scowl and motioned me toward a seat. "What makes you think so?"

"My son was taken from me July of '44."

"*Taken?*"

"My son's father, an Italian, hired a pair of—guides, they called themselves—to get us across the border into Switzerland. When the time came, they took only my son. All these months I assumed he'd been reunited with his father."

"A common enough hoax in those days," she said tersely, as if the whole business offended her. "I suppose you paid them?"

"Everything I had."

"If you're hungry there's the soup kitchen."

"Thank you, but I've found work. It's my son. From what I've been able to gather, he spent time in Visegrád in what might have been an orphanage. After that, I don't know. But he's a bright boy and a wily one. He may well have found his way back to Budapest. Perhaps you've some record of him?"

Again, the scowl. "There were so many like him—thousands, tens of thousands—and conditions what they were ... Who could think about names and numbers? They had to be fed. There wasn't enough food in Budapest, so we put them on trains for the countryside. The farms needed hands, the children needed homes." She snapped her ink-stained fingers. "Problem solved."

I felt my composure ebb. "You've given away my son?"

"If, indeed, he's alive."

"He's alive. Just tell me, where do I begin to search for him?"

Wearing her mourning like a suit of armor, she faced me squarely. "First things first." Touching the tip of a biro to her tongue, she thumbed through her ledger and made a few notes. "You'll need a special pass, the *propusk*, to travel outside the capital. I'll arrange it." She opened the topmost drawer of a filing cabinet and drew out a stamped and sealed document. "Here's the directive: *children to be sent to outlying villages along the borders of Ukraine and Romania... farmers to be notified in advance of their arrival.*"

"I see, but what exactly was the procedure for placing the children in these families?"

"Procedure? Simple. The children would get down from the train, and the farm wives would choose whom they wanted and take them home."

"But most of these children had never seen a farm before."

"What hadn't these children seen by then? Would you rather we had left them on the streets? Out in the country, they could learn to work."

"Cleaning out stables, feeding pigs?"

We paused to collect ourselves, she snapping closed her ledger, and I feeling for my lump and finger-combing a lock of hair over it. Clerks in starched lab coats ferried coffees and manila folders among the desks.

The widow was the first to speak. "I'll get you the pass, but let's be realistic. It's a big country. A country whose borders are in flux and whose infrastructure has sustained damage—how severe, I can't tell you. There are trains that run and trains that don't. Your son might be in any village east of the Zagyva."

"How soon can you have the pass ready?"

"Come back on Monday," she said and stood to see me out. "We can't be responsible for your safety, you understand. There are the Russians, of course. And something else—" Her voice abruptly lost volume. "We get scattered reports of violence toward... certain groups." *Pogroms* (why not call a thing by its name?).

"I know how to defend myself." Something the maestro might have said, did say, long ago.

♪

I began my forays into the countryside at once, leaving the office early on a Friday afternoon and returning on a Monday or

Tuesday. The Keménies asked no questions, would only say, "My, but you're sunburned," or "Let me ice that leg."

Conditions on the road were bad, as I knew they would be. The earth lay scarred, trees splintered, houses missing windows, walls, whole rooms, and the people I met edgy, jockeying for position in a new order yet to show its true face.

I showed my clipping to stationmasters, priests, school-teachers, to anyone willing to pause a moment and glance at a faded photograph of a crying boy. I had no reason for optimism. One after another these strangers shook their heads, turned away, and· yet, so long as a jot of road remained before me, I paraded my son's image. Staring out from every window, down from every fencepost, just beyond the next mile marker he would be waiting for me, a little older, but unmistakably his father's son, and mine. Mine in the way the maestro's songs were, a piece of myself set free.

Wherever I searched, night always came too soon. I would find a solitary spot, a patch of dry ground, and lie down, my only roof a canopy of stars, the cicadas chirring. Knowing better than to sleep, I lay alert waiting for sunrise.

Until one night, too tired to battle sleep, I dozed off on the outskirts of some logging town that smelled of pine and whose fields were soft with fallen linden flowers. I slept, not long enough to dream. When a hand came out of the darkness and clamped itself tight across my mouth, my first impulse was to bite.

"Aie! You hurted me, you old witch." The hand withdrew, replaced by a foot, bare, that kicked hard at my jaw and ribs.

Rearing up, I trapped the foot, tugged, and brought my attacker down.

"Let me go or I'll call my friends."

"Call your friends, and I'll wring your neck."

We wrestled, both panting like dogs in summer. My assailant didn't weigh much for a man, made little use of his fists, favoring his elbows and knees. We writhed and rolled, neither able to pin the other. The moon strewed puddles of light across the dry, indifferent earth.

"You're nothing but a mean old witch," my attacker said and began to whimper.

As my eyes adjusted to the light, I made out a pale, dirty face with convex cheeks framed by a tangled mop of carrot-red hair.

"Why, you're just a child." My hand rose to wipe away his tears.

"Got any bread?"

From one end of Hungary to the other, children roamed in packs, slept rough, begged or stole—was my son one of them? Hatvan, Heves, Devaványa… the sorts of places that had inspired Bartok, ramshackle, full of flies. War had spared the flies.

I walked on. All eyes followed me, the stranger in the second-hand overalls, asking at every turn, *Is there a school nearby? A church? Have you seen this boy?* And the Russians swaggered by in twos and threes, clumsy when sober, rapacious when drunk. How many pigs had they dragged off, how many family heirlooms pocketed? I knew the litany. A hundred times, a thousand, I listened to some peasant lament, *"They took my sow,"* but never once, *"The Nazis took our Jews."* And yet they were gone. For hours, for miles, I would trudge through this absence, the last leaf on the tree of life hanging by a fiber.

With cloth to barter, I might return to Budapest with a wedge of cheese or slab of bacon. Just as often I returned hungry.

"How long can you go on like this?" Klára once asked.

"Has Oszkár complained? Am I neglecting my job?"

My friend bent at the knee to plant a kiss in my hair. "No one is complaining. To the contrary, Oszkár and I marvel at your business acumen. It's just that—do you remember, Manci, how you said we'd be two fine ladies after the war?"

"Once the maestro comes, we will be. All this will seem a bad dream."

She angled away, and I could see a single blue tear bead on her lashes. "He'll take you home?"

"When the time comes. Pasquale's a master of timing."

"We'll walk along the Via Veneto—"

"We'll *strut*, Klári."

"Of course, my dear, only... he will come, won't he?"

Winter set in and with it woolens, hundred-yard bolts shipped in from Yorkshire. I sewed my mother a stylish dress. She, slow to regain her girth, took to packing a hot-water bottle in my knapsack.

Wearing the map of Hungary etched in calluses on my feet, I ventured north. Polgár, Tokaj, Kisvárda... slicks of mud and snow punctuated by church steeples. The peasants fattened their geese for Christmas. They had not seen my son, could only point me toward the cemeteries. A nun in a gray habit murmured, "Our days are swifter than a weaver's shuttle."

Back in Budapest, my mother felt my head and sighed. "You're burning with fever. Get into bed."

"You know I can't."

She crossed her arms beneath her bosom, a posture that had once quashed all argument. "These journeys—can't you let off until spring?" She raised a crinkled hand to my cheek and cupped it. "You're even paler now than when you returned from that camp."

"I feel stronger every day."

"They say the thaw will come early this year."

For me there would be no spring until my son nestled safe in my arms. "Do you remember how Cesare used to march around in that awful uniform?"

Szidonia's eyes misted over. "I held onto to that uniform for dear life, held on as if my grandson were still in it." The shirt had fetched a kilo of flour at the *Piac*.

Hajduhadház, Màtezàlka, Nyíregyháza... The patchwork of dialects, the generalized confusion, told me I had reached a border. I wandered among donkeys and beggars, and eventually reached the city center, a cluster of buildings left intact, a dozen or so cars. My instincts told me to find a church, but instead I came upon a synagogue—or what had once been. A caretaker unlocked the gate and let me in, saying, "What brings you here? The rabbi's dead, the Torah scrolls burned, and anyone who returned alive they've run off."

I stated my business, and he drew me inside and relocked the gate.

"Your son? We've had children pass through here. No use for them in the city." He motioned me into a cluttered office. "The Germans turned the synagogue into a hospital," he said sadly, "took our holy books and left these in their place. " He elbowed aside a heap of bedpans. "I have a map here someplace."

"The town I'm looking for had to have had a train station."

"Only a few of those out this way." He unfolded a yellowed Baedecker and pointed: Apagy, Zàhony. "Last I knew, the border lay here." He etched a line with the tip of his index finger. "The Russians seem to be settling down," he added, "not that you can trust them."

I thanked him and started for the door.

"Wait," he, waxing chivalrous, called after me, "I'll get my friend's cart."

He took me as far as Apagy, a pig-farming region of unfinished roads and scrubby pastures, stopping short of the town center. "Better they not see you with a Jew," he said, beginning to fidget with his whiskers. "If you should come back to Nyiregyahàza, you know where to find me. I thought I might remarry."

Another soul left halved.

I slogged into town, if a town that welter of sties could be called. A man dressed in overalls identical to my own and carrying a staff led me to the barn that served as a schoolhouse, where class was about to let out for the day. A matron with palms dusted in chalk stepped out to greet me.

"Pardon," I felt obliged to say, "have I come at a bad time?"

The question brought a smile to her eyes. "Only two of those, planting and harvesting."

"You've had some rain, I see."

"Come get warm. I'll put on tea." We went inside, and she fueled the wood stove with twigs and set about heating water. Only once the tea was ready did she glance in my direction and ask, "Something I can help you with?"

I presented my clipping.

She took it in both hands and brought it to her nose. "Fuzzy," she murmured, took a pair of reading glasses from a desk drawer, and put them on. "That's better."

"Have you seen the little boy?"

"Looks familiar. If I didn't know better—" She bolted to her feet and made for the door. "Wait here."

I hadn't long to wait. Within moments my hostess returned, leading by the hand a little girl with wiry hair and unmatched shoes.

"This is Anna Babály. She will take you to Gèza."

"Gèza?"

The little girl lisped through the gaps between her teeth, "He had a funny name when he first came to live with us. A funny way of talking."

"He lives with you? He's well? Dear God!"

I don't remember how I arrived at the little mud house beside the train station. In memory I am surrounded by barefoot children, by pigs and geese and guinea hens... the children dancing circles about me, the livestock pawing and pecking the moist earth. I sit on a wooden bench with my heart so light it might be a helium balloon, rising. The Babály daughters race off crying, Gèza! Gèza!" And then I see him: my son grown tall and reedy, browned by the sun. How fast and sure he runs on his new grasshopper legs.

"Cesikém." My Cesi.

"*Anyám*," he says in the same nasal dialect spoken by his adoptive family, "they told me you were dead."

What I replied to him I don't remember. It seemed necessary, urgent, to take his hand and study it. He had always had the maestro's hands, mimetic, blunt in the fingertips, but now dirt caked beneath his nails, calluses studded the palm.

Mrs. Babály stood at a distance, her eyes glassy.

"*Anyám,*" repeated my son, turning in her direction, "can she stay with us? Will we all live together now?"

The farm woman stepped briskly to the stove and busied herself with a brick of lard. "Wash up. Show your mother the orchard. I'll wait dinner."

♪

I stayed with the Babálies for two weeks, living as they did, getting to know the little man my son had become. Have I described their home? Its earthen walls and floors; the hearth around which the family clustered to eat, sleep and wash; the straw mattresses spread across the floor at night and taken up again the next morning at first light. It was spring, and the fields lay in furrows. My son had learned to sow potatoes, marking the rows with a stick, burying the spuds at just the right depth. Mornings he'd herd the pigs to pasture at the town's edge, calling them by name—Attila, Péter, Gizi…

"Do you remember your father?" I asked him.

"The photograph next to the bed, you mean?"

"How he'd lift you in the air and you'd laugh? How he'd play songs for us on the piano? Remember the songs?"

He put an unwashed finger in his mouth and chewed at a callus. "A man fell out of the sky in Visegrád and spoke to me in Italian. The priests hid him in a storeroom, and I was the only one who could speak to him."

"A paratrooper?"

"The other kids thought he was an angel."

"Maybe he was. An angel sent by your father, so you wouldn't forget him."

He nodded skeptically as if to indulge me. Had he already stopped believing in miracles, or was it his father's devotion he had begun to doubt?

My son taught me to milk the cows, to catch a goose and

wring its neck. The fetid stalls, the sight of blood, did not deter him. Muscle brought out his swagger. He wore the same homespun shorts as the other farm boys, the same woven cap, and nothing else—no underclothes, no socks, no shoes.

"Is that how you go to school?"

The question seemed to puzzle him. "We take turns going to school. Someone has to stay with the pigs."

At dinner the Babálies would assemble at a long plank table, say a few words of grace, and help themselves from assorted earthenware pots and platters, potatoes most nights, but also noodles and the occasional sliver of fowl. The family, having raised the livestock and grown the tubers that filled their stomachs, ate with gusto.

"Gèza was so thin when he first arrived," recalled Mrs. Babály, "no one else would have him. Erzsi found him alone on the train platform after everyone else had been chosen, the little runt, and brought him home."

Mr. Babály, slower of speech than his wife, puffed out his barrel chest. "He's fattened up nicely, our Gèza, no?"

My son, his fingers shiny with grease, tipped back his chair. "The big boys don't bully me anymore."

The youngest daughter, Anna, gazed at him with undisguised adoration. "Before Gèza came, we thought of nothing but Sàndor and Andràs, spoke of nothing but Sandor and Andràs."

"Our sons," explained Mr. Babály, "our eldest." A third son, Józsi, not much older than Cesare, sat dozing over his plate.

"They haven't come back from Russia yet—when did we last have a letter?"

Dignitaries might sign treaties, but wars never end. Oil dries up and bombs run out, but never a mother's tears. "I wish I could do for your sons what you've done for mine."

Mrs. Babály averted her eyes. "Wash your faces," she ordered the children. "Get ready for bed."

I waited for the others to wander off and then followed her to the sty, where we scattered the table scraps.

"I don't suppose you keep animals in the city?"

"We ought to. There's so little in the markets."

"It takes hands to run a farm. Gèza wasn't made for this work, can't even lift a bucket of water from the well, but he does his share. He fits in. We've never thought of him as an outsider."

"He's Italian," I felt obliged to remind her.

"He fits in."

Too well. His coarse country manners would raise eyebrows back in Rome. "He hardly seems the same person." *Zug nischt.* Why burden this stranger with a memorial to the boy I raised?

"The children have taken to him."

"From the time I realized my son hadn't reached his father, I've prayed, let him not be hungry or cold, give him courage." That he be loved would have seemed too much to ask.

Mrs. Babály turned away. The pigs trailed after, lapping at her bare heels. She waited for me to leave the pen and then secured the gate behind me.

"There's no repaying what you've done for my son, but if there's ever anything I can do for you ... "

"We were getting on before the war. My eldest boys knew all there was to know about farming, they had their eye on the future—crop yields, mechanization."

"Your sons will come home," I said, convincing neither her nor myself.

"The Russians don't give back."

In the end we were each half right. One son would return, years later, to his natal home—only to die in his prime, mangled by a tractor.

"I can't stay much longer."

She had to have known this, yet she winced.

"Cesare—Gèza—needs to return to school. But I promise to send him back to you for the harvest, as soon as classes are out."

"That will make it easier." Angling away, she raised the hem of her apron and discreetly daubed her eyes. "For the children," she hastened to add.

The moment called for something more than words, but Mrs. Babály kept walking, an empty bucket thumping against her skirts.

♪

The morning of our departure, the Babály children all stayed home from school. Mr. Babály went alone to pasture. Mrs. Babály left his unfinished breakfast on the table and loaded a sack with bread and onions, smoked sausage and bacon—there was no curbing her generosity. Into the sack went a mason jar filled with elderberry jam, another with plum, a hard-shelled squash... As we dragged this bounty the few hundred meters to the train platform, Józsi zigzagged toward us with a plump young goose flapping in his arms.

"My father wants you to have her," he said shyly. "We call her Lili."

I was about to refuse the gift when I thought of my mother, her unnatural thinness, her flair with a goose liver.

Józsi deposited the fowl into my son's arms, and the creature squirmed and nosed his chest.

"I hope Lili likes trains," I said, catching sight in the distance of a weathered locomotive.

My son wrestled the bird still. "Leave her to me."

The Babály boy gave Cesare an affectionate punch on the arm and headed at a trot for the fields. Mrs. Babály, her hands white with flour, stepped out from her house and called, "We'll expect you this summer, Gèza. Godspeed!"

As the train chugged nearer, the Babály girls clung to their adopted brother, sending the goose into paroxysms of pecking. Bloodied fingers; feathers borne aloft on gusts of steam; a last glimpse of Mrs. Babály, her hand outstretched and flour rising from the palm like cedar smoke.

The train wheezed to a full stop. No one got off. I kissed the girls goodbye and boarded, hefting the burlap sack onto a shoulder. Cesare wrestled the goose onto the uppermost step.

"You'll forget us," sputtered Anna, throwing herself at his

knees. "You'll go back to your fancy friends and your fancy ways and forget all about us." Erzsi tugged her sister down onto the platform. Anna began to weep. "I'll wait for you, Gèza. I'll keep your place at school. It will be just like before..."

As the train pulled away, we watched her race along the platform, mouth round as coin, arms thrust forward as if snatch us back. She ran in the steam's wake, her wet cheeks filling with soot.

"Gèza! Gèeeza!"

Cesare stared after her, unable to lift a hand in farewell.

The reeds grew tall alongside the tracks, taller than little Anna, whose voice whistled through them. At the first bend all sight of her vanished. And then Lili began to honk, to honk louder than the sum of all sorrows, so that all Apagy might hear her.

"We'll be home soon," I told my son.

Cesare said nothing, only gave me his skeptical smile. For a long time he gazed back through the grimy window, stretching his sunburned neck, until finally his chin dropped to his chest and he slept.

We took Lili back to my mother's flat and barricaded her in a corner of the kitchen. Cesare would feed her from his own hand, smooth her feathers, coo to her in a language all their own. When she topped the scales at twenty kilos, my mother took her to the kosher butcher to be slaughtered. I worried that my son might resist the inevitable, even beg for the goose's life, but he did neither. Hunger had taught him the value of a good meal.

"It is the end of a day that will never return
Sunset killed the light but not the memories."

"Il Tramonto"
The Sunset

♪ *Five*

I never danced again after the war. I still had the musculature, and with practice might have regained my suppleness, but I could see no light on the horizon toward which to direct my steps. We waited for József to return home, but he never did. We waited for friends. Through a searing, hungry summer I waited for the maestro, soaking the beans there was no fuel to cook. The Russians dug in for an extended stay. Evenings the drunken soldiers would kick in the door and storm up the vestibule, pawing the women, toppling them into corners, humping anything with a bit of flesh still on her bones. Summer ended, and having nothing to bury, we carried the lost in our hearts. Still we waited. We waited until we weren't sure anymore what we were waiting for, and then we waited some more.

"Where's papa?" Cesare once asked.

"On his way."

"What's taking him so long?"

"The roads have been blown up, the bridges."

He nodded and went back to his model airplanes, but the skepticism that had crept into his expression never left it. Having exhausted his childhood by the time he cut his teeth, he knew better than to ask again.

I hired a tutor for my son, bought my mother a kerosene stove, sewed curtains, and thought of Italy and another life, the life I had chosen on a piazza in Milan when the maestro got down on his knees and begged me to have him. But hunger doesn't care what we desire or contrive, hunger finds the pit of our stomachs and mocks our hollowness. I had a son and a mother to provide for. A woman might spend her whole life waiting turns at the bread shop, sparring for crumbs.

One morning, too early for the chestnut vendor, someone knocked at the door, a mere flurry of fingertips, unlike the soldiers who pounded with both fists. Szidonia and I raced to the foyer. "Who could it be?" she asked in a voice at once hopeful and tinged with dread.

I opened the door a crack. "You? I thought you were—"

"Dead?" Gyula gave a strangled laugh. "Say it: you thought I was dead."

"Wait, I'll get a robe."

My mother and I quickly wrapped ourselves and let him in. He carried a felt fedora in his hands and wore heavy canvas pants with the zigzag crease that marked men as widowers. We settled him in the armchair.

"When did you arrive?"

"Last night. Truck. I hitchhiked—but first there was the hospital. I'd caught something."

"And József?"

Gyula lowered his head.

"We had hoped…we thought maybe, still…"

"I know how that is."

"People do turn up. Even now."

"They put us to build an air strip in the middle of nowhere," he began to recount, dusting his shoes toe against heel. "They needed a place to land their fighter planes. They worked us twelve hours, fourteen hours … The front was coming nearer, the ground had frozen, and they worked us. I don't know how long. There wasn't enough to eat, scraps. We were in a bad way, the lot of us. You don't want to know."

"We got a letter from József in '43. I have it here." She turned away and dug it out from her brassiere. "Read it to him, Margit. I don't have my glasses."

I did as she asked. *"My dears, how are you and what are you doing? What's new at home? I ask that in the next postcard you not write to me here because I will have another address. I am fine and in good health. With lots of love, I kiss you all. Your loving son and brother, József. "*

"We had to write those things, that we were well, that conditions were mild. You'd think we were on holiday at Lake Balaton! Only it wasn't like that. You don't want to know."

My mother opened her arms. Gyula, having returned from the dead a softer man, curled onto her bosom. He had lost his own mother, his wife, his child, and couldn't bear the thought of going home. We put him to bed with Cesare, washed his socks and vest, set a place for him at the table. For months he came and went, emptying the coins from his pockets into my son's piggybank, leaving offerings of eggs and walnuts on the woodstove. I saw little of him, indeed barely noticed him, until one sabbath he had too much plum brandy and cornered me in the pantry.

"Help you with something?"

He was not drunk exactly. The alcohol had settled in his eyes, giving him the startled look of a jellied trout. "I've always admired you, Margit, but you knew that, didn't you? If you hadn't left for Italy, I'd have made a fool of myself and asked for your hand."

"That was a long time ago."

"You haven't changed as much as you think." He had come too near, his breath warm and acrid on my cheek.

"Tell me what happened to József."

Gyula took a step backward to brace against the wall. "József had a hurt foot." He paused, staring into a mason jar, fingering its lid. "You couldn't afford to get hurt, not once things got bad. At the beginning, some of the others might help, might share their bread, but not later on. They'd take advantage, steal from the weakest. And the sergeants worked us, worked us... The Nazis got their airstrip, they landed their planes, and when they'd drained the life out of us, they made us dig one last trench—our grave. We dug our own grave." He emitted what was meant to be a laugh, short and sharp. "What do you think of that? Tell me, Margit, lover of all things beautiful."

"You had to have lost your mind."

"We put down our shovels and lined up to be fed. Instead, they shot us. It was better than waiting for the cold to finish us off."

"And József?"

"He was lucky. He didn't have to crawl out of that pit."

I made to step past him, but he clamped a hand to my waist.

"This is no life we're living."

"No life? You wake to a new day and sit down to coffee and look out over the treetops and yet say you have no life? You're wrong about József. *We* are the lucky ones. What wouldn't he have given to come home?"

"Home to *what?* Rubble and beans, beans and rubble..."

"Let me go, Gyula. It's late. Cesare should be in bed."

He only tightened his grip. "Marry me, Margit."

"But I *am* married."

"Not in any way that matters. I'll take care of you. I'll be a father to your son."

"My son has a father."

"Don't be too proud to let yourself be saved. I have relatives in America. They'll sponsor us. We'll leave this cesspit and start again. Think of the opportunity! Broadway, Hollywood—Hungarians own Hollywood—Coney Island and mansions and motor cars—the Cadillac, the Chevrolet coupé..."

217

How we left the pantry I don't remember, but later, once the sabbath candles had burned low, Gyula got hold of the bread knife and tried to slit his wrists. He stayed with a cousin after that.

When spring came, I bought another piano and saw to it that my son had lessons. Having been sired by a maestro, surely he would have the gift. But every key he touched seemed to bleat. The music teacher despaired of his fumbling fingers and wandering concentration. "He can't string together three notes," the teacher uttered, tapping out a dirge, ending with a sigh on E flat. "You waste your money, madam."

I let the teacher go. "Don't worry, Cesarino, your father will teach you himself when we get to Italy. There is no finer pianist than your father."

Even under communism the maestro's songs arrived in Hungary. We'd hear them on the radio, melodies so sweet they seemed to issue from the flowers, from the green hills beyond the sooty skyline. When night went on too long they enveloped us like a silk cocoon.

♪

With the last frost Ádám dragged home to Budapest. We made a show of celebrating, but our toasts and tears only seemed to tire the young man with the old man's face.

"He'll be more... more himself after he's had a rest," Klára rationalized, but Ádám did not rest, did not recover. The fever had gone to his soul.

"They're sending people to camps again, the Russians are." He rarely spoke above a whisper. "Nothing has changed, only the uniforms." Pocked and emaciated, he retreated into his books.

The next I knew he was in Sàrospatak prison.

"Guards nabbed him at the border near Rics," explained Oszkár, not troubling to dissemble his growing contempt of the regime. "He was traveling with a Zionist group, children mostly, pretending to be Pioneers. Three months, they gave him. He'll try again. If there's a way out, he'll find it."

Who wasn't plotting escape by then? Bewildered, we watched the city of our birth sprout monumental statues celebrating heroes we would sooner spit upon than honor. Andrássy út, the street that had once contained the whole of my world, rechristened itself Stalin Boulevard. *Stalin*, who starved our livestock and carried off our factories while we queued for bread.

No sooner was Ádám released than he stowed aboard a freighter bound for Austria, intending to gain asylum and continue on to America. The passage, spent wrong side-up in a crate, nearly killed him. Discovered by an Austrian customs agent, he was treated as a common criminal, placed in detention, and again repatriated.

"You'd think we were lepers," he mused in a whisper, fingering the chin stubble he had given up shaving. We were alone, his sister Eva having become popular, Ádám's few friends avoiding him. I prepared coffee.

"You'll try again?"

"It only gets harder. The Moscovites have secured the borders, twenty-five hundred miles from the Baltic to the Black Sea mined and wired."

"There must be ways?"

A knowing look overspread his tired face. "One hears things, but it's a young person's game—evade the roadblocks, outrun the dogs…"

My mother, however strong-willed, had never regained her old stamina.

"Szidonia won't make it," Ádám said flatly.

The conversation was over. We drank our coffee in silence, each chained to a separate hurt, a dying dream, and the day dimming.

Long after Ádám had quit trying to escape, he made it out, sent by the regime to lecture on semi-conductors at the Friedrich-Alexander University near Nuremburg. It seemed an odd destination, but the communists had a short memory when it suited them, and Ádám couldn't refuse the appointment. He told us Germany was finding its conscience, a notion impossible to fathom, that a nation could murder millions of Jews, millions of Poles, millions of Russians, and yet become home to the homeless.

But that was how it was after the war. You stopped expecting things to make sense. You stifled the urge to speak and listened, turning the radio down and pressing your ear against the speaker. If you thought about love, you denied it, sucked the feeling down into your gut and bore it in silence.

♪

The opera house looked shabby, its frescoes faded, floors unwaxed. Even its paired marble sphinxes had lost their hauteur. Having called ahead to arrange a meeting with my old classmate Margit Horvath, I entered the lobby unimpeded, passed through the smoking parlor, and took a seat, noting as I did a change of scent. Gone was the bouquet of lemon wax. In its place, antiseptic and the faintest hint of (unthinkable in my day) sweat.

Ballerinas—toe-shoes slung across their shoulders, faces flushed from exertion—began to trickle out of class in twos and threes. No one I recognized. Too young, most of them, to remember ballet before Russia clamped its iron fist on it.

"Waiting long?" I wouldn't have recognized Horvath either, not because she had changed, but because she hadn't. We had once been the same age. "Rehearsal tonight," she reminded a passing student and then sat down beside me in a posture of apology. "I'd invite you to lunch, but—" She gestured with a pinky toward the wall clock.

"Long day?"

"How else to turn out dancers?" She kept her tone light, cordial. "You must come to our next performance. I'll reserve you a ticket."

"With pleasure, but it's not a spectator I wish to be."

Horvath subtly stiffened. "If it's work you're looking for, the opera house gives preference to Party members." She crossed her legs, reached down to massage an ankle. "You may have better luck outside."

"But there's no getting out."

"Outside Budapest. That is to say, the provinces." She glanced up and down the hallway and then lowered her voice. "We're treated no differently than factory laborers—the work books, the political meetings. It's not the ballet you knew."

"You speak as if I had a choice. Ballet chose me, not the other way around. You, of all people, should know that."

She faced me, her anger thinly veiled. "Why else would I be here?"

"Listen to us. We were friends once."

"If you want to get on, my dear, don't blame your friends, or even your enemies. Blame *the system*."

A handy evasion, but I knew better. Every edict, every lapse into barbarism, wears a human face. "This building was once a wonderland to me, from the moment I'd lace up my toe shoes... the world outside would disappear. It can be so small and dark outside."

Horvath tapped a finger to her painted lower lip. "There was talk of an opening not long ago."

"Where do I apply?"

"You don't change," she said with a brusqueness I could only interpret as approval. Testing her sore leg, she rose. The lipstick had migrated to her chin. "I'll put in a word, just don't expect too much."

The last of the students swept past, their step so light they might have been treading air. I watched their supple backs recede down a maze of corridors. Bankrupt and bullying the system may have been, but if ballet had a future, then I would coax perfection from the next generation of ballerinas. I would keep the dream alive.

♪

Years, it took, to count the murdered: József, Mano's nephews, Szidonia's Viennese cousins, old Mr. Feininger who had crafted my ballet slippers... Eventually, someone would turn up with a story and one more ghost would be added to "the List."

It was the famous ones that stunned us, the famous ones whose names we stumbled over. *Rene Blum?* No, surely they didn't get Rene Blum! Wealth, talent, influence meant nothing to the Nazis. It was enough that the victim be a Jew or gypsy, a homosexual or communist. And so Rene Blum died with all the others, taking with him the dazzle that had left audiences breathless. Another stage went dark.

The List grew beyond our ability to fathom it.

Nearly as hard to fathom were the reappearances, years later, of people we had taken for dead—people like Gabriel Saunders, whose face I had once seen in the flame of a *yortsite* candle. Nineteen forty-eight it had to have been by the time his letter arrived from Palestine (or was it Israel by then?).

The Austrian informed me he was well and living with his daughters in Tel Aviv, having lost his wife in 1940. He did not waste words describing his flight from one hostile country to another. He had found a home in Zion, a position, pride, and he wanted me to have the same. *"My dear Frau Wolf, imagine a country where Jews decide for themselves which works will dignify their stages. Your talents are needed here. Our girls have an innate grace that cries out for classical training."* A more passionate recruiter the young state could not have ordered, but my future was spoken for. *"My dear Herr Saunders,"* I wrote in response, *"your news fills me with hope for the next generation of Jews who will grow up free to express what is best in themselves. As for me, my place is with my husband and son. At the first opportunity I will return to Italy."*

And here memory blurs... the endless hours at the Italian consulate filling in form after form, my son outgrowing his clothes. Did I say that Cesare came to resemble his father? Around the mouth especially, not to mention the brow. He even lost his hair prematurely—but that was later. As a boy he was baby-faced, a fact he compensated for by playing tough. When he turned fourteen, I secured a place for him at the Polytechnic, bribing the director with a pair of diamond cufflinks I had picked up on the black market.

My son had the scientific turn of mind prized by the regime. A nation building itself back from the brink of ruin could ill-afford to trod its youth underfoot—or so I told myself each time another rumor surfaced demonizing the AVO, a secret security force much whispered about at the time. Our neighbor, Mr. Matrai, was one of them. One night, stepping out from their lair in his spruce black uniform, he would be shot dead.

♪

When Stalin died unmourned in '53, my son graduated with honors, hung his diploma on a wall, and waited. There were still rumors of abduction and torture, the periodic disappearance with only questions to fill the void, but Cesare had lost the habit of sleeping. We all had by then.

And then Teréz reappeared. Teréz of the ungovernable derriere, who had danced her way into an advantageous marriage. She returned to Budapest on the pretext of attending a soccer game, the famous rematch against Britain. Seven to one the Magyars smeared them, a feat never to be repeated. But that is a lesser miracle. My childhood companion of the *Pas de Quatre* spotted me walking down Andrássy and took off in pursuit, fleet of foot even in her Ferragamo heels.

"Margit, dear Margit, we feared the worst." She wore burgundy silk, yards of it. To embrace her was like swimming through wine. "Come, let me invite you to lunch." A note of charity blighted the invitation.

"I've already eaten." A fib.

"Coffee then."

She linked her arm in mine and drew me close, so that her painted lips grazed my ear. "Is it true what they say about spies?"

"It's all true."

We found a table at our old haunt, the Lukács, which had retained just enough of its luster to recall better times. "I used to love this place," murmured Teréz, looking glamorous and lost. With a dancer's conscious poise, she reached into her purse and removed a gold cigarette case. "Smoke?"

I took a Blonde.

"How are you, darling? You look well."

"We manage. I teach, choreograph." Years it had taken before the regime deemed me worthy to return to ballet.

"Russian school?" said Teréz with undisguised scorn.

"My own." The apparatchik assigned to monitor my classes would not have known the difference.

A waiter plodded to the table, and we ordered espressos. "How shabby Budapest must look to you after all these years." Its dingy facades and outmoded shop windows, the dour faces and nervous tics.

She glanced over a shoulder before responding, "Dante would have felt right at home."

"You've been to the opera house?"

"I stopped in to say hello to Margit Horvath—who else is left? Place was crawling with Cossacks."

"Do you see the others?"

"Karola and I talk. She made it to La Scala, you know, as a teacher. Always was the brash one. Ilona I saw before she left Italy. There was nothing to keep her after Ferretti decamped, and high time, too. Nearly ruined her."

"You've done well for yourself."

"I'm comfortable, if that's what you mean. But the stage—there's nothing like it. Those were good years."

"How many times did we threaten to wring Buffarino's neck?"

"That was part of the fun. Those dives he booked us into!"

"We were compromising everything we had worked for."

"Admit it, Manci, you enjoyed the attention. I did. The way the audience caressed us with their eyes."

"I got used to it. After a time there was no going back."

"Or forward either." She sighed then, and despite her finery looked a very ordinary woman. "When I left the tour, I thought I had broken free—from Buffarino, from the pressure of having always to be skin-and-bones perfect. But who was I kidding? When I stopped dancing, I stopped dreaming. In the place of dreams I had only small indulgences: a morning at the hairdresser, a carriage ride through the park…"

I could neither envy nor pity her.

"We tried to have children, couldn't. My fault, I suppose."

"No one's fault."

She sat back and surveyed the room, expectantly at first, and then with a glum stare. "We heard such horrible things after the war. Things beyond belief. Why didn't you write?" To my friend's credit, she didn't wait for an answer. "The three of us were always asking, 'Have you heard from Margit? No, have you?' Not a single letter."

"I don't suppose you've seen Pasquale?"

"Pasquale. Always Pasquale." She gave a backward wave of the hand, the same gesture I'd once seen her use to dismiss a servant. "If you must know, Karola ran into him outside Cinecittá. He'd lost the rest of his hair, she said."

There were questions I might have asked, but why risk the answers? My husband inhabited a land of mist beyond sight and touch.

Teréz, her torso suddenly intent, leaned across the table. "Is there something I can do for you?"

"Not for me. For Cesare."

She sat chain-smoking as I told the story of the security police. Irked by my son's refusal to assume Hungarian citizenship, they had banned him from university, relegating him forever to the proletariat.

"What's he to do," my friend seethed between puffs, "work a machine? Drive a truck?"

Either that or land in a gulag. "There's only one place for him: Italy. In Italy he'll get a proper education."

"Is that what the boy wants?"

Who but a woman swaddled in imported silk would think to ask such a question? "He'll do what's sensible."

"And Pasquale?"

"Pasquale longs for his son. He'd do anything for him."

"What makes you so certain?" A verdict. When I made no attempt at persuasion, Teréz took a last drag of her cigarette and exhaled languidly with her chin in the air. "I'll talk to my husband," she said finally. "Old Boselli knows how to pull strings."

♪

Bureaucrats do not take kindly to intercessions. Their one satisfaction in life is to keep us waiting in line, begging for that last signature. In the end it was Monsignor Angelo Roncalli, soon to become Pope John XXIII of the Catholic world, who rescued my son from the regime's clammy grip. *Old Boselli* had known him as a parish priest, had bankrolled the restoration of his first church.

"Is this what you've come for?" The clerk with a fondness for puzzles slapped the stamped and sealed visa onto the counter with a loser's ill temper. "You may know someone on high, *signora*, but favors run out. You won't find the consul very well-disposed to your requests in future."

"Then my son is free to leave?"

"That's up to the Hungarians." Picking the scab from a shaving nick, he stepped away from the glass partition.

Within the week I had my answer: an official letter from the Hungarian Ministry of the Interior, ordering my son to leave the country. Twelve days they gave him, a grace period during which, it was suggested, he might wish to "put his affairs in order."

Szidonia read the fine print through a magnifying glass. "Affairs? Since when does a twenty-year old boy have affairs?"

"The son of a maestro mustn't return to his homeland looking like a refugee. He'll need clothes, gifts."

My mother's brow filled with ledger lines. "Can't his father buy him clothes?"

I strode to Cesare's closet and examined its contents garment by garment. "Outmoded. Poorly cut. Tatty."

"But you bought him that suit only a year ago."

"It won't do. Have the tailor make him a new suit, something Continental, and a tuxedo—no, two tuxedos—one white and one black, each with a pleated cummerbund. And half a dozen shirts, not cotton but silk."

"In twelve days?"

"He'll need bed linens, of course—sheets, pillowcases. Have them monogrammed with his initials, by hand not by machine, and large, say three inches—no, make that four inches. And a quilt of the finest satin to match."

Whatever I had managed to put aside, I spent for the pleasure of sending my son off looking like a prince. How proud the maestro would be! Cesare, though he did not play music, had an avid ear. Mention an opera and he could recount its libretto, a symphony and he could hum it. True, his Italian had grown rusty (as had my own), but this did not concern me. The language was in his blood; he had only to get his tongue around it.

The day before his departure, he put on his new clothes and we went together to the photographer to have a portrait taken. I still have a copy somewhere: Cesare unsmiling, trying to look grown-up, and I angled just so, to hide my lump. The image my son would carry away with him and hang on a wall.

I accompanied him to the train station. A bulging duffle bag slowed his gait, and his collar, starched for the occasion, chafed. He spoke little. Having purchased his ticket in advance, there was nothing to do but wait.

"*Anyám*," he began.

"*Parla Italiano.*"

"*Mamma...*" His composure shattered, that hard knot of will that had kept him alive from the time he could run. He did not weep exactly, only quaked, like a volcano about to erupt.

I might have held him, but I didn't. "We're strong people," I said, "and strong people don't cry."

The struggle to contain himself made speech impossible.

I ran my handkerchief along his shined brogues, removing the least speck of dust. "By now you know what kind of world we're living in. Study hard. Make something of yourself."

Cesare gazed down the tracks, up at the wall clock, and said nothing.

"Look after your father."

"But *anyám*—"

"*Parla Italiano.*"

"Who will look after *you?*" he blurted and bit down on his lip.

I slicked back his cowlick, straightened the handkerchief in his breast pocket. Another few moments and he would get his emotions in check. Avoiding my eyes, he looked again at the wall clock. The train was late.

Softly, as if to salve a wound, I placed my hands atop the crown of his head and recited, "*Ye'simcha Elohim ke-Ephraim ve'vhi-Menashe...*"

The grimy locomotive wheezed to a halt and he boarded, dragging his baggage after him like a penance. I glimpsed his face behind the glass. He seemed to be struggling with the window, wanting to open it, perhaps to tell me something, but the pane would not budge. The platform moved beneath me—the train, pulling away. My son, the song of my flesh, gone in the time it takes to blink back a tear.

♪

Open that drawer, *signorina*, and I'll show you something. See that envelope? Hand it to me. Don't bother with my reading glasses, I know it by heart.

"*Carissima mia, I suppose we should count ourselves lucky, having survived this filthy war. Legs, arms, necks intact. A roof over our heads. People, wherever I go, sing my songs, but I can't sing them. I compose only to let the sorrow flow out. Take care of our precious bambino. See that he keeps his Italian, so that one day we may speak of all this. As for you, my faithful Manci, if I were a better man I would release you, but that I can never do. Pasqualino.*"

A touching missive, yes? An ending worthy of the silver screen—only, our story didn't end that way. I wrote the letter myself. I wrote it when the waiting became too hard and the silence so crushing I could no longer dig out from under it. I wrote it in order to go on.

Eventually I even returned to Italy, as you see, returned with nothing but the grooves of my skin, the regime having relieved me of every last trifle and trinket. My mother accompanied me, though she was sick by then. We moved in with my son at Turin, where the maestro also lived. Once I had put together the necessities and settled-in, he came by for a visit, older and much changed, it's true, but hardly diminished. He smelled of Cassis and mentholated tobacco, his vices of choice, laced with a smooth French cologne. The music hall brashness hadn't left him, it was just better clothed.

"Manci," he said when we were alone, and again, "Manci…" He spoke my name as if the sound of it pained him, a barb tearing at his throat.

I said nothing at all.

He cocked his proud head. "How was the journey?"

"Fine, thank you."

"Have you everything you need?"

"Certainly. My son has made provision."

"*Our* son," he whispered and the rasp returned.

"I heard about your marriage." To another dancer, the estranged wife of the comedian Macario. A woman whose alimony was also her dowry.

He turned away and walked heavily toward the window. There was something tragic about him from behind. The skin of his nape creased and bunched like old upholstery.

"Nineteen fifty-four, wasn't it, the wedding?"

"Dates." He had always been hopeless at remembering them.

"You've done well—the film scores, the hit songs, the marble penthouse... Bravo, maestro!"

"Bravo?" he echoed bitterly. "Thankless business, music. What was all the rage yesterday, today won't buy a plate of linguini. If only I had composed that ballet... but then, for whom would I have composed it?" His neck sunk lower on his shoulders, and he turned for a moment to glance at me, a look not so much tender as raw.

"Your songs were on the radio. We heard them, we memorized the tunes, there's not a single one we don't know. "*Tu solamente tu non ritorni piu...*"

"Don't! Please."

"*Du immer weider du, flustert mein mund zartlich dir zu.*" It's lovely in German, don't you think?"

"Don't."

"Your songs can only be lovely. I believed every word, you see. I thought it was your way of speaking to me."

"Speaking? I was screaming into a void."

"I was sure you'd come in '46."

"Impossible."

"People who love do the impossible all the time."

He swatted the remark away. "Every song tore pieces from me. What was left to tell after '38? What was left?"

I could have gone to him, but I didn't. He could have turned back, taken me in his arms, but what would it have changed? Across the sun-freckled room his fragrance wafted toward me.

"What was left, *babuci*? A dirge? You had taken my future. I would never watch my son grow up." He veered and one manicured hand shot up as if to strike a blow. "*Porca miseria*, why did you have to leave me?"

"Why did you let me go?"

Hardly an answer, but it was all I could say. Have I disappointed you? Life is so much shabbier than cinema, so many loose ends. A woman might spend a lifetime trying to knit them together, only to land in a place like this. Not that I'm complaining. I've always loved Naples—the light, the show, the unending petulance. What better place to die?

But look, we have a visitor. Just look at him, stamping water across the floor, wringing out his cuffs.

"Ladies," the newcomer says in greeting, bows a few inches, and reaches behind him for a chair.

"Joining us for a spell?"

The young woman and sopping man exchange a look, and I wonder if they might be flirting.

"It's your son, *Signora* Wolf."

But of course, Cesare always visits when it rains. "Come kiss me, Cesarino. How I have missed you! Ages it's been."

"I was here day before yesterday—wasn't I, *signorina*?"

I smell a conspiracy, but there's no use arguing. For all I know, my son and this Babes-in-Toyland are already lovers. Cesarino has lost most of his hair and let his midsection go to jelly, not that decay ever stopped a man from carrying on. "How is your wife?"

"*Mamma*, you know Magda is dead. She died three years ago."

"Of course, dear. Such a fortunate woman, she could have done better than to run off with that drunkard."

The girl blushes to the roots of her hair and slips from the room, soundlessly closing the door.

"Who was she anyway?"

"Magda?" Cesare flicks raindrops from his eyelashes. "Your daughter-in-law, of course."

"Not Magda, *that* girl. Such a patient listener, never said two words."

"A volunteer of some sort. I think she's from the convent school."

"You really oughtn't ogle her, you know."

"I wasn't ogling her. I don't *ogle*." He's like that, contrary. Whatever I say he contradicts. "Next you'll be accusing me of corrupting the morals of a minor." He walks his umbrella to a dry corner.

The rain has stopped, leaving the sun to overflow the sills. The gauze curtain ripples with breeze and something more.

"Listen. Hear the music? Stravinsky—no, Delibes—but where's the orchestra?" The melody draws me up from the iron bed with the starched sheet trailing. I cannot put words to the tune, only a color—smoke gray, the color of night trains—only a lightness in my ribs, time falling away. I glide about the floor tiles, testing my legs, venturing a glissade, then a pirouette, and another. The music hums in my pores.

My son's arthritic index finger points to the wall clock. Two o'clock.

But I've lain long enough in this stale bed in this stuffy room, watching my companions wait for death, watching them die, and not ready to follow. I rise to my toes, lift and extend into an arabesque. The body forgets nothing.

And now Cesare is beside me, linking his arm through mine. "*Siesta*," he chides and leads me back to the iron bed.

"Oh, how the suitors used to line up at the stage door! Your father had names for them: Lord Toupee, Daddy Greenbacks, The Salamander…"

My son stifles a laugh.

"Neanderthal Nino, Paddy from Cincinnati, *Capitano* Missed-the-Boat."

Just once I wish he would throw back his head and let fly one of those unruly hee-haws that were his father's signature, but he only expels air. "Little chilly in here. Shall I shut the window?"

"No!" There's a burning in my lungs, and I try not to breathe, but the reflex is involuntary. Close your mouth and your nostrils suck up air just the same. The poison clouds are out again. "See, there. See how the gas seeps into the room through the electrical sockets? I don't like this room."

"But it's the best locale in the sanatorium. Just look at the view! You can see Capri from this window."

"And the light bulbs—sniff. It's gas, I tell you, poison gas. We can't stay here!"

"Please, *mamma*, you're safe. The director has changed your room a dozen times, remember? You started in the far wing, upstairs, downstairs... there's nowhere we haven't tried."

"They find you, you know."

"Who finds you?"

"Don't pretend you don't know. *Them*. You think you can blend in, disappear, you think if you keep out of the way and don't call attention to yourself that they'll leave you alone. But they never do."

"Has anyone been unkind to you—the nurses, the doctor?"

They have him fooled with their plaster saints and tepid assurances about sanitation and the sanctity of old age. The good life has made him soft.

"The war's over. It's 1998. You're safe."

"They didn't let me dance! I was impure. I corrupted the stage. When my legs were good, I could soar like a bird, like a bird... and they made me clean toilets. The world threw roses at Markova's feet. The queen paid court to her. Why couldn't they love me?"

"But they did. In England, in France, in Germany, through the darkest years of the war they sang about you. I've collected the sheet music, the recordings. They may not have seen your face, but they prayed for you, wept for you. You were the embodiment of loss, every loved one they would never embrace again, every dream snatched away."

I had been right about "*Tu Solamente Tu*." It will outlive its composer and muse both, elegy to two lives briefly one. Some small consolation, if I let it be

233

"Next week I'll bring the old phonograph and we'll listen together, eh?"

This kind, measured man my son has become, so like someone I used to know. And that old phonograph, still spinning out refrains… "I'm so tired. I can't take another step."

"You don't have to, *mamma*. Rest. I'll sit beside you."

For once he's right. And even if he weren't, I haven't the strength to tussle. How soft the light this time of day, as if the sun had drawn a silken veil about itself and knelt to look in on us. Beside me the maestro stirs—is it time to put the coffee on? I'd like to speak his name—Pietro? Paolo?—but better to lie still and let the light skim along the twin peaks of his shoulders, better not to force the dawn. It's enough to have him near.

Eulogy Never to Be Delivered

My mother died last night, and I feel more alone than if I'd never been born. I stand in the shower long after the water has run cold and cannot bring myself to reach for the taps. The water just keeps falling.

Margit was lucid at the end. With the last of her strength she clasped me by the shirtfront and made me promise to take her home to Budapest to be buried beside her father, the tailor Mano Wolf. I haven't the stomach right now to make the arrangements, but I will. I'll take her. It will be icy this time of year, the earth hard to move, but if souls find one another again, father and daughter will rest whole.

It's the wrong time to review accounts, especially those that can never be settled, and yet I find myself thinking of all the people who thwarted my mother's talent, starved her body and soul, the people who took and took and took. Had she not raised me to reason, I would trap them like rats and roast them alive in their snug little houses, but her memory denies me even revenge. The water needles down. My mother's remains lie bagged in cold storage, waiting for me to give them rest. I must get a grip—

Her face, once life had left it, might have belonged to a young woman. She was ageless, radiant. I'd once seen a photograph: she wore a tutu and stood high on her toes, not smiling but radiating happiness. She had to have been in love.

Already I miss her, though she was not much company these past years, more of an anchor. Her gaze held me fast. I couldn't bring myself to close her eyes—the nurse did it, mechanically, with rubber-gloved fingers. And then it was over, her life and the part of mine that had drawn force from its constancy. I went back to my apartment and called my daughters, listened while they cried, promised to send airfare. I hope I was some comfort.

The water keeps falling. My mother died last night, and I'm an eggshell in a hailstorm. It will be worse in Budapest—everything is—with the abyss of memory newly excavated and nothing to do but heave a clump of earth onto her casket. Why she would want to lie in such patchy soil, I'll never understand, with the stench of the Danube forever in her nostrils. This final request pains me. Not for the exertions it will cost me, which are nothing measured against what I owe her, but because I was so utterly unprepared for it. Had she said, throw my body into Vesuvius, I couldn't have been more stunned. I'd like to think that I knew my mother, not the facts of her life, about which she never spoke, but an inner essence. I took her for a person who never looked back.

She returned from the camps unbent. Only the number on her arm—1369, unlucky—marked her as a survivor. For years she rubbed at the digits with a pumice stone, inflaming the skin, bloodying herself. The tattoo refused to go away. She took to wearing long sleeves, even in July, when other women strolled fresh and aloof in their summer dresses.

And then the hallucinations started, fleeting at first—informers trailing us, enemy planes loosing deadly gas above our heads... I moved her from one flat to another, from city to city. Everywhere peril. She lived to escape, from the doctors and caregivers who tried to protect her, from the policemen who fished her off the streets. Anyone in uniform was suspect. Anyone who dared lay hands on her met with kicks, punches, a blind will to endure that defied age and reason both. Once, when I was out-of-town on business, she lost her way and fought her rescuers with such fury that the authorities hauled her off to an insane asylum. Days passed before the chief doctor found her and brought her back. Bruised, unbathed, her white hair matted, she marched through the entranceway with an orderly on each arm and never uttered a word.

Hers was not the only silence. The painful retellings she spared me I also learned to hold inside. If her life was less acid for my secrets, then I'm glad to have kept them.

What purpose would it have served to talk about the corpses I awoke beside the winter of '44? Children's corpses. Playmates who had lain down to sleep and died of hunger and cold. Should I have told her about fashioning shoes for myself out of horses' feedbags? About eating the corn that spilled from their mouths? She had her own dead to contend with, her own privations. I, at least, was nobody's enemy—not that my innocence stopped the bullet that tore through my knee as the Russians liberated Visegrád. Would the wound have stung less if my mother had been there to embrace me? For all I knew, she had no arms.

An armored vault she may have been, but did she need to know that I felt myself an orphan long before I became one? That I gave up all hope of seeing family again, of returning to school, and resigned myself to the life of a pig farmer?

Not that my expectations were much brighter after she rescued me from Apagy. The security police taught me what I could expect of the future: terror. Should I have described to her the hours spent at the headquarters of the AVO, squatting with my nose against the wall, my hands bound to my back, my heels raised—the games they would invent! They were patient, these cops, enjoyed their work. It wasn't so much the beatings they liked as the building-up to them—the insults, the accusations. *What sort of name is Cesare? Name of a dog.* Of what was I guilty?

Could my mother have told me? Had she already formed a theory of her own about arbitrary cruelty relentlessly applied?

I learned to read her eyes, her gestures, the posture she'd strike as I entered a room. I read her silence the way others read mystery novels. Speech was a mere movement of the vocal chords, unavoidable, but not to be indulged.

When I put her in the care home, it took a scant few hours to clean out her old studio. What had she ever possessed that wasn't stolen from her? I found no valuables. Her clothing I took to a charity shop, her pots and pans I threw away. She had already removed the one object that mattered to her: a battered tin box of no particular distinction. The head nurse released it to me this morning. Locked inside was a sheath of yellowed letters—letters from my father.

For maestro Pasquale Frustaci I have kept my blackest secrets. Oh, he was good with words, my father. His letters, had they been set to music, would have topped the charts. "*Your sadness has a limit. Mine has none. I have here close to me your portrait and the one of Cesare, and next to it are all of his toys: the bear, the ball, the tiny chair. These objects are endless tortures for me. I cannot find peace.*" And later, once his star had begun to rise, "*You have made me a different man with different feelings, and I am infinitely grateful to you. You will see what I am capable of doing in time and you yourself will say, 'Bravo!*'" And later still, after "*Tu Solamente Tu*" brought him the fame he had lusted after, "*No one can take you and Cesarino away from me. Only God can divorce us.*" How my mother cleaved to these pages! How she trusted.

Should I have told her about the night I spent in Milan in '56, dressed in my best clothes, my new shoes spit-shined, waiting in a hotel room with my Aunt Elena and Uncle Peppino for my father to come from the theater and claim me? Eighteen years I had waited to embrace the great maestro, and he didn't come. My aunt called the theater, called again, called through the night. We sat staring at our own feet, nodding asleep. In the morning we were still waiting. We had run out of things to say, not that I knew much Italian then.

Palsied with ire, my aunt stormed the theater, interrupted my father at rehearsal, and told him, 'Come get your son or I'll deliver him to the *comandante di polizia* and you can answer to *him.*'

Toward evening he arrived at the pension, and not bothering to knock, stepped heavily into the room. Here was the father for whom I had endured torture: a soft balding man with a showman's smile and in whose eyes I saw the fear of a trapped animal.

"Papa..."

"*Discrezione,*" he said, touching a buffed fingernail to his lips. "Someone will hear."

Did my mother need to know that, for years after our reunion, my father introduced me as his nephew? That he skimped on my allowance and cut me off the day I turned twenty-one? That he used me as a chauffeur to shuttle him among his various lovers, who were leggy and stupid and made me ashamed to have been sired by such a hound.

She wept when he died, something I never saw her do before or again. He died married to another woman, yet it was my mother, grown brittle in the space of a day, whose tears bathed his fat, embalmed cheeks.

Should I have told her about the second son who inherited his copyrights? A son born to a certain Maria Consiglio, whom the maestro married in Naples in '27—and to whom he was still married that giddy day in Tripoli, when he put a wedding ring on my mother's finger and recited the sham vows. Should I have intruded on her mourning to say, you weren't the first wife of Pasquale Frustaci? Legally speaking, you weren't his wife at all.

And if that disclosure hadn't sufficed to shatter her heart, should I have treated her to another? Should I have shown her the 18-karat gold Doxa wristwatch my father entrusted to me for safekeeping after my stepmother threatened him with a carving knife? He hadn't thought to hide it from me. The inscription on its casing was so shallow I had to hold it to the light to read: *A Greta, Con Amore. Capri 1946. Pasqualino.* That the Greta in question was Garbo, I know from a certain Count Biancoli, who for the price of a brandy was only too happy to recall their tryst: my father at the keyboard, Garbo, still waspish at forty, draped over a fainting couch keeping time with a Spanish fan. It had been summer. The countess would retire to her room early each night, leaving her guests to their sport.

About my father, what more is there to say? He left me nothing when he went, and his widow would not part even with the conductor's baton I asked for. My only memento is this solid gold watch, which I take from its pouch once each year and polish for no other reason than to see myself in it.

Margit died last night as luminous as a saint, forgotten but for a song. The maestro's portrait beside her on the pillow. I would have liked to sit with her through the night, but they rolled her away after no more than an hour, something about hygiene and preparations, and shouldn't I get some rest?

It's my mother's turn to rest, not mine. Arrangements must be made. The mortuary has suggested a freight train, but I'd prefer to accompany the coffin. It's a long way to travel alone. The milestones outside gray as ghosts, the stations passing... Must you go, *mamma?* Must you take from me what even hatred spared? I will miss our silences.

Cesare Frustaci Remembers

It was August 1956 and I was on my way to Italy, the only passenger in the train wagon. Beside me rested an enormous hand-made duffel bag holding all the finery my mother had custom-ordered for my journey—black and white tuxedos, silk shirts, a satin quilt... However torn or jittery I might feel, I would, at least, look the part of a maestro's son.

As the train neared the Austrian border four armed Hungarian guards entered the wagon and demanded my documents. Confident that my papers were in order, I handed over my passport.

"What's in your luggage?" asked the one in charge.

I watched, helpless, as they overturned the duffel bag onto the floor and began like vultures to pick through its contents. Every item had been pre-approved by the authorities in Budapest and noted on an official list. I gave them the list and was ordered to a far corner of the wagon, where I was forced to sit in silence while they pillaged.

"There are too many shirts, underwear and shoes. Choose three of each."

"But the list was approved for the exact quantity I am carrying," I protested.

"The regulations have changed."

All argument was futile. In the end, I sat back and let them steal what my mother had taken such pains to acquire. But the ordeal was not over.

"Now get up and undress," the head man ordered.

"What do you mean undress?" I knew perfectly well what they meant and could not contain my indignation. Under their beady gazes I took off my jacket and the rest of my clothes and stood there barefooted with only my boxer shorts on.

"Those too," snapped the guard, pointing vaguely in the direction of my fly. "We have to check everything."

He passed each of my garments to the other soldiers, who palpated every inch of fabric. The search took half an hour.

"Now tell us, how much money do you have?"

I stated the obvious. "You have checked my pockets and have in front of you the 30,000 lire the Hungarian National Bank permits me to export (roughly the equivalent of $50.00)."

"Are you hiding any up your ass?"

At last they left me alone and I dressed and sat in my assigned seat, a twenty-year old who could not remember ever having been free. I thought of my mother, thought of her so intently that I could hear her voice.

"*Tu sei forte.*" You are stronger than they are.

Just hearing her voice made the pain subside. It was my greatest inspiration. It never failed. Her words, her ubiquitous presence, had helped me through the most difficult situations-- the lonely nights on the streets of Budapest during the war, the frigid winter in Visegrád, the torturous interrogations at Andrássy #60...

The train passed through the notorious Iron Curtain, two rows of soaring barbed wire between which stretched a minefield. Attack dogs skulked the length of the barrier from one surveillance tower to the next. Anywhere I turned, I seemed to be looking up the barrel of a gun. Finally, like waking from a bad dream, I reached the West. My first thoughts were of my father, the stranger whose songs had been my lullabies.

Nothing had prepared the maestro, newly married to a second (or third) wife, for the shock of my arrival. When he finally came for me and took me to the Teatro Lirico where he was rehearsing *La Febbre Azzurra*, he introduced me to the orchestra members as his *nipote*, the son of a brother. Later, he introduced me as his son, only to add with inflated irony, "*Un errore giovanile.*" An error of my youth.

Eighteen years earlier, this same man had referred to me as the reason for his life.

The maestro never knew what my mother and I had endured during our long absence; he never asked. His career gradually declined, and with it his health. On the back of a photo he sent to me in the early 1950s he described himself as "old, tired and sad," yet he smiled for the camera.

I recall, a decade later, an occasion in Vienna when my father and I attended a gala performance at the Volks Opera. Formal dress was required, but my father had spent the afternoon in a grey turtleneck sweater and did not feel like changing into a tuxedo. Instead he vanished into the men's room and inserted a white handkerchief into the front of his sweater, fashioning a priest's collar. As we approached the ticket usher he raised two fingers on his right hand and made the sign of the cross, reciting aloud in Latin, "*Dominus vobiscum...*"

After university my relationship with my father warmed. We both lived in Torino by then, and sharing a passion for art and music, became frequent companions. Once I completed my university studies, he missed no opportunity to introduce me as his son, the professional electronic engineer. In the 60s, when the RAI (*Radio Televisione Italiana*) commissioned my father to record a 21-episode program on the history of musical theater, we pooled our record collections and set to work, I translating the jacket covers from English to Italian and recording the tracks, and my father providing commentary. I would like to think we made a winning team.

My mother and grandmother, having at last broken free of the communist regime, joined us in Torino in 1964. I cannot say that the four of us formed a family in the conventional sense, but there remained between my parents a mutual affection and respect that was apparent to anyone who saw them together.

My parents' reunion lasted only as long as their estrangement had. In 1971 the maestro died in Naples of a lung ailment and we—my mother, wife and young daughter—drove south for his funeral. During the ten-hour journey my mother did not speak a single word, but when she approached my father's coffin I thought I heard her whisper, "*Ora non devo dividerti con nessuno.*" Now I do not have to share you.

In closing, I would like to revert to memories of childhood. My earliest recollection of my mother is quite vivid. I can clearly visualize the room in my grandparent's flat where my mother and I slept. Every night without exception, before going to bed she had me kneel by the bedside to say my prayers. She taught me to say the Lord's Prayer first and then made sure I asked God to bless my father and keep him well and safe.

Another memory makes me smile. Every time we approached a public place she would bend over and straighten my clothes, wet her fingers with saliva and slick down my hair, and push back my shoulders saying, "*Stai dritto, togliti le mani, dale tasche, e saluta.*" Stand-up straight, take your hands out of your pockets, and say hello.

She guided me until her last days. She still does.

By telling my family's story, I hope my children and grandchildren will know and appreciate who Margit Wolf was and find inspiration in her example. As Americans, they enjoy opportunities my mother could barely have imagined. With pride I urge them forward—shoulders back, hands out of their pockets—to seize their dreams.

Cesare Frustaci has made a mission of sharing his story and insights at schools, churches, and synagogues around the world. If you would like Cesare to speak with your group, email him at cesarefrustaci@msn.com.

Acknowledgments

I met Cesare Frustaci at the home of mutual friends, Hungarian émigrés, in the winter of 1990. My first impression was of a cultured middle-aged man, friendly, if guarded.

Reflecting later upon that meeting, I identified Cesare's defining feature: regardless of where he made his home, he was unplaceable. He spoke with an accent, not Hungarian exactly, but not Italian either. Unlike his fellow émigrés, he had no wistful memories of Hungary, no desire to return.

I remember sharing a meal with him in a restaurant. There was something about the way he ate I had never before observed: although his table manners could not have been more refined, he appeared to be starving. Immediately upon finishing a course, he would signal the waitress and order a second helping—only to cancel the order moments later.

As we got to know each other, details of his childhood began to emerge—the malnutrition he suffered during World War II, the "shoes" he fashioned for himself from horses' feedbags, the corpses alongside which he would awaken each morning... He seemed to be describing the perils of an orphaned waif abandoned to his fate, yet he was the son of Pasquale Frustaci (aka "the Italian Cole Porter"), a composer and conductor whose star, while the war cast Europe into darkness, had never shone brighter. How then, from the age of seven, did Cesare end up alone on the battlefronts of provincial Hungary in the midst of the worst carnage the world has known?

The answer would arrive in my mailbox fifteen years later: a videotaped oral history Cesare contributed to Yale University. It told the story of a gifted Jewish ballerina who inspired a universal anthem to longing only to fade from history without a trace. I sat riveted, as if hearing the libretto of a classic ballet or opera, but this was memory—the memory of a hungry boy searching for his parents.

To Cesare, my eternal thanks for entrusting me with his story and never once impinging on my creative freedom. Thanks also to Cesare's wife, Judy, for enduring our endless interviews with indefatigable good humor.

David Liss, my stellar first reader of many years, who traveled half the world at my side and believed in me every step of the way, deserves to be knighted.

Many scholars and archivists have aided in my research, among them historian Doreen Eschinger, Ferenc Katona of the United States Holocaust Museum, Dr. John Botos and Mihaly Csato of the Hungarian Holocaust Memorial, Nora Wellman of the Hungarian State Opera, and Alan Cass of the Glenn Miller Archives.

In Italy the entire Frustaci family contributed stories, notably Carmine Pettisani and Giuseppe (Pino) Letizia. Raffaelo Cossentino added missing songs to Pasquale's prodigious discography. Count Lucio Biancoli shared an eyewitness account of the maestro's meetings with Greta Garbo.

In Hungary revelation flowed from Margit's cousin Dr. Gyorgy Hahn, Eva Kemény Sos, and Anna and Jozsef Babály (who received Cesare like a brother after an absence of more than 60 years and passed away shortly after their reunion, blessed be their memories).

My thanks to literary agents Rob Weisbach and Jake Bauman for taking-on an idiosyncratic work of fiction in an impossible market, and to Pale Fire Press for defying the odds.

I am humbled by the talented artists who took time to read and endorse *You, Fascinating You*: Susan Jaffe, Kinga Nijinsky Gaspers, Janet Panetta, Elana Altman, Elizabeth Evans, Howard Allen, Georgia Reed, and Jim Bencivenga.

And then there are the countless friends and supporters who buoyed me up through the long, circuitous journey toward publication. Space allows me to name too few: Vera Marie

Badertscher, Jeannine Relly, Eric and Jane Force, Larry and Marilyn Shames, Marilyn and Rusty Shteir, Peter and Terri Held, Aryen Hart, Victoria Lucas, Shay Salomon, Arlene Kellman, Jane Heil, Alice Pringle… and others, whom I hope to thank properly next book.

Last and foremost, thanks to you, my readers, for helping me give a forgotten ballerina and great soul her moment in the spotlight.

To dance! To music! To love!

Germaine Shames scours the globe in search of compelling stories. Shames is author of *Between Two Deserts*, two earlier nonfiction books, and three feature screenplays. A former foreign correspondent and contributor to *Hemispheres, More*, and *National Geographic Traveler*, she has lived and worked in such diverse locations as the Australian outback, Swiss Alps, interior of Bulgaria, coast of Colombia, Fiji Islands, and Gaza Strip. With *You, Fascinating You* the author returns to her roots in the performing arts to reveal a hidden story painstakingly researched across three countries over the course of five years.